MELINDA

MELINDA AND THE MASTER

Susanna Hughes

First published in 1993 by
Nexus
332 Ladbroke Grove
London W10 5AH

Copyright © Susanna Hughes 1993

Letter from Esme copyright © Esme Ombreux 1993

Typeset by TW Typesetting, Plymouth, Devon

Printed and bound by Cox & Wyman Ltd, Reading, Berks

ISBN 0 352 32890 8

This book is sold subject to the condition that it shall
not, by way of trade or otherwise, be lent, resold, hired
out or otherwise circulated without the publisher's prior
written consent in any form of binding or cover other
than that in which it is published and without a similar
condition including this condition being imposed on the
subsequent purchaser.

This book is a work of fiction.
In real life, make sure you practise safe sex.

One

Melinda was a very beautiful woman. Her husband knew it, her friends knew it, and what is more, she knew it. It would have been difficult not to, after all. She could not ignore the evidence of her own eyes. Now, for instance, as she finished drying her body after her bath and walked through into the bedroom, she caught sight of herself in the cheval mirror that stood in one corner of the room. She stopped and gazed at her reflection. Her flaxen blonde hair was cut short and combed back off her forehead, its natural waviness tucked behind her ears and bunched in curls at the nape of her neck. Her face was soft and feminine, her cheekbones round, her nose small and slightly retroussé, her mouth full with thick pouting lips. Under her neatly plucked blonde eyebrows, her eyes were large and green; they sparkled with life.

Her body was slender. She was not particularly tall, but her legs appeared long and elegant, with strong thighs and shapely calves. Her hips were generous, rich curves of flesh, her buttocks plump and round, divided by a dark chasm that cut deeply between them until it met the slit of her sex. Her labia were fat and rubbery and prominent, exposed by the fact that Melinda's pubic hair was no more than a thin downy blonde fleece; soft and silky and almost totally transparent. Above the triangle of this fleece her belly was

1

flat and her waist distinctly slender. Her breasts were not large, but were round and full and needed no support. They rose proudly from her chest, two perfect orbs topped by pink and almost disproportionately large nipples.

Melinda liked looking at her body. It made her feel excited. Over the years it had often provoked her to masturbate. She masturbated frequently; she was good at it. If she dipped her finger now – down between those wrinkled, creased, exposed labia – she knew she would find herself wet with the first stirrings of her sexual pulse.

But tonight, she told herself firmly, there was no time. Melinda had her clothes laid out on the bed. A full-length black strapless evening dress in a material woven with a silvery thread that glittered under the light. A black basque in satin and lace to hold her breasts and display a firm cleavage above the dress, and sheer dark stockings, their nylon also spun with an element that made them shine. Not that anyone would see much of them. Except for a glimpse at her ankle, the long skirt of the dress concealed her legs. But she would know. It was to be her little surprise for her husband.

Melinda hooked the basque into place, its tight elasticated panels moulding her soft flesh, constricting her body. She loved the feeling of being held so tightly. She sat on the bed and took the stockings out of their cellophane packet. Pointing her toe, she pulled the fine nylon over her foot and up over her calves and thighs, transforming her creamy naked skin from white innocence into dark veiled mystery. When both stockings were in place, she stood up to pull them taut and clip them into the long, black satin suspenders of the basque. The front suspenders needed adjustment to hold the stockings more tightly. She moved the little metal hoop that doubled the elastic material until she was satisfied it would pull tightly enough, then clipped it back through the darker nylon on the welt of the stocking.

She looked at herself in the mirror again. The basque and the stockings bisected her body, leaving bands of white nakedness across her shoulders and thighs, contrasting with the blackness of the lingerie.

Her downy pubic hair was still exposed, framed by the bottom of the basque and the two suspenders at the front of her thighs. The blonde fleece looked innocent. It did not hide the top of the crease of her sex.

As she looked in the mirror she felt a throb of sensation, like a mild electric shock. Almost before she realised what she was doing – before she could tell herself there was no time – she spread her hand over her navel and slid it forward, so her forefinger eased between her labia and onto the little knot of her clitoris. It was swollen and wet. It responded immediately to the intrusion of her finger, sending out a wave of pleasure as she stroked it with practised ease.

She watched in the mirror, watched her finger moving; tiny almost imperceptible movements that made her whole body quiver. She watched as though it were someone else. Another person. It was easy to imagine. She rarely wore such exotic underwear. It felt so different. It made her feel so different. The way the basque squeezed her body excited her.

'I look like a whore,' she said aloud. 'A very expensive whore.'

The words thrilled her. She pushed at her clitoris and once again, before her mind had realised what she was doing, before it could talk her out of it, her other hand had found its way down over her arse and

3

into the crease of her sex from the other side, plunging two fingers into the silky, welcoming flesh of her cunt.

'Like a whore . . .' she said again.

She fell to her knees, no longer able to think of anything but the needs of her body. Her hands worked at her sex, probing, kneading, stroking. She closed her eyes. In her mind she was always blindfolded, a white band of silk tightly bound over her eyes, so tight she would have felt the silk pressing against her eyeballs. In her mind she was always held down. Hands held her wrists, her ankles. Hands pinched and kneaded her breasts. Hands and mouths and tongues and teeth. Biting, pinching, licking, penetrating. In her mind she never struggled. Though she knew she was being violated, she never tried to escape. She let them take her, let them carry her over to the bed and, one by one, take her. One in her mouth, one in her cunt. They held her flat and open, wide open.

That was her dream, her fantasy, her masturbation rite.

Her orgasm cascaded through her body; she heard herself gasp with pleasure. The fantasy was so real, that she was surprised, when she could open her eyes again, to discover she was alone.

Slowly she got up off the floor. She went into the bathroom to wash her hands. They were soaking wet. Then she sat down at her dressing table to hurriedly put on her make-up. She wanted to have the dress on before her husband got back. She didn't want to spoil his surprise.

'You know how important this is,' he said as she adjusted his black bow tie.

They were both dressed, their overnight bag packed with a change of clothes for the morning.

4

'Mark, you've told me a million times.'

'If I get this contract, it'll change our lives. Literally. I mean Hammerton's company is the fifth biggest in the States – '

'And he's going to spend five million setting up in Europe. I know. You've told me.'

'You don't seem to realise – '

'I do. I do. I'll be on my best behaviour. What do you think I'm going to do; get drunk and take all my clothes off?'

His tension visibly lessened and he smiled. 'That might not be a bad idea.'

He pulled her into an embrace, but she turned her head aside when he went to kiss her.

'Can't get lipstick all over you. People might talk.'

'Car should be here soon.'

'What's he like anyway?'

'Charming. But hard. Eats executives for breakfast if there have been mistakes. But he's very generous. His parties are supposed to be fabulous. The best of everything. No expense spared.'

'Wonderful. I can't wait.' By all accounts their invitation to dine with Walter Hammerton was going to be quite an evening.

At exactly seven o'clock the Rolls-Royce glided into their driveway. It was, Melinda was assured by her husband, who took an interest in such things, a long-wheelbased Silver Wraithe. Its chauffeur made no attempt to ring their doorbell, assuming, correctly, that they would see the car. Instead, as soon as the front door opened, he got out and went to the rear passenger door, opening it and saluting smartly as Melinda slid into the luxurious leather interior. Her husband locked the house, handed their case to the chauffeur and joined her.

5

'I love the smell of leather,' Melinda said. The interior of the car, all leather seats and walnut veneer, was redolent with an aroma that suggested elegance and wealth.

The car journey took no more than ten minutes. Walter Hammerton's staff had rung Mark's secretary. The nearest suitable landing place for a helicopter had been researched, permission obtained, flight plans filed. Everything arranged.

The car glided effortlessly through the traffic, its engine noiseless, the ride soft and smooth. Mark poured himself a whisky from a crystal decanter that was neatly housed in a custom-made walnut bar.

As they approached the helicopter, its rotor blades were already turning. The chauffeur parked as close as he dared to the concrete helicopter pad, and rushed round to open the rear passenger door. A quick dash and they were both aboard and strapped into the Belljet Executive. As soon as their overnight case was aboard, the doors were secured and the helicopter lifted into the dusk, just as the sun was setting to the west.

The aircraft headed north. Melinda soon adjusted to the noise and vibration, and concentrated on picking out landmarks as they flew over central London. Buckingham Palace, Park Lane and Hyde Park passed underneath them. The traffic below was horrendous, long snakes of stationary headlights heading down all the major routes. Unable to stop herself from grinning as they flew over the gridlocked cars, Melinda decided a helicopter was definitely the only way to travel. She could certainly get used to this, she thought.

It was no more than ten minutes later when, after a course change to the west, the helicopter descended onto a brightly illuminated circular concrete pad, set in the four-hundred acre estate that had become Walter Hammerton's European headquarters.

As soon as the helicopter had settled on its skids, a uniformed servant opened the doors and helped Melinda and Mark out. A Range Rover waited, its doors open.

There was not enough light to see much of the estate, but the driveway up to the house was lined with cedars. The house itself, a vast Tudor mansion, was fully illuminated by powerful floodlights. It was an impressive sight, the complicated Tudor brickwork in a herringbone pattern, off-set by an ancient and still vigorous Virginia creeper, its leaves half-coloured by the dusky red that would one day overtake the whole growth.

Walter Hammerton, like the good host, was standing by the front door in black tie and evening suit, his cummerbund a deep burgundy red.

'Welcome. Welcome,' he said in a soft, lilting American accent, shaking Mark's hand firmly.

'This is my wife Melinda,' Mark said by way of introduction.

'Delighted,' Walter said.

Melinda presented her hand. Walter took it in both of his and pressed it to his lips. His eyes, having followed the progress of hand to mouth, then looked up, under the brow of his bowed head and into Melinda's green eyes. As they met hers she felt an almost physical shock.

'You are a beautiful woman, my dear. Your husband is a very lucky man.'

She looked into his eyes. They were hypnotic; the lightest blue she had ever seen. They looked straight back at her, unwavering and unblinking. The little

7

tableau lasted too long, Melinda's hand held in his. The world had stopped.

The noise of the helicopter rising over the house broke the mood.

'One more set of guests to pick up,' Walter said, dropping Melinda's hand and looking at her husband.

He led them through into a large reception room. A Tudor fireplace was ablaze with massive logs, cut, no doubt, from trees on the estate. Ten or twelve people stood drinking cocktails, the women all wearing expensive designer gowns in silk, satin and lace.

Walter introduced Melinda and Mark to the nearest set of guests then drifted away. A waiter paraded through the room with a silver tray of champagne. While Mark talked to another couple, Melinda watched her host. He had made an indelible impression on her. He was a tall man and powerfully built. Though he was sixty and his hair completely white, he exuded a sense of power and energy. Every movement he made – his walk, a gesture of the hand to illustrate a point, lifting a glass of champagne – was made with an elegance and economy of movement. Melinda found it difficult to take her eyes off him. The look they had shared at the front door seemed to have bored into her. She could feel it.

The pre-dinner small talk continued. Melinda found herself next to a young and attractive brunette, her long hair pleated to hang down between her shoulder blades, her dress no more than a long tube of vivid-yellow silky material that clung to the ripe contours of her body.

'Have you been here before?' Melinda asked.

'Yes. Are you on the A-list or the X-list?' the brunette replied.

'Sorry, what does that mean?'

'You're on the A-list then.'

'I don't understand.'

'If you don't know there are two lists you're only on the A-list. I'm surprised. You're definitely Walter's type.'

'What's the X-list?'

'I'd bet it won't be long before you find out.'

'Very mysterious.'

'Walter has two sorts of parties. One sort like tonight. Respectable. Dull. Business. All that. That's the A-list.'

'And?' Melinda's curiosity was rampant.

'There's parties that are ...' She searched for a word. 'Different.'

'Different?'

'You have to be on the X-list.'

'And how do you get on the X-list?'

'Walter asks you.'

'Are you on it?'

'Yes. I'm glad to say.'

'Sounds fascinating.'

'It is. Very.'

The noise of the helicopter rose to a crescendo then died away. A few minutes later the final three guests were greeted by Walter. Another round of champagne and canapés was distributed by the tail-coated waiters. Then a butler announced, like a character from a West End play, that dinner was served.

Walter led the way into the panelled dining room. At one end of the room another log fireplace burnt in a huge brick inglenook. Along the centre of the room, a massive oak dining table was laid with white linen, Georgian silver, and white porcelain plates. Each plate setting was set for five courses, a crystal glass in different sizes for each course. On the side plate of each lady's place lay a corsage of orchids. A solid silver flower pin was part of the gift.

The table was lit by candles mounted in Georgian solid-silver candelabras. The room sparkled with flame from tallow, wick and wood.

The meal matched the surroundings. As did the wine. Mark had been right. No expense was spared. Caviar, lobsters and grouse were served with Montrachet and Château Petrus. As the meal progressed the volume of noise increased, the food and wine loosening inhibitions in the presence of the 'Master', as Walter Hammerton was known to his friends on Wall Street and recently to the august pages of the *Financial Times*.

Melinda chatted happily to the man she had been seated next to, a balding unprepossessing accountant. But her eyes were on Walter. She watched as he talked to the large-bosomed lady on his right. She watched as his eyes turned to look directly at her, like two powerful spotlights suddenly brought to bear, and felt the same sensation she had at the front door, as though the whole world had stopped. He looked long and hard. He did not smile. His expression was questioning. She did not know what the question was, but she knew her answer would be yes. She would never be able to refuse those eyes.

A legion of waiters cleared away the glasses and plates after each course. After the cheese, Melinda excused herself from the table to find the loo. Outside the dining room she asked one of the waiters the way. He pointed down a long hallway and told her to take the stairs at the end. She would find the ladies' cloakroom at the bottom of the stairs on the left.

As she walked along the corridor, she thought

about what the brunette had told her and wondered what on earth she had been talking about. She thought about Walter too. If Mark's firm was engaged to do all the legal work for his corporation they would no doubt be invited to this palatial house again. Perhaps they would get onto the X-list, whatever that meant. Perhaps the X-list comprised people who were on the payroll, so to speak.

Melinda picked up the long skirt of the dress as she walked down the wide, richly carpeted staircase. A large lion, its claws holding some animal prey, had been carved into the newel post.

At the bottom of the staircase, Melinda looked in vain for a door. Instead there was only a long, narrow corridor. Puzzled, she set off down the dimly lit passage expecting there to be a door on the left at any moment. In fact, there was no door on the left in the oak panelling that lined the walls. She was about to turn back when she noticed there were three identical doors on the right side, just before the corridor came to an abrupt end.

They did not look like the doors to a cloakroom. She listened for any activity. There was only silence. She couldn't even hear the noise from the dinner party upstairs any longer. She was alone. She should go back and retrace her steps. She must have taken the wrong turn. There must have been another staircase she'd missed.

But she did not move. Something made her want to look into these rooms. Was it just curiosity? Or something else? Her hand grasped the handle of the first door. The door was locked, but even in the dim light of the corridor she could see the key was in the lock. Now she hesitated. Actually unlocking the door was a far more fundamental step than merely blun-

11

dering into a room by mistake. It required a conscious effort.

Melinda turned the key as quietly as she could. It rotated with a sharp grinding of metal that echoed down the corridor. She opened the door. The room beyond was dark. There was no light switch. As far as she could tell the room was empty.

What had she expected? It was just an empty room in the basement of a huge house. She closed the door again, relocked it and started back down the corridor. As she did so, something stopped her and drew her back to the second door. It was an extraordinary feeling, like the invisible pull of a magnet. For some reason she suddenly saw Walter's eyes. She could hear his voice too. She could not hear what it was saying, but she realised she was excited and trembling with anticipation. Where did she get these feelings from, and why? She had no idea.

The second room was as empty as the first.

She did not hesitate to open the third door. It was locked. She turned the key and did not flinch at the noise it made as the barrel of the lock retracted and the door opened. A strange bluish light, seemingly transfused with a smoky mist, leaked out of the room as the door swung back. As it was lighter than the corridor her eyes took a moment to adjust.

She stepped through the door, closed it after her and leant against it. Another extraordinary feeling filled her mind, as though she had done this before. Déjà vu. She felt she had opened this door before, seen this peculiar light. Had she dreamt it?

What she saw in front of her eyes was like a dream.

The room was lit by a single spotlight set in the ceiling. Its strong beam of light was directed onto a small circular dais about two feet off the ground.

Standing on this dais was a naked woman; naked, that is, apart from a pair of white, patent leather high heels. The heels were so high, her feet were almost on tip-toe. They needed to be. The woman's hands had been strapped into a pair of padded white leather cuffs, suspended from a chain of bright chrome links dangling from the ceiling above her head. Without the shoes the woman's feet would hardly have touched the base of the dais.

The woman's body had a strange hue, a bluish-white all over. As Melinda's eyes got used to the light she realised that this was only partially caused by the colour of the spotlight. In fact the woman's body had been covered in a thick white pancake of make-up. Even the triangle of her pubis, which had been completely shaved, was as uniformly white as the rest of her body. At first Melinda thought the woman's head had been shaved too until she realised that her hair had been tucked up under a tight-fitting white rubber cap, like a swimming cap. The cap emphasised the woman's remarkably beautiful face, her high cheekbones and strong fleshy lips.

Tentatively, Melinda walked towards the woman. She should have fled, run back upstairs to the party and forgotten she'd been in this room, or seen what she had seen. Instead, in a daze, her heart beating so fast she could hear it, she walked forward. Her excitement was absolute, her body shivering.

The woman's eyes looked at Melinda. There was no way of telling whether she was blonde or brunette, but her eyes were a dark brown. They looked on with no expression, showing no interest, no concern, and surprisingly, considering her position, no pain.

'Beautiful, isn't it?'

The voice startled Melinda so much, she jumped back in alarm.

'I'm sorry, I didn't mean to startle you.' Walter stood in the shadows. The room must have had another entrance as he had not come in by the door behind her.

'Yes,' was all that Melinda could think of saying. She tried to get her breath back.

'Woman in White,' he said as though announcing the title of a sculpture. 'Tell me what it makes you feel.' He said 'it' instead of 'she' as though the woman was only an object.

It was Melinda who should be asking the questions, she thought, not Walter. Her mind was full of them. She looked into Walter's hypnotic eyes again. Even in the shadows she could see them clearly like they were their own light source.

'Please tell me . . .' he said.

'You want the truth?'

'It would interest me a great deal.'

'The truth is it makes me incredibly excited.' Melinda used 'it' too.

'Why?'

'I don't know.'

'Yes you do,' he said firmly.

Melinda knew precisely. She said nothing.

Walter extended his hand. He ran his forefinger down between the white woman's breasts, and then up round over her breast to her nipple. The nipple was caked with make-up, more so than elsewhere so as to transform its darker brown to the same white as the rest of her body.

'Tell me why.'

'May I touch?'

'All good sculpture should be touched. Didn't your Henry Moore say that?'

'Sculpture?'

14

'These are my sculpture rooms.'

Melinda cupped her hand to the woman's breast. Her breast was large, fat and heavy. Melinda had never felt the weight of a woman's breast before. She felt a surge of excitement course through her body. When she let go her hand was smeared with the white make-up. Her body was throbbing. It felt like it did during sex.

'Please tell me,' Walter persisted.

'What?'

'You're turned on, aren't you?'

'Yes.'

'Tell me why.'

She didn't need to think. She knew. 'Because I wish it were me. Tied like that.'

'You find that exciting?'

'Yes.' It was true.

'Good.'

'Why good? What is all this?'

'I wanted you to see it. I had the staff direct you down here.'

'I might not have opened the doors. I nearly didn't.'

'But you did. That was the choice. Your choice.'

'I don't understand.'

'You are a beautiful woman, Melinda. And I am a very rich man.'

'What has that got to do with it?'

'Rich men are used to getting what they want.'

'And what do you want?' She looked into those hypnotic eyes again and immediately found herself under their spell.

'Some rich men collect art, rare books, postage stamps. I collect women.' He paused. A thousand questions welled up in Melinda's mind but his eyes stilled them all. 'Tomorrow I'd like you to have breakfast with me. Just the two of us. Alone. I have a proposition I want to put to you.'

'A proposition?'

'I'll explain everything in the morning.'

He looked at the Woman in White. As soon as his eyes left her, she felt as though she had been released, suddenly cut loose from her bondage, freed to think for herself. She remembered what the brunette had said about the X-list. Was that all part of this?

'I think we'd better go back to the party,' he said.

'What do you want from me?' Melinda said bravely.

'Tomorrow . . .'

'Tell me now.'

'Look at her.' For the first time he said 'her' and not 'it'. 'That's what I want from you. Your submission.'

Melinda felt a flood of emotion overwhelm her. It was as though Walter had walked into her dreams, read the books of her secrets. She felt exposed. Open. Prised open.

'How did you know?' she mumbled, not at all sure she wanted to know.

'I knew from the first moment I saw you.'

Walter took her hand and led her out of the room, into the dimly lit corridor. He locked the door behind them.

Two

'Unzip me, darling, I have a surprise for you,' Melinda said. She had told her husband nothing about what had happened between her and Walter. She hadn't the slightest idea why not.

'I think he's going to do it, Mel. I really think he is. Last thing he said to me was that he's looking forward to working with me. His exact words. That must be good.'

'Great,' she said.

He pulled the zip down. He was searching for his pyjamas in their case. He stopped when the dress fell to the floor.

'Oh Mel,' he said.

'You like?'

'Magnificent.'

They were in the west wing of the house, a huge bedroom complete with its own log fire and an antique carved four-poster bed. Melinda saw her husband's eyes on her body. Hooking her thumbs into the thin sides of the lacy knickers she pulled them down her thighs until they reached her knees and fell, of their own accord, to the floor. She stepped out of them.

Her excitement surged. She knelt on the floor, her hands resting on her knees, her head bowed. It was the beginning. Mark would know what it meant. It was a ritual; their ritual. And tonight, with her mind full of the Woman in White, of Walter's eyes, she needed it, needed the comfort of knowing. She felt her body trembling with her need.

'Where are they?' her husband snapped, his voice cold and hard, as she wanted it to be.

'On the bed,' she replied almost in a whisper.

She had laid the six white silk bands out carefully on the foot of the bed.

'So they are.'

She could not see him, but she heard him pull off the rest of his clothes. She knew he would be erect.

He picked up one of the bands of silk and came round behind her. She raised her head and he slipped the silk over her eyes. Almost more than anything that followed, she loved this moment. Deprived of sight, plunged into darkness. It was her dream after all. He tied the silk tightly. She could feel his cock nudging between her shoulder blades.

'Open your mouth,' he said.

She obeyed. She heard him walk over to the bed and return with a second band of silk. He fed it into her mouth. She could feel the silk on her tongue. It became wet instantly. It was not a proper gag. It did not physically prevent her from speaking. It symbolically prevented her, however. That was enough.

Mark's cock must ache, it was so hard. It had become moist. Their ritual always made him hard.

'Stand up,' he ordered.

Melinda obeyed immediately.

'Walk forward.' In front of her was the log fire. She had no way of knowing how many steps away it was. She walked without hesitation, trusting him. 'Stop,' he said.

She could feel the heat of the fire on her naked thighs, and on her belly and breasts under the basque.

'Come on, Melinda, you know what to do.'

Immediately, she parted her legs, planting her feet wide apart. Then, bending over, she grasped each ankle in her hands. In this position she knew her sex was completely exposed, her labia opened, the corona of her anus on view. She could feel the heat of the fire on her shoulders.

He took his time. He always took his time. That was the point. The stockings and the black basque made the position she was in more alluring, the tight black suspenders straining to hold the stockings, her plump arse so white by contrast. He would be able to see a wetness glistening between her legs.

Melinda wanted to beg. The wet silk in her mouth reminded her that she must not.

Mark found what she had tucked away in the side pocket of the case. She heard him take it out. Her back began to ache, but it was a pain she welcomed. It was a pain she revelled in. She grasped her ankles tighter, feeling the harshness of the nylon on the palms of her hands.

She heard his feet on the carpet. He stood right behind her. He poured the oil onto the neat round target of her anus. It was cold. In her position it was able to pool there before it overflowed the banks and ran down into her labia. She could not suppress a moan. He dipped the tip of the vibrator into the middle of the little puddle of oil.

'This is what you want, isn't it?'

She moaned a 'yes'.

Slowly he pushed the vibrator down into her arse, twisting the hard plastic shell in his hand, inching it down. It filled her as it always did. Violated her, a violation she wanted. It made her gasp for breath. When it was deep inside her he turned on the motor.

19

Vibrations coursed through her body. She felt her clitoris, only inches away from the source of vibration, quivering. Her cunt quivered too. She could hardly bear the pleasure. Her breasts had fallen out of the bra of the basque. They seemed to be shaking too. She knew she could not stop herself from coming. As she felt her orgasm powering into every nerve in her body, her mind saw the Woman in White, saw her eyes, saw her submission.

Melinda screamed as her climax locked her muscles and she fought not to collapse onto the floor.

Mark turned the vibrator off. He did not take it out. It stuck vertically up like the stump of a tree. He was wanking himself, using the fluid his cock had produced. She knew better than to move until he ordered her to do so. Little aftershocks of orgasm trembled through her.

'A four-poster. Very convenient. I think it's time for you to please me, don't you?' He removed the hard plastic phallus.

She straightened up. The pain in her back was so close to the feelings in her sex that they seemed to be joined. She felt her nerves kick out another shock of pleasure so strong that it took her by surprise.

He took her hand and guided her to the bed. She lay down on her back. Immediately she felt the white silk being tied round her wrist. It felt cool. She was hot. The heat of the fire and the heat of her body had made her hot. Her arm was dragged by the silk up over her head, then out to one side. In the darkness she felt a surge of passion. Silk being wound around her other wrist. Cool silk. Tied tight. Her other arm jerked up. Both arms were spread apart and tied to the posts of the bed.

Now her ankles. She kept her legs pressed together.

When he pulled her leg over to the bed post to be tied, she moved the other leg too, stretching herself across the bed to keep her thighs closed.

He wound the silk around her other ankle. Knotted it. Then he pulled, forcing her legs apart, opening her. It was the moment she loved. Her heartbeat surged, her breath coming in shallow pants. She struggled to keep her legs together, but inexorably they were opened. He tied the silk to the last bedpost. She was spread-eagled on the bed.

He tortured her. Was it torture? His fingernails pinching at her nipples. His fingers wanking the hard, swollen knob of her clitoris. His tongue in her ear. Never knowing where he would touch her next. She writhed on the bed, unable to control herself, arching her body up towards him, trying to use it to ask him to take her. His mouth kissed and licked and sucked at her. It was hot and wet. It sucked on her neck, on her thigh, on her breast. It sucked at the satin and lace of the basque, at the shimmery nylon of her stockings. It made her want.

In the darkness behind the blindfold she saw Walter's eyes. She heard his voice. 'Your submission . . .'

She was on the brink of coming again but she knew he would not let her. His finger would not stay long enough on her clitoris to bring her off. It would tease. She struggled against her bonds, loving the feel of them holding her so tightly. She shook her head from side to side, wanting to scream at him to put his cock inside her, to fuck her, to take her. But instead she only gasped.

He knelt between her bound legs. He wanked his cock slowly in his hand. As always there was so much temptation. He could come over her belly, watch his spunk shooting out in great white gobs, let her feel it

21

splash onto her flesh. He could push his cock into her mouth, past the white silk. He'd done that before. Or he could plunge between her legs, into that hot, wet cunt.

She arched up off the bed again, her limbs fighting her bonds to allow her cunt to get nearer to his cock. The silk was so tight, so unyielding. She was so close to the edge of the precipice of her orgasm that she only needed the faintest of touches. She tried to bring her thighs together to give herself that touch, but her legs were tied too far apart.

He looked down at her struggles. Her cunt lips were wet, wet from the oil that had trickled from her anus, and wet from her own excitement. The long crease of her sex, from puckered anus to pink clitoris, glistened.

He had no real choice. He could feel her cunt radiating heat. He couldn't ignore it. With all his strength he threw himself onto her bound helpless body, his cock instantly finding passage; sliding into her cunt like part of a well-oiled machine. She was lubricated with her own wetness and he had never felt her so hot. As his cock hit the neck of her womb, she came. He felt her body shudder, felt the walls of her cunt contracting around his fleshy sword; heard her wail, helplessly, hopelessly, every muscle of her body locked, fighting her bonds. In seconds, in three or four quick-darting strokes, he was coming too; jamming his cock as deep as it would go, its base grinding against her clitoris, then waiting, not moving at all, letting his cock spasm to jet his spunk deep into her dark, wet cunt.

There were two cameras. Neither Melinda nor Mark had seen them. They were well hidden. There were

22

four microphones equally well hidden. The sound quality was exceptional, but then he had specified that it should be. He wanted to be able to hear every word. And what Walter Hammerton wanted, he got.

He watched with intellectual interest but he was not, as the moment, excited. He lay on his bed in a silk robe, propped up against his pillows with the remote control beside him allowing him to switch from one camera to the other, and zoom in on the figures on the screen.

He had sensed something in Melinda when he had first seen her. Something rare. Now he saw it confirmed. He smiled to himself in anticipation of pleasures to come. She was an exquisitely beautiful woman. Her unusual sexual proclivity was an unexpected bonus. Most women had to be carefully trained. They all had the potential but not all realised it. Melinda was a natural. Walter knew she had initiated the ritual he was watching now; her husband enjoyed playing his part but this was a game played by Melinda's rules. She would need no training.

Walter concentrated on the television monitor as Mark rolled off the prostrate body of his wife. Picking up the remote control again, he had the camera zoom in on her open sex, exposed so graphically by the bondage of her legs. The gash was red, wet, wrinkled and used. It filled the screen, her labia so thick and puffy they looked almost unreal. Walter felt a pang of excitement. Melinda lay completely still, not struggling now.

Opening his robe, Walter circled his cock with his hand. It was slowly unfurling.

He switched to the second camera as Mark untied the white silk gag and pulled it from his wife's mouth.

'I'm not finished with you,' Mark said.

23

'No, please,' Melinda said quietly.

'I'm going to leave you like this.'

'No, please. You're hurting me. No more please,' she said, meaning the exact opposite.

'That's what you like,' Mark said. He found the vibrator. He held it up in front of her eyes.

'Please . . .' She struggled, the silk cutting into her flesh.

'You have no choice.'

Mark positioned it between the open lips of her cunt. Walter switched cameras again and zoomed in to watch the hard plastic shell being pushed between her labia.

'Nooo . . .' she screamed, as it drove into her over-sensitised body.

Walter was completely hard now. He wanked himself aggressively. He could have picked up the phone and had one of half-a-dozen women come up to his room instantly to do whatever he bid, but this was private. Melinda was special. He wanted to be alone. He could hear the vibrator hum, the sound muffled by Melinda's sex, as Mark turned its motor on. He could see her body beginning to tremble again, filling the large television screen.

He watched intently as Mark knelt over her face, holding the vibrator with one hand, feeding his cock into her mouth with the other. His cock was still flaccid, she sucked it all in eagerly. She reeled in the balls, until they were both in her mouth, and her lips were up against his pubic hair. Walter could see her using her tongue, and watched as her cheeks bulged, as Mark grew rapidly. It was not long before her mouth could not contain him all. His balls spilled out between her lips. The camera picked up every detail.

Walter saw Melinda's body arching up off the bed,

24

her muscles taut. The vibrator was bringing her off again. She was helpless to prevent it, to prevent anything that was done to her. That was, Walter knew, the feeling she loved. She wanted to be free to tear the vibrator away. At the same time the feeling of being unable to, of being helpless, of having no will, no control, was the feeling that swamped her body, as it did now, making her come hard over the head of the unyielding plastic shell.

As he watched her orgasm rake through her nerves, stretching her like an elastic band against her bonds, Walter smiled to himself. He had trained so many women to love these pleasures, to allow themselves to be bound and spread and opened, to free themselves as a result of their bonds.

The Master – Walter liked the sobriquet and encouraged its use – watched as Mark pulled his cock out of Melinda's mouth and started to wank. As soon as her orgasm subsided, and Mark let the vibrator slide from her body of its own accord, she reached up to lick at his balls. His balls were obviously sensitive. Mark was coming again, wanking himself while Melinda licked his balls. He knelt above her face, staring down at her spread-eagled body encased in black satin and lace, her legs sheathed in stockings pulled taut by suspenders, her fine pubic hair now wet with sweat. Suddenly, his cock spat spunk out over her breasts and the lacy constraints of the basque.

Walter spunked too, almost at the same moment, his fist hammering at his cock. Hot, pearly-white spunk flooded over the circle of his thumb and finger, like lava from a volcano, flowing out from the summit . . .

The sun shone brightly through the gaps in the heavy

25

curtains at the bedroom windows. It was the beams of light that woke Melinda from a light unsatisfying sleep. She stretched her body like a cat. She felt a soreness in her muscles, which was not surprising considering how they had been abused last night.

But her first thought was of Walter. His deep, calm voice, those ice blue eyes, and his 'proposition'. She could not suppress a shiver of anticipation.

Melinda slipped out of bed without disturbing Mark, who was still sound asleep. She found a black silk teddy and pulled it over her naked body, then wrapped a matching black negligée over her shoulders. The lace panels of the teddy, on either side of her hips and over her breasts, gave tantalising glimpses of her milky flesh when the negligée wafted open.

She had no idea how she was going to find Walter, but as soon as she stepped quietly out of the bedroom door the problem was solved for her.

'This way, madam,' a white-coated servant said. Presumably Walter had stationed him outside the door to wait for her emergence.

Melinda followed him along the beamed Tudor corridors into the central part of the house. After a considerable walk they finally arrived at two large oak doors. The servant knocked on one as a prelude to opening it. He stood aside to let Melinda through, then closed it after her.

Walter's bedroom was vast. He was sitting at a circular rosewood breakfast table in front of the main window, overlooking the gravelled drive and the two wings of the house on either side. The strong August sun was streaming through the leaded glass, backlighting his head and making his white hair appear like an iridescent halo.

26

He got up immediately. His eyes locked on hers.

'My dear, how lovely you look. Please . . .' He indicated a chair at the table, and pulled it out for her. She sat down. 'What can we get you? Coffee, orange juice, champagne?'

The idea of champagne appealed. This was such an unlikely adventure, champagne for breakfast seemed somehow an appropriate way to begin it.

'I would love champagne,' she said.

Walter picked up the cordless phone on the table and ordered quickly.

'Coffee meantime?' he asked.

She nodded.

The table was already set for breakfast. A large Georgian silver coffee pot sat on a small electric warmer. Walter poured steaming black liquid into a white porcelain cup and passed it to Melinda. As she took it, he noticed a red ring around her wrist.

'What have you done to yourself, my dear?' he said solicitously.

'Nothing,' she said quickly, managing not to blush and keeping the other wrist, which was equally marked, out of sight. Unconsciously, she crossed her marked ankles too. The marks never lasted long, but last night she had struggled harder than usual. She knew why. The reason sat in front of her.

'Well, it is a beautiful morning.' Walter did not pursue the subject of her wrists.

'Yes.'

'Did you sleep well?'

Before she could answer, a knock on the door heralded the arrival of a servant. He brought in a bottle of Krug, in a silver wine cooler. He set it on the breakfast table with two champagne flutes. The bottle was already opened.

27

'I'll pour,' Walter said, dismissing the servant with a wave of his hand. He poured the wine without spilling a drop, his hand steady. They clinked their glasses. 'Chin, chin. Isn't that what you say in England?'

'Not any more.' She smiled, sipping the wine. 'So good . . .'

'I'm glad you like it.' He paused for a moment, then continued, 'In business, I like to come straight to the point. Would you mind if I do the same this morning?'

'No.' She had hoped he would do just that.

'My proposition. I find you a very beautiful woman, as I said to you last night.'

'You hardly know me.'

'Beauty is something that appreciates with time, I agree. But it is my experience that initial impressions never lie. I wanted you from the moment I set eyes on you.' His eyes looked into hers again. She felt their incredible power. 'I would like you to become part of my collection. To be with me. Exclusively. For one year. You will do whatever I tell you to do. Without question. I will ask you to do some unspeakable things. You saw an example last night. I don't want you to have any illusions.'

'What about my husband?'

Walter studied her face, leaving a long pause before he spoke. 'That is an interesting question, my dear. Of all the questions you could have asked, you ask only about your husband. Not about my demands. Not about what will happen to you. Only about your husband. Why is that?'

Now it was Melinda who hesitated. 'The truth?'

'You were truthful last night.'

Melinda thought carefully for a moment, trying to analyse why she was feeling so excited again, why her heart was beating like a steam hammer under her ribs.

'The idea ...' She hesitated, then started again. 'You are a very attractive man. Very knowledgeable. Very worldly-wise. The idea of giving myself to you makes me feel ... alive. I don't want to know the details.'

'You must give me control.'

'Yes, I know.'

'You will have no will, Melinda, no ability to choose.'

'That's what I want.'

Her heart surged again. She had lain awake all night thinking about Walter, about the woman bound in the special room in the basement, about what it all meant. She had played games with her husband, games she loved but in the end they were only pale shadows of what she craved for, what her body wanted, and what her mind had, for so long, cherished and cultivated in fantasy. The truth was, her fantasy was about to become reality.

'And my husband?' she said.

'Leave your husband to me.'

'If it were a few weeks. But a whole year ...'

'Shh,' he said firmly. 'I will tell your husband that you are going to work for me for a year. I will tell him I have decided to give him my legal work. If he does not wish to lose you for a year then I will find another firm of lawyers. There are many. Not all with such compliant wives.'

Walter sipped his champagne.

'He won't believe you,' Melinda said anxiously.

'Look into my eyes, Melinda,' he said firmly. She obeyed. Suddenly she forgot everything. She saw the Woman in White, her arms stretched above her head,

29

as though she was reflected in those ice blue eyes. 'I will make him believe me. I can do that. Do you understand?'

'Yes. I think so.'

He looked away. For the second time, she felt as though she had been released from invisible shackles.

'In one week.' His tone had changed. They were no longer equals. 'You will come to my London house. You must wear nothing of your own. Nothing. Not a hair-pin. No make-up. No nail varnish. The servants will bring you clothes and shoes to wear before you leave. You must be punctual. If you have not arrived on time, I will assume you have changed your mind. Will you change your mind?'

'No.'

'Now go back to your room and tell your husband to come and see me.'

He handed her a white card. On it was printed an address. Written by hand were the words, 'Seven p.m. 26th.' It was exactly one week from the day.

'Go now. I won't see you again before you leave. Next time, the circumstances will be different.'

The words thrilled Melinda. She got up and went to the door.

'You could make me, couldn't you?'

'Make you what?'

'Make me come to the house. Anything you wanted.'

'Yes.'

'Why don't you?'

'Because, my dear, that would be no fun at all . . .'

Mark could hardly contain his excitement. He used the phone in the Rolls that had picked them up from the improvised helicopter pad to book a table at their favourite restaurant. Getting Walter's business was cause for a major celebration, he told Melinda. Like Walter's party, no expense spared. The whole journey home he talked endlessly about Walter's company, Walter's ambitions, Walter's money, and Walter's magnetic personality and charm.

Melinda inserted the odd word of approbation into Mark's monologue. But they were unnecessary. Mark's enthusiasm was total. It was not until they reached home – and were no longer in the company of Walter's employees – that she thought it safe to broach the other aspect of Walter's offer.

'Did Walter mention me?' she asked tentatively.

'What do you mean?' Mark said as they unpacked their overnight bag in the bedroom.

'He said he was going to . . .'

'Oh that. Yes, yes, he did.' He made it sound as though it were something of no importance.

'And?' Melinda persisted.

'Well, it's good, isn't it? I mean you wanted to go to work again. I'm sure you'll find it fascinating.' His tone of voice had changed. He spoke as though repeating lines he had learnt.

'You don't mind?'

'Why should I mind?' He looked astonished at the thought.

'I'll be away . . .'

'Walter explained all that, darling. He explained everything. Everything. It will be wonderful for you. An opportunity. And I'm going to be so busy. All the work I'll be doing. I mean it's ideal really, isn't it? Ideal.'

Melinda could see Walter's eyes, see him coaching Mark, getting him to repeat the perfectly reasonable grounds for making no objection.

31

'Did he tell you what I'd be doing?'

'Sort of personal assistant. It'll be so interesting for you. Exciting.' But his voice reflected no feeling. It was flat and unemotional.

Melinda hesitated, wondering whether to push it any further, but fascinated to know what else Walter had said.

'You'll be starting in one week's time,' Mark continued in the same tone. 'Seven p.m. on the 26th.'

'Yes,' she said quietly.

'It's an opportunity. And I'm going to be so busy. All the work I'll be doing. I'll hardly miss you at all.'

'For a whole year.'

'Yes, seven p.m. on the 26th, for a year. That's the agreement. Walter explained everything.'

'He's a very persuasive man, isn't he?'

'Oh very. Very charming. Did you notice his eyes?'

'Yes.'

'So blue . . .' Mark said. He had hardly moved since they had begun the conversation, standing by the foot of their bed, staring out of the window, not looking directly at Melinda. He lapsed into silence.

'Mark . . .'

'It's all right, darling. Walter explained everything.'

Melinda felt a sudden chill. Walter Hammerton was a powerful man in every sense. He had done what he said he would do. He had convinced Mark that the sudden absence of his wife for a whole year was something to which he should make no objection. Mark was not going to save her from herself.

'Unzip me,' she said, turning her back to her husband. She had worn a light, flowery, yellow cotton dress for the return journey, its long zip extending down her back.

'Oh . . . sorry.' He snapped out of his trance-like state. He pulled the zip down.

32

Melinda shucked the dress off her shoulders and let it drop to the floor. She was not wearing a bra. Her breasts trembled as she stooped to pick up the dress, her silky white panties clinging to her pert firm arse. They were cut high on the hip, the band of material that passed between her legs not wide enough to cover the whole plane of her crotch.

'I'm going to have a bath,' Mark said.

The thought of Walter had started an engine running in Melinda's body. She could feel it throbbing like the engine of a ship, deep down below deck.

'Take your clothes off then,' she said, unbuttoning his shirt, then pressing her naked breasts against his hairless chest.

'Melinda,' he protested.

'What's the matter? Don't you like to feel my tits?'

'Stop it,' he said, pulling away.

Melinda cupped her breasts in her hands. 'I'm getting wet,' she said, squeezing the round hillocks of flesh as though they were made of sponge. 'Look how hard my nipples are.' As if to demonstrate, she took each one between thumb and forefinger and held it up, suspending her breasts by them, stretching them out till she felt the delicious sharpness of pain.

Mark's eyes watched her.

'No . . .' he said.

'No what?' she asked innocuously.

'We can't.'

'What do you mean, we can't?' She released her tortured breasts and stepped into his arms again, her hand feeling for his cock under his trousers. It was flaccid.

'We can't. It wouldn't be right.'

She squirmed her hand against his crotch. 'What are you talking about?'

'Stop it.' He pulled her hand away.

'What's the matter, Mark?'

His face was creased in a worried frown. His eyes looked shifty, moving from side to side as though he expected, at any minute, someone to burst through the door.

'It wouldn't be right. You know that.'

'Why on earth not?'

'Not now.'

'Now?'

'Now. Now you're going to work with Walter. He explained it all to me. It wouldn't be right. It wouldn't be proper. We can't.'

'Walter?'

'Yes. It wouldn't be right. That's what he said.'

'What's it got to do with Walter?'

Her words hung in the air. Mark did not meet her eyes. He turned and fled into the bathroom, closing the door firmly behind him.

She could answer her own questions. She could guess precisely what Walter had to do with it. Everything. For the next year Walter was going to be her life. He would own her and control her. His power would be total. And it had already begun. He'd extended his power into their bedroom; no other man was going to take Melinda, not even her husband. Not now.

Melinda shuddered – someone running over her grave, as her father used to say. But it was not her grave that was being interfered with. It was something deeper. Walter Hammerton had reached into the depths of her sexual psyche and found her secrets. They lay open and exposed in front of him, in front of those ice blue, cold, unblinking eyes. The Master's eyes.

34

Three

Melinda unzipped the small black nylon bag, like an airline bag, that the servant had delivered to her room before they left Walter Hammerton's estate. It had sat in the corner of the bedroom for the last week, a silent reminder of what was to come.

The week had seemed endless; each day dragging by, each hour a new lesson in tedium. But now, at long, long last, it was time.

What she found in the bag was not a surprise. She'd examined its contents as soon as she'd been left alone in the house after their return from the estate. There was a black velour tracksuit, in a very plain design, black cotton bra and knickers, both equally functional, and a pair of simple, soft black suede shoes with a low, almost non-existent, heel. Carefully, deliberately, she laid all the items out on the bed.

It was six o'clock. She had already bathed and washed her hair. Remembering Walter's specific instructions, she had carefully removed the nail varnish from her fingers and toes. Now she sat down at her dressing table and meticulously removed all traces of her make-up, going over her eyes twice to be sure of stripping every trace. When this was done, she took out the small stud earrings from the pierced lobes of her ears and took off her rings. She took off her wedding ring last of all.

It was a strange feeling. She felt free, liberated, unmarried. But at the same time she knew her freedom was born in an act of singular submission. She was unbound only to be, she knew, bound more securely than ever before.

Exactly what was about to happen to her she did not know. But her imagination had run riot all week. Wherever she had gone, whatever she had done, Walter Hammerton's eyes had followed her, boring into her, fuelling her speculation as to what he planned for her.

She had not tried to make love to her husband again. How he had done it she did not know, but clearly Walter had planted the idea in Mark's mind that he should not, must not, have physical relations with his wife. In fact Mark's attitude to her had been altogether remote. Even this morning, when she had attempted to say goodbye with more than usual ardour, bearing in mind he was not to see her again for a year, he merely pecked her on the cheek and went off to work with no more than a casual farewell.

Strangely too, though Melinda had previously practised and enjoyed masturbation, her attempts in the last week had proved totally abortive; despite all the provocation of her encounter with The Woman in White, an image she found impossible to forget. She had lain on the bed several times with every intention of bringing herself off as she saw that naked, white-painted body, felt that heavy breast, looked into those passive, pliant eyes; but she had no success. Her first tentative movements, her fingers straying between her thighs, nudging exploratively at her clitoris, had led not to tension and excitement, but to a feeling of lethargy and relaxation. A short circuit in the mechanism. The first couple of times Melinda had

36

thought nothing of it, but after the fifth or sixth attempt she had begun to suspect that her husband was not the only one under the influence of Walter Hammerton's mesmeric powers.

Stepping out of the towelling robe she was wearing after her bath, Melinda picked up the black cotton knickers and stepped into them. She pulled them up over her hips and smoothed them into place. They were a very old-fashioned design, wide at the sides, and low cut, the elasticated waistband seating on her natural waist. Her whole navel was covered at the front, and her buttocks were covered at the back. The bra was similarly full, hiding her breasts completely, its straps thick and functional.

Melinda looked at herself in the full-length mirror of the wardrobe door. She was used to wearing sleek, minimal modern lingerie; satin, silk and lace concoctions cut to display and flatter. This underwear looked as though it came from a prison.

Quickly, she slipped into the tracksuit. This too was not cut to flatter, but at least did not appear as institutional as the underwear. She poked her feet into the shoes. Despite the fact she had given no one her size, everything, including the shoes, was a perfect fit.

She looked in the mirror again checking she had not missed anything. That she wore 'nothing of her own'. She looked at her face, scrubbed clean. She looked young, innocent even. There was nothing innocent about what was going on in her head.

Downstairs she took the house keys from her handbag and a ten pound note for the taxi. She looked at her watch. Damn, she had nearly forgotten her watch. She unstrapped it and tucked it away in a drawer of Mark's desk. Her heart was beating rapidly in alarm at her mistake.

It was six-thirty as she walked out of the house and locked the front door, posting the keys back through the letter-box. As she heard them drop on to the mat she felt a shiver of excitement she could not control.

Already everything was different. She could never remember going out with nothing, without a handbag, without keys, without even her purse. It was an extraordinary feeling. Wasn't this what they did to you in prison? Stripped you off, showered you down, gave you clothes to wear? It made her feel somehow exposed and incredibly vulnerable.

At the end of the street she picked up a cab, the ten pound note crumpled in her hand. She gave the driver the address on the card.

Sitting back in the black leather seat, she could feel her heart pounding against her ribs. Her excitement was so intense, she felt almost alienated from herself, as if the body sitting in the cab in these anonymous clothes did not belong to her. She stared out of the window but saw nothing of what passed by.

She sat with her legs crossed. It was some minutes before she noticed the discomfort. The soft sensitive flesh between her legs began to itch. Rapidly the itch turned to a sting, as if she was sitting on a bed of nettles. She uncrossed her legs and tried, surreptitiously so the driver would not see the manoeuvre, to pull the crotch of the knickers out of the crease of her sex. But it didn't help. The stinging increased. Only then did she notice her nipples. They felt sore too: the same itchy feeling turning to a sharp stinging. They had puckered and were hard. She could not resist the temptation to scratch them but that only made matters worse, increasing the contact between the material of the bra and her tender skin.

She realised it was something in the underwear that

was doing this to her. She hadn't felt anything un-toward when she'd first put them on, but it was obvious now that the crotch of the knickers and the cups of the bra were not normal cotton.

She squirmed on the seat, trying to ease herself into a more comfortable position. In the rear-view mirror she could see the eyes of the taxi driver watching her with curiosity. She wriggled like a cat on heat. Nothing worked. No position eased the discomfort.

Well, at least she could undo the bra, she thought. Trying to shift into a corner out of range of the rear-view mirror she reached behind her back under the loose tracksuit top to the clip of the bra. Her fingers felt the familiar hook and eyes and deftly, with years of experience, performed the little pinching move-ment that usually resulted in the elasticated strap of the bra springing free. Nothing happened. She tried again. Still nothing. The hooks refused to disengage from the eyes. Melinda repeated the action, straining her arm up behind her back. But the bra was firmly locked in place. Short of stripping down and pulling the whole thing off her shoulders there was nothing she could do.

The irritation was getting worse. It was making her hot. She could think of nothing else, nothing but the stinging sensation in her nipples and labia. Between her legs it was even worse; the crotch of the knickers seemed to cling to her, working its ways up between her puffy lips until she felt it was right inside her, the stinging spreading right up into her cunt itself.

She was hot. Sweat was running down her neck into her bra. Beads of sweat ran down her face. If she had been wearing make-up it would have run.

She tried a different tactic. Instead of squirming she tried to remain perfectly still, hoping this would reduce the friction of the material against her flesh. It didn't work. The stillness only seemed to increase the pain.

It felt like a thousand bee stings, a throbbing, poisonous, feverish pain. Then, as suddenly as it had come, the sensation changed, changed from the angry heat of pain to the pulsing tempo of pleasure. It happened so quickly, so unexpectedly, the line between pain and pleasure crossed so rapidly, that Melinda moaned aloud.

'You all right, luv?' the driver shouted back to her.

'Yes, fine,' she managed to reply. She grabbed the handle on the side of the taxi for grim life, as her body drowned in sensation. Her sex felt as though, instead of stinging, a thousand bees were kissing it, crawling over it, applying the gentle touch of their fragile wings to the most delicate of her nerves. They touched everything: her cunt; her clitoris; even the corona of her arse. Her nipples too sung with pleasure.

She reached behind her back, found the material of the knickers and pulled them tight into the crease of her sex, wanting more contact now, not less. As the material bit into her labia she gasped, trying to gag the sound but not at all sure she'd succeeded.

'Oh my god . . .'

'Do you want me to stop, luv?' the driver asked, seeing her face beaded with sweat, her body squirming involuntarily on the leather seat.

'No . . . no . . .'

That was all she could manage before the orgasm flooded through her body, rolled her eyes back and blanked out the world, as wave after wave of hot sweet pleasure broke over the tortured, tenderised flesh of her sex.

When she opened her eyes again, when the long, seemingly infinite orgasm had freed her finally, the taxi was stationary.

'You sure you're all right?' the driver asked, turning round in his seat and looking concerned.

'Yes. Sorry. Bit faint,' she mumbled. 'I'm fine now. You can go on.'

'This is it.'

'What?'

'We're here.'

'Here?'

'The address you gave me.'

'Oh. Oh right.'

Regaining her senses, Melinda stumbled out of the cab and handed the driver the ten-pound note. It was crumpled into a ball and distinctly damp.

'Keep the change,' she said.

'Thanks. You sure you're all right? You look a little shaky.'

'I'm fine,' she replied, turning to look at the house he had deposited her outside. The cab pulled away, the sound of its noisy diesel engine gradually fading into the distance.

As she had expected, Walter Hammerton's London house, like his country estate, was vast. A long, sweeping gravel driveway lay behind tall wrought-iron railings. Beyond, a beautifully manicured garden – lawns interspersed with shrubberies and carefully planned flower beds surrounded the house, which was largely hidden from the road by three or four mature and majestic oak trees.

An entryphone was mounted on the side of the railings beside the wrought-iron gates. Melinda pressed its chrome button. Immediately, she heard a whirr of electric motors. She looked up to see the security

41

camera mounted at the other side of the gates swivelling round in her direction. The lens zoomed in.

'Yes,' a female voice said from the speaker of the entryphone.

'Melinda Elliot,' she said, looking up into the camera.

The entryphone went dead. Another, much louder, whirr of machinery filled the air, and the two wrought-iron gates began to open, swinging inwards.

Melinda's heart was beating fast again. The release she had experienced in the taxi had only temporarily dulled the soreness between her legs and at her breasts. They still throbbed, making her intensely aware of her body, and in particular of its sexual components. She knew, of course, it was no accident, no chance allergic reaction to the material of the underwear. The lining of the bra and knickers had been coated with something – she had absolutely no idea what – that had produced these feelings. It was deliberate. The irritation had narrowed her consciousness down, and made her capable of feeling and thinking of nothing, on the way to the house, but her sex. From the moment she had stepped out of her house she had been under the Master's control. What she was reduced to in the back of the cab was, she knew, a measure of what her life was about to become.

Which did not mean she hesitated. She walked through the gates confidently, wanting whoever was operating the camera to see that she was not afraid. As soon as she was clear of their track, they reversed direction and closed with a clung of iron that made Melinda start. Despite the finality of the noise, she did not look back, though she could not suppress a momentary panic. She increased her stride and the panic abated. She was committed, there was no turning back.

The gravel crunched under the thin suede shoes. She spotted two more security cameras mounted in the shrubbery along the driveway. They moved to follow her as she passed. As the drive curved round to the left she saw the whole house for the first time, an eighteenth-century double-fronted mansion with a columned portico. The house was painted white, with an ancient wisteria dripping across it in a diagonal stripe. Trees and shrubbery hid most of its depth, but it had obviously been massively extended at the back. The panelled front door was painted black, with a highly polished brass door knocker in the shape of a lion's head, its individually crafted teeth holding the ring of brass.

As she approached, Melinda glanced at her watch, only to be greeted by the sight of her bare wrist. There was no way to know whether she was exactly on time. But it was, she estimated, five to seven.

She stood in front of the black door under the portico. The moment she had waited for, the moment that had seemed so far away all week, had, at last, arrived. Her fevered imagination had supplied her with a hundred scenarios of what lay behind this door. Now she was to be faced with reality. Without hesitation, she reached up to the lion's head and rapped on the door twice. Her heart was knocking just as hard inside her chest.

It was only a few seconds before the door swung silently open.

'Come in,' the woman who opened it said.

'I'm Melinda – '

'I know who you are,' the woman cut in chidingly. She was over thirty, Melinda thought, and strikingly attractive. Her long, very black hair was pinned up into a neat chignon on the back of her head to emphasise her slim, sinewy neck. The neck held her head high. Her face was strong, marked by high cheekbones, dark brown eyes below thick black eyebrows and a complexion that was flawless. She wore the expression of someone who had seen and done everything, for whom the world held no surprises. She was the same height as Melinda and her figure was equally slender. The tight, knee-length skirt she wore covered an iron-flat navel and a well-rounded bottom. A simple white blouse delineated an ample bust. Under it, Melinda could see the outlines of a lacy bra.

'Follow me . . .' she said, not sparing Melinda more than a glance.

They walked into a large vestibule floored in white marble, inset with black slate diamonds at the corners of each tile. A curved double staircase, its balustrades carved from wood, led up to the first floor. An elaborate crystal chandelier hung above their heads.

The woman led the way under the arch of the staircase, and down a long marble-floored corridor. She was wearing black court shoes with remarkably high heels which clacked loudly on the marble floor, in contrast to Melinda's flat heels, which made no noise at all. Her legs were sheathed in sheer black nylon and were long and shapely, her ankles pinched, her calves neat and slim, the line of her thighs clear under the clinging black skirt. Her hips rolled from side to side as she walked.

They were in a long courtyard now, where the back of the original house had been extended and attached to what was clearly once a stable block. The courtyard between the stables and house had been glassed in to form what was virtually a huge conservatory.

The whole area was littered with exotic plants, flourishing in what was nearly a hothouse atmosphere.

The woman reached a small door at the nearest end of the long, narrow building that had formed the stables. It appeared now to be the only entrance. To the side of the door was the panel of a computer lock. The woman punched in four numbers and the door sprung open.

Inside, Melinda saw a long corridor, its floor covered in the sort of wood flooring used in gymnasiums, its walls painted white. At regular intervals down the length of the passage were a series of doors, each with a computer lock identical to the one outside. On each door a number had been painted in a delicate white script.

The woman strode right down to the end of the building, her high heels echoing once more on the flooring. Melinda followed, her mind blank, her heart in her mouth, the incredible tension of anticipation making her tremble slightly.

Near the end of the corridor, the woman stopped in front of one of the doors. Its white number read '20'. She punched the computer panel and the door sprung open.

'In here,' the woman said, standing aside to let Melinda enter first.

The room was completely bare, its walls painted white, its floor covered in the sort of fibre usually used for front door mats. There was one other door in the room, but no window. The only furniture was a small three-legged wooden stool no more than a foot high. Above the door they had entered, a video camera was mounted in the corner, just below the ceiling. The room was illuminated by a fluorescent light panel set in the high ceiling. In fact, the room was higher than it was long. It was narrow too, no more than six or seven feet wide.

The woman closed the door behind them. It made a heavy clunking sound as the lock engaged.

'Take your clothes off,' the woman said. Her voice was hard and unsympathetic.

Melinda's mind was not working properly. She felt as though she was experiencing everything at one remove, so far was all this from normal reality. It took some seconds for the woman's words to sink in.

'Do as I say . . .' the woman prompted crossly.

'Sorry,' Melinda said, hastening to obey. She pulled the top of the tracksuit over her head. She took her shoes off. The coir matting prickled the soles of her feet. Quickly she pulled the tracksuit bottoms down to her ankles and stepped out of them. The woman's eyes did not leave her for one second, scanning every inch of her body critically.

'The bra's stuck,' Melinda said, suddenly remembering her experience in the taxi as she was about to reach behind her back to unclip it.

'Don't speak unless you're spoken to,' the woman rebuked. She stepped up to Melinda and pulled the straps of the bra down over her shoulders. Melinda co-operated, pulling her arms out of each strap in turn. The woman tugged the bra down until it fell to Melinda's waist, freeing her breasts. 'Now down over your legs,' she said as if talking to a stupid child.

Melinda pulled the bra over her hips. It fell to her ankles. She wanted to ask if the clip was deliberately made not to undo, but dared not. She knew the answer anyway.

The woman was looking at her breasts. Melinda was expecting them to be red and raw after whatever

46

irritant they had been exposed to, but when she glanced down at them they appeared perfectly normal.

'Your knickers,' the woman chided again.

Melinda had stopped undressing. It was not hesitation. She had simply forgotten the knickers. Was that her mind's way of telling her it was acutely uncomfortable? She hooked her thumbs into the high waistband and drew the black cotton down her long legs.

The clothes lay in a heap on the floor. There was nowhere to put them.

'My name is Marion,' the woman announced, with no warmth. 'Hold your hands out.'

Melinda obeyed. The woman inspected her nails, then ran her hands through Melinda's hair and examined her face carefully, obviously looking for any trace of make-up.

Casually, her hands ran over Melinda's body, down over her shoulders and arms, around her back, down over her breasts, along the distinct curve of her waist and over the flare of her hips.

'Open your legs,' she ordered.

Melinda parted her feet. The woman stood so close at her side that Melinda could smell her heady perfume. One hand delved between the cleft of Melinda's buttocks, the other over the downy hair of her pubis. The fingers met over her labia. They parted the puffy thick lips and Melinda gasped as one, then two, then three fingers penetrated her body. There was no resistance. Melinda was already wet. It was the first time in her life she had been touched intimately by a woman.

'You experienced an irritation here?' Marion asked, her fingers deep inside Melinda's silky flesh.

'Yes,' Melinda said breathlessly, trying to control her feelings.

'And on your breasts?'

'Yes.' She hardly managed to pronounce the word, her breathing was so shallow.

One of Marion's hands left the crease of Melinda's sex to cup her breast. Melinda looked down as the long carefully manicured fingernails, varnished a bright flame red, found her nipple and pinched it between the nails of her thumb and finger. At the same moment, she thrust her other hand up deeper into Melinda's sex, with such strength that she was hoisted onto her toes. Melinda gasped.

'I can see why he wanted you,' she said, looking straight into Melinda's eyes. Her face was consumed with what looked like anger and jealousy. 'Well, if you make a mistake it will be my job to punish you. I will take pleasure in that.'

She pulled her hands away from Melinda's body. The fingers she had used to penetrate her sex she brought up to Melinda's mouth. 'Suck them.'

Melinda opened her mouth and sucked the three fingers she was offered. She sucked greedily, feeling the long nails against her tongue. She tasted herself. It was a familiar taste. She had often sucked her juices off her own fingers. She had never sucked them from the fingers of another woman. The idea excited her.

Marion read her mind.

'You have never had a woman, have you?' She extracted her fingers from Melinda's lips.

'No.'

Marion's expression changed. For the first time, the hardness seemed to melt slightly.

'The rules are very simple,' she said. Her hand stroked Melinda's cheek tenderly now. 'Obey. Obey anyone who gives you an order. Anyone. Without question. Speak only when commanded to speak. Never address the Master by any other name, if he commands you to speak. They are the only rules. They are absolute. Obey, and you will be punished only for the entertainment of others. Disobey, and you will be punished for your own sake. Disobey repeatedly, and your contract here will end and you will be sent away.'

Her eyes searched Melinda's face looking for her reaction. 'Do you understand?'

'Yes.'

'You will call me "mistress". And any other woman who commands you.'

'Yes, mistress.'

As she said it the words sounded strange, like a word that had suddenly acquired a new meaning.

Marion was looking at her body again.

'You are a beautiful woman. Aren't you?'

Melinda phrased her reply carefully, wanting to please. 'If you say so, mistress.'

'Will you like being used by women?'

'I don't know, mistress.'

Marion felt a sharp ache of desire. She hoped she would be allowed to initiate Melinda into the pleasures of female love.

'Stand where you are,' she ordered, snapping herself out of her reverie and returning to the business in hand. She strode out of the room.

Though completely alone, Melinda stood stock-still, bound as firmly by Marion's words as she would have been by physical restraints. The soles of her feet hurt, the short fibres of the matting cutting into them as sharply as pins.

The video camera appeared to be trained on her, but she had not seen or heard it move since she came

49

into the room. There was no way of telling whether it was on or off.

It was only seconds before Marion returned. She was carrying a black leather harness, an arrangement of wide leather straps connected by bright, strong, chrome chains. The leather was thick but supple, and smelt strongly of itself.

'Raise your head,' Marion ordered, coming to stand behind Melinda.

'Yes, Mistress,' Melinda said, for no other reason than wanting to hear the sound of her own voice: so obedient, so submissive.

'Don't speak unless you're told to,' Marion snapped. She slapped the palm of her hand down on Melinda's rump to emphasise the point.

Melinda felt a wide leather collar being wrapped around her neck and buckled tight. It was not tight enough to affect her breathing, but the hard leather grazed the flesh of her throat uncomfortably if she lowered her chin. She could feel the coldness of a metal chain hanging down between her shoulder blades. Something was attached to the end of the chain.

'Hands behind your back.'

Melinda only just managed to stop herself from saying 'yes, mistress'. But the words were in her mind. They made her sex pulse. She knew she was wet. Bondage always made her wet. And she could feel Marion's fingers in her cunt; they seemed to have left an impression there like a key pressed into soap.

The chain at her back was attached to a pair of leather cuffs. Marion lifted Melinda's hand up into the cuff bending her elbow at an acute angle and quickly folding the leather around her wrists; buckling it tight. The other wrist followed. The harness was uncomfortable. It held her hands high in the small of her back, forcing her elbows out to the side, her arms straining against her shoulder blades.

But that was not all. Melinda could still feel something hanging down from the harness, down the cleft of her arse until it almost touched the floor. It was a thin leather strap no more than the thickness of a rope.

Melinda felt Marion's hand pick the leather up. It was attached to the metal link that held the two cuffs together. Parting Melinda's thighs, Marion drew it up between her legs – allowing the strap to cut into Melinda's sex – up over her pubis and navel, between her breasts.

'Now you must sit on the stool,' Marion said, still holding the end of the strap in her hand.

Looking over her shoulder, Melinda moved back to the stool. Without being able to use her hands for balance, it was difficult to lower herself onto the stool, but she managed it without falling over. Immediately, Marion pulled the strap tight and buckled it into a small loop of leather that hung down two inches from the front of the neck collar. The thin leather bit into Melinda's sex.

In Marion's experience, and in these matters it was great, this was the point at which most women rebelled. The Master's persuasive technique took them so far and no further. It got them through the gates, up to the house, into this room. It got them to undress, to be inspected. But after that, the tentacles of fear began to grip them, loosening the Master's hypnotic gifts. They had perhaps imagined the Master waiting to greet them, waiting to take them straight to his bed. They had not imagined this. Some rebelled when Marion's fingers probed them, some at the first touch

51

of the leather collar on their throat. But the majority left it until it was too late, until their bondage was complete, until this last thin strap was buckled tight, girdling their body lengthways, pressing up into their sex.

They would discover, if they tried to get up, that the leather strap would cut them in two. They had no choice but to sit on the stool and wait. The more violent their rebellion, the longer they had to wait. It took some longer to learn than others. It was the first step in their training, a training that would lead them to submission and ultimately to pleasure. Rare pleasure. Marion knew, because she had been one of the first to undergo the Master's techniques.

But Melinda was different. Melinda had not hesitated. She had not rebelled and would not, Marion knew. She could sense that Melinda's body was already on fire with excitement. Melinda was a natural; just as the Master had said she was.

Marion looked down at her, kneeling uncomfortably on the tiny stool. Then, feeling a sudden envy of the sensations Melinda was going to experience that evening – the newness of it, the not-knowing, the anticipation and suspense – she turned and without a word left Melinda alone, locking the door behind her.

Melinda thought she could hear Marion's heels clacking on the wooden floor in the corridor outside, but it might have been her imagination. The noise faded and there was silence.

It was the beginning . . .

Four

Melinda sat crouched on the hard wooden stool. In this position, with the seat of the stool being so low to the floor, her legs were almost doubled up underneath her. She had quickly discovered she could not stand up; the long leather strap cutting deeply into her sex the moment she tried to raise her head.

She managed to ease the pain in her knees by wriggling her legs around so they were straight out in front of her. But, though this helped her calf muscles, it put all her weight on her buttocks, which soon protested as painfully as her legs had. This was to say nothing of the ache from her arms and shoulders, held so awkwardly by the leather harness, or her feet, still tortured by the prickly coir matting.

But the discomfort only revved-up Melinda's excitement. Along with everything else: the way Marion had touched her; the way her fingers had examined her as if she were some sort of animal being prepared for market; and most of all, the look in Marion's eyes. Her lack of interest had changed, Melinda knew, to something else. She hoped it was desire. Though Melinda had never had a sexual experience with a woman and never imagined she would want one, she knew that Marion had aroused her. She ached to feel Marion touching her again.

A noise attracted Melinda's attention to the video

camera above the door. A little electric motor had whirred to change the focus of its lens. Someone was watching her, ordering a close-up of her body. She stared into the camera proudly, wanting to show whoever was watching that she was not afraid, that she accepted her fate; gloried in it even. Perhaps it was the Master, his ice-blue eyes watching her naked body on a television screen, somewhere in the depths of the house. She saw and heard the lens being moved again, zooming out she thought, so as to view her whole body. She held her head high, ignoring the aching pain this caused in her shoulders, and the bite of the strap as it was pulled deeper into the tender flesh of her sex.

Suddenly, though she had no way of knowing for certain, she had the impression that the camera had been switched off. She was alone.

It was not true to say that Melinda's expectations had been fulfilled. She had none. She had imagined vividly all sorts of fanciful things, but there was a difference between imagination and expectation. She had truly not known what to expect, and still didn't. Nor did she really want to know. She had imagined what she would feel like. She'd graphically imagined her excitement. And in that respect her mind had let her down; the feelings she was experiencing now were out of all proportion to anything she had imagined in her wildest dreams.

The leather cuffs bit into her wrists, her elbows stretched back. The thin leather strap between her legs had worked its way up against her clitoris; a constant reminder of her situation. If she dipped her head slightly forward, she could ease the pressure on the strap a little, but only a little. Too far forward and her hands were pulled up by the collar, increasing the pressure on her shoulders and pulling the strap tight from the other direction. If, on the other hand, she moved her head back to ease the pressure on her arms, the long leather strap was pulled up at the front, and once again bit sharply into her delicate flesh.

By shifting her weight Melinda found a subtle way of dealing with the constant constriction in her limbs. Each time she brought about a momentary relief, it was a cause of delight. However, it did not last for more than a few precious seconds.

She had no means of telling the time. Time ceased to have any meaning. She could measure it only in the minutes it took for the ache in the limbs to become unbearable; before she needed to ease them, however temporarily, by some small movement.

Despite the pain, or more truthfully, because of it, Melinda's body throbbed with excitement. The thin leather strap rubbed against her clitoris whenever she moved even slightly. She realised that, by rocking back and forth, she could move the strap between her labia. By straightening up, she could get it to go deeper. She had started doing this before she realised what she was doing. She eased the strap right up against the swollen bud of her clitoris, sawing it back and forth, the harsh leather moving against the engorged flesh. She looked down at the black strap emerging from between her legs, bisecting her pubis and rising between her soft, plump breasts. With a little effort, she twisted around so that one of her nipples rubbed against the thin leather, as she rocked her body from side to side. The sensation was pleasurable but not pleasurable enough.

She wanted to pinch and torture her nipples; to squeeze and knead at her breasts. She wanted desperately to plunge her fingers into what she knew would be the soaking wetness of her cunt. She wanted to play with her labia, and hammer at her clitoris; all the ritual things she did when she wanked, all the things she knew so well, that brought her off. But she could do none of them. Her hands were no longer her servants. They no longer belonged to her. She had given them to someone else.

She felt her excitement increase another gear. She pulled her head back, harder and further, and felt the leather dig deep, pressing her clitoris against her pubic bone. Oh, how she wanted to touch herself, and how she almost swooned with the knowledge that she could not. Rhythmically, she rocked her head back and forth, the leather sawing up and down, her whole body concentrated on that little knot of nerves the leather so cunningly caressed. She knew she was coming. She watched the black leather between her legs as it moved up and down, glistening with her juices.

Her orgasm began slowly at first: big waves gradually mounting higher and higher; gathering height and weight; seemingly hovering in mid-air, unwilling to crash down and release her. But, at that moment, out of the corner of her eye, Melinda saw the camera lens move again. She was being watched. This time she *knew* it was the Master. She could feel him. See his eyes. Immediately she thrust her head back, right back as far as it would go, cutting the strap right up into her body. That was the final release. She felt the wave of orgasm crash down over her, enveloping her, gathering up all her feelings, all the pain in her tortured body, all the pain she welcomed, into one, feeding on it, and on the images in her mind, her excitement, her situation.

Her whole body shook, testing her bonds, trembling out of all control, feelings that seemed to go on forever. Naked, bound, helpless, available. It was her fantasy after all. What she wanted, what she had craved ever since the first time. Ever since then . . .

He had been handsome and strong. Very strong. Long, thick black hair falling over his forehead as he walked or talked. Long black eyelashes too, the longest she'd ever seen on a man. He always wore the same clothes. White T-shirt, jeans, a black leather jacket. The picture of the rebel he was.

She'd never been out with a man like him. She had never been short of men. She used her beauty to get the men she wanted. She took them to bed occasionally, let them fuck her. Sometimes, they even made her come, the more experienced men, the ones who knew what to do.

But he was different. There was something about him, something unpredictable, something very different. He was dangerous.

He took her to his flat. She would have been devastated if he hadn't. But he'd kissed and stroked her all evening, and on the dance floor she pushed herself up against him and felt his penis harden. She'd squirmed against it, wanting him to know she liked it. Wanting him to know she wanted it, that she wasn't afraid. And she wasn't.

The flat was sparse. He led her straight into the bedroom. The double bed had an old-fashioned brass bedstead. A single bedside lamp was draped with a red cloth to dim its light.

'I want to fuck you,' he said, drawing her into his arms, his broad chest squeezed against her breasts.

'Yes,' she said.

'But you have to do as I say.' His voice was serious. 'Exactly what I say.'

The words made her feel peculiar, stronger than she had ever felt in her life. The dampness she had felt between her legs turned instantly to wetness. Her knees were hardly capable of holding her.

'Will you?'

'Yes.'

'Say it.'

'I'll do exactly what you say.'

'Good. That's what I need.'

He swept her off her feet and, carrying her over to the bed, laid her down on the sheets. They were black.

'Take your clothes off.' The authority in his voice was absolute, no room for discussion.

She unbuttoned her blouse and threw it aside. She slipped off her shoes and pulled her skirt down.

'All your clothes,' his voice demanded.

She reached behind her back and unclipped her bra, hardly able to believe the level of her excitement. She had to keep reminding herself to breathe. Her breasts quivered as she peeled the bra away. His eyes never left her body as she arched her hips off the bed and pulled her panties down. His eyes never left her as he stripped off his clothes. He pulled down his pants and jeans together, his cock bobbing out, already fully erect.

His cock was big, circumcised, a tear of fluid formed at its tip. She reached out a hand to touch it.

'No,' he said, the rebuke delivered so smartly it felt like a slap in the face. He pushed her back and over until his face was inches from hers. 'You do what I say.'

He opened a drawer in the bedside table. At first

she didn't realise what it was he took out – a piece of material shaped like a party mask, but with no holes for the eyes. A blindfold. He was going to blindfold her. As the realisation struck her, another wave of exquisite sensation rushed through her body. She was trembling, but not with fear.

He fitted the blindfold over her eyes, the tight elastic holding it firmly against her face, the material moulded to her nose and cheeks. Darkness descended. She would never forget that sensation for as long as she lived. She felt a rush of pure sexual passion. Now she could only hear and feel. She could hear her heart beating so fast she thought it might explode.

She heard a rustle of material and felt something being wrapped around her wrist and knotted tight. Then her wrist was pulled back over her head and to one side. It was tied down. The experience was repeated with her other wrist. Then her ankles. He spread her legs wide apart; so wide she could not close her thighs at all. He tied her tight. Spread-eagled. Spread open. She was helpless.

Noises stopped. There was only silence. And the blackness.

There was only the beating of her own heart, and the sound of her shallow breathing.

There was only sensation. Her breasts heaving, her clitoris alive. It felt like a tiny snake between her legs, hot and hard. It felt like it was moving.

She knew he was looking down at her. She knew he was standing at the foot of the bed, his eyes on the long crease of her sex which lay exposed and open to him. She wanted him to see it. She arched her hips off the black sheets pointing her cunt at him, her young wet cunt, so sparsely covered with hair that he would be able to see every detail, every line. She wanted to tell him to look at it. But something told her she should not speak.

That was when she came. Suddenly, unexpectedly, an orgasm coarsed through her body like a current of electricity, flashing out from her throbbing clitoris to every nerve in her taut, bound body. Spontaneous combustion. A gasp of pleasure escaped her lips. She rolled her head from side to side. She fought her bonds, wanting to feel their constriction, that feeling sending another shock of sensation sizzling through her prone body.

She would never have believed it possible. To come like this, without even being touched. Only his eyes had touched her.

'Take me, take me. Fuck me,' she wanted to scream, but knew she must not.

Like a bolt of lightning, his finger touched her clitoris. No other part of her body, just the tiny snake that still throbbed with the aftermath of her orgasm. He was not gentle. He pressed it down hard against her pubic bone, then, with equal force, pushed it up and down.

'Ah . . .' she moaned, pulling against the bonds, her body as taut as an archer's bow.

'You like it,' he said. It was not a question.

'Yes, yes, yes.'

He was bringing her off against his finger; relentlessly, unyieldingly. She felt her body arch again, the sensation too much to bear, the orgasm stronger, harder, higher. She screamed aloud, unable to stop herself. It was the bonds that were doing it, her bondage, her inability to do anything but take.

'Bitch,' he said, 'you love it you little bitch.' He took his finger away. 'Don't you?'

'Yes, yes, I love it.'

He fell on her like a wolf on its prey. His cock plunged into her cunt, right up so deep she thought it would fill her entirely. He moved so rapidly she could hardly believe it. In and out like a piston, faster and faster. She could not believe the feeling, the heat of his cock, her own wetness. Her cunt felt like a river; felt like she'd spunked. In the blackness she felt everything: felt every inch of his hard shaft; felt the stem banging at her clitoris; his balls at her arse; felt the glans at the neck of her womb. She could feel his hands groping for her tits, then pinching her nipples.

She met every stroke, pushing off the bed as far as the bonds would allow. He was so deep. The first time, she kept saying to herself, it felt like the first time. As if she'd never been fucked before. It was so perfect. It had never felt like this before. She had never come like this before.

She was coming again, rolling her head from side to side again. She fought the bonds that tied her to the bed, knowing now that the constraint was turning her on, intensifying all her feelings. She loved it. Loved being bound, being taken, not having a will.

'Oh, oh . . .' she gasped.

'I'm going to spunk in you,' he said, his voice as hard as his cock.

'Do it,' she begged.

She felt his whole body tense. He pushed his cock as deep as it would go, arching his back so it would penetrate as deep as he could get it. She moaned again. Then he pulled it back slightly, found a place and stopped. He waited. With all her strength she squeezed. Deprived of her ability to use her lips, she concentrated on her cunt, squeezing it around the hot flesh inside her, swooning with pleasure as she did. He was as hard as a bone.

'Yes,' he said.

She felt his cock jerk and his spunk splash out into her cunt. In her mind's eye she could see it, pulsing and spurting great gobs of white spunk into the sticky depths of her body. She felt her body trembling, from tip to toe; trembling and quivering, as another orgasm was wrung from her nerves by the hot spunk shooting inside her.

'Oh god,' she screamed, her body stretched taut by her bonds, unable to do anything but cling to his cock and feel her orgasm raking through every nerve she possessed.

It was a long time before the feelings ebbed away, before her body went slack and his cock slipped from her cunt. But he did not untie her.

'You want more?' he asked, pressing his lips into her ear and speaking in a whisper.

'Yes. Yes,' she said passionately, never having wanted anything so much in her life.

He got up off the bed. She heard him crossing the room and opening a cupboard. He came back to the bed.

'This is only the beginning . . .' he said. And it was.

Melinda had lost track of time. Her whole mind was concentrated on the discomfort of her body. Just as in the taxi, her consciousness was restricted to purely physical concerns. She could not think of anything beyond ways of easing the constant aches in her legs and shoulders. She could not begin to think about what was going to happen to her next.

The door opened suddenly, making her start. She hadn't heard any footsteps in the corridor outside. Marion strode into the room. The expression on her face was restored to one of unconcern. She did not look directly into Melinda's eyes.

'You are required,' she said, leaning over to un-buckle the thin strap from the front of the collar. 'Stand up.'

Melinda obeyed. Her aching muscles protested at this sudden activity. She could not suppress a moan.

Marion stood behind her and began freeing her from the rest of the leather harness. If she noticed that the thin leather strap was stained and wet where it had rested between Melinda's thighs, she made no reference to it. She freed Melinda's arms and pulled the collar from her throat, dropping it on the pile of clothes that still lay on the floor. Gingerly, Melinda lowered her arms. The rush of blood to her limbs was a surprisingly pleasant sensation.

Marion went to the inner door in the room and unlocked it. The door revealed a small bathroom. The walls were covered in large white tiles and it con-tained a cubicle shower, a toilet, a wash basin and a small dressing table and chair. It was roughly the same size as the room in which Melinda had been imprisoned: one of the old stables divided in two down the middle.

'Shower. Use the toilet,' Marion ordered.

Melinda walked through into the bathroom. She sat on the loo and peed, not realising her need had been so urgent. Marion stood in the doorway, watch-ing her. Even this most private of activities was to be public from now on.

A little uncertainly, Melinda turned on the shower. Having been deprived of the ability to do anything for herself, even stand up, it suddenly felt strange to be free to reach out and adjust the mixer tap. She stepped under the cascade of water from the powerful shower and let the spray play over her body. It was not a freedom that would last for long, she knew.

'Quickly,' Marion snapped.

Melinda soaped herself with a bar of soap from a little tray at the side of the cubicle, then rinsed the lather away. She stepped out of the shower and took the single bath towel that was on a towel rail by the wash basin. In a few minutes she was dry.

Another woman had entered, and was standing behind Marion, watching Melinda dry herself.

'Ready?' the woman asked. The question was addressed to Marion not Melinda.

'Yes,' Marion said, standing aside to let the woman into the bathroom. She was young, no more than twenty, with long fair hair tied in a ponytail, and a small round face. Her body was small too, short and very slim. She was dressed in a pair of shiny yellow Lycra leggings over a leotard in the same material. The V-neckline of the leotard revealed little cleavage. She was carrying a black plastic box, like a tool box, which she set on the dressing table and opened. Inside a concertina of compartments were stuffed with every description of make-up.

Marion took the towel from Melinda. 'Sit,' she ordered, indicating the chair.

'She's a pretty one,' the make-up woman said. 'Good figure.'

Marion did not reply. Melinda sat on the chair in front of the dressing table.

'How long have I got?'

'They've only just started,' Marion said. She turned, and paused before leaving the room. 'You know you are not permitted to speak,' she said to Melinda. Melinda nodded.

Marion left the two women alone. The outer door of the room slammed shut.

The make-up woman pulled an elasticated towel-

64

ling band over Melinda's forehead to keep the hair off her face. As it went on Melinda's face was tilted back and she noticed the bathroom too had a video camera set in the junction of wall and ceiling. It was pointed at her.

'Now then,' the woman said, like a painter looking at a blank canvas.

The woman began to apply make-up to Melinda's face. She worked quickly, expertly. Eyebrows, eyeliner, mascara, a blusher for her cheeks. It felt strange not to be able to see what she was doing. There was no mirror in the bathroom. The woman worked on her fingernails, coating them with a red varnish, a deep crimson red. She applied the same varnish to Melinda's toes, kneeling on the floor, paying, apparently, not the least attention to Melinda's nakedness. Last of all she applied lipstick, brushing it on thickly.

'Very good,' she said to herself, standing back to admire her work after she'd brushed out Melinda's shining blonde hair. She adjusted the eye shadow slightly on one eye, and added a little more colour to the blusher on one cheek. 'That's it,' she declared, packing the tools of her trade back into the plastic box. She closed it, and without a word walked out of the bathroom, leaving Melinda on her own. She heard the outer door open and close.

Throughout the procedure, Melinda had remained totally still, sitting with her hands folded in her naked lap, except when they had been required for varnishing. The make-up woman had worked on her as if she were inanimate, inert. She had looked at her as a piece of work, but she had not seen her as a person.

Alone, but this time unbound, Melinda did not move. She remained totally passive, as though her body was bound by a thousand invisible cords. That was what she wanted. To move would involve a conscious act, a decision, however trivial. But decisions were no longer hers to make. She had gifted them willingly to someone else.

She looked up into the video camera. She could feel the make-up on her face but had no idea what she looked like. She imagined her lipstick matched the crimson red of her finger and toe nails, but what else had been done to her she did not know. She had been made-up to conform to someone else's idea of how she should appear. Her face, like her body, no longer belonged to her. It was for someone else to determine how she should look, what she should wear, when she bathed, when she used the toilet. None of these decisions belonged to her any more.

To be done to, not to do.

Five

Time passed. With nothing to measure it by, Melinda had no way of knowing for how long, but it dragged by more slowly than when she had been bound in the harness. Then, she had had pain to contend with, to take up the slack. Now, she had nothing but her own determination to remain perfectly still.

The outer door opened.

'Come in here,' Marion's voice ordered.

Melinda obeyed, walking back into the bare room. Marion closed and locked the bathroom door. She had changed her clothes. Her shapely figure was now wrapped in a full-length black velvet evening dress, its halter neck leaving her arms and back completely bare. Her make-up had changed too. Her eyes were much heavier and darker, her mouth a rich red. From the hem of the long dress, the toes of a pair of satin evening shoes glittered with diamanté.

'Put your hands behind your back with your wrists crossed,' Marion said.

Melinda obeyed at once, and gladly. She knew it meant she was going to be bound again. She welcomed it. She was uncomfortable with freedom.

Marion wrapped a white silk rope around Melinda's wrists, tying them tightly together. She produced a black velvet choker. The choker was, in fact, made of leather for strength, and covered in velvet for the sake of appearances. Marion buckled it around Melinda's throat. At the front it had a small chrome ring.

'Turn round to face me,' Marion ordered.

Melinda turned. Marion took a bright chrome leash and clipped it into the ring of the choker. The cold metal hung down between Melinda's breasts. Her nipples instantly puckered to erection. The end of the leash reached the apex of her thighs.

'Put those shoes on.' Marion indicated a pair of black patent leather high heels she had set down on the floor. The heels were precipitous, higher than anything Melinda had worn before. Marion held her arm, knowing she would need support, as she slipped one foot and then the other into the shoes, and gained five inches in height as a result. The shoes tightened her calf muscles and tilted Melinda's pert arse into a distinct pout.

Marion did not release her arm. For a moment she looked into Melinda's eyes. There was something there that excited her. Something she had not seen in the eyes of the other women, the many other women, she had trained for the Master. Melinda displayed no fear, only acceptance. An all-embracing acceptance. She would rebel, Marion knew, one day. One day they would take her too far and she would struggle and beg and plead for them to stop. They all did in the end. But for Melinda, Marion knew, that day might be a long time coming.

Almost without realising what she was doing, she cupped Melinda's breast in her hand, feeling its warmth and weight.

'I want you,' she whispered. And she did. She ached to take her, to try her, to test her submission, to order and command her, to make Melinda her own.

This was not the time, however. She would have to wait for such pleasures. The Master and his guests were waiting, and Marion, in the end, was as much the Master's slave as Melinda. There would be time enough for her own pleasure, Marion told herself. The Master would want it. Want her to teach and explore, to introduce Melinda to sensations she had never experienced before, to submit to a woman's body. Marion felt a surge of passion as she looked at Melinda's fine, proud body; seemingly more naked and exposed by contrast to her own clothed figure. She let her hand fall away from Melinda's breast and pushed such thoughts aside. For the moment, at least.

Picking up the chain leash, Marion pulled Melinda forward.

'Follow me,' she said unnecessarily. Melinda could do nothing else.

Melinda trailed Marion out into the long corridor. The high heels prevented her from taking long strides, but Marion appeared to be aware of this and walked slowly, the leash held in her left hand. Their heels clacked on the wooden floor.

The dress was perfect for her, Melinda thought, as she admired Marion from behind. Her back was flawless, the scapulas of her shoulders well defined, the long line of her spine straight and clear. She moved with grace and elegance, her hips swinging her plum-shaped arse from side to side.

Marion unlocked the outer door into the courtyard. They then walked through into the main house, and out under the double staircase into the marble-floored vestibule. Here, Melinda could hear voices in the distance.

Marion led her through a large reception room dotted with sofas and armchairs, its walls covered with Impressionist paintings, and out into a short hallway panelled in walnut. She stopped outside a pair of doors, also walnut and panelled. Now the voices were loud, the noise of a dinner party in full swing behind the double doors. Glasses and crockery clinked, and laughter rang out. Conversations, one on top of another, created a hubbub of sound.

'Kneel,' Marion said.

Melinda obeyed, but slowly and awkwardly. The height of the shoes and the inability to use her arms made the manoeuvre difficult.

A small brass ring was set in the wall beside the door, at what was now the same height as Melinda's head. Marion threaded the chain of the leash through it, pulling it tight until Melinda's cheek was forced right up against the wall. Knotting the leash securely, Marion stroked Melinda's fine blonde hair once, then turned and entered the dining room, closing the door behind her.

Melinda was alone again. The floor of the hallway was marble; cold and hard against her knees. The leash pulled her over to one side, straining her neck and distributing her weight uncomfortably. She rested her cheek against the panelling, but she could not ease the pain in her knees by straightening up or crouching down. She was half kneeling, with her buttocks a foot above her heels. The position of her arms, tied securely behind her back, pushed her naked breasts out prominently.

Excitement buzzed again through her body. Part of her mind floated away so she could see herself, from somewhere way above, kneeling on the marble floor, naked but for the black shoes and the velvet choker, her buttocks curled, her legs bent double, her thighs thick, the deep cleft of her arse running down to join

70

the crease of her sex. Naked, prone, two feet away from a room full of people. She was wet again. She hoped it would not show, but she feared her juices were already leaking out onto the puffy thick lips of her cunt.

She heard footsteps behind her, but could not turn her head to see who was coming. She felt the brush of air as a man in a tail coat walked past her and opened one of the walnut doors, closing it again behind him. He did not look at her.

A few minutes later the door opened again, flooding the corridor with the full volume of sound from inside. The tail-coated butler emerged. Once again he did not look at Melinda, and strode past her down the hall.

He had left the walnut door ajar, and the gaiety and conversation of the dinner party inside spilled through, together with the smell of expensive cigars, high-class perfumes, and heat. The marble floor made the corridor cold. Melinda could feel a wave of heat radiating from the open door, warming her body.

More footsteps behind her. Two men and two women, followed by the butler. They were all dressed in servants' uniforms. As they passed, one of the women, in a plain black dress and white apron, glanced down at Melinda. Their eyes met for an instant. The woman giggled, nudging the other waitress in the ribs. But her companion did not look down.

The staff went into the dining room and quickly emerged with trays of empty and half-empty dishes, wine glasses and plates of half-eaten desserts. They paid no attention to Melinda. The waitress who had looked before did not look again. Eventually, after several trips, the dining table must have been cleared because the traffic stopped. The walnut door was closed from the inside by the butler. At the same time, a sudden silence descended on the dining room.

Melinda could hear a single voice speaking but could not hear what it was saying. Her physical discomfort was becoming acute. Not only did her knees ache, but her toes, crammed into the shoes and bent by her position, protested at their prolonged constriction. Her back ached too, unable to straighten properly. The pain was the accompaniment to her situation, to her acceptance. It was real, tangible, proof that she would submit. And that, after all, was what she wanted.

The single voice stopped and the butler opened the walnut door again. But conversation was not resumed. There was an expectant silence. The butler bent forward to untie the leash from the brass ring. The sleeve of his jacket brushed Melinda's breast, but he did not look into her eyes, nor did he say anything to her. He merely jerked the leash upward to indicate she was required to stand. Supporting herself with her shoulder against the wall, Melinda struggled to her feet, her knees unlocking with a sharp pang of pain.

For one half-second she saw the butler's eyes on her body, flitting down from the roundness of her breasts to her blonde, wispy pubic hair. He was a middle-aged man, white-haired, with a ramrod straight back and dark hooded eyes. He allowed himself no further indulgence. Pulling on the leash, he turned and led Melinda into the dining room.

Set in the middle of a large spacious room was a huge rectangular dining table laid with white linen. Around it were sitting, in what looked like genuine Chippendale dining chairs, twenty people. At its head sat Walter Hammerton, the Master. One wall of the room was formed entirely of French windows over-

72

looking the garden, which had been lit like a stage set; floodlights under the mature trees, small spotlights in the more colourful shrubs, the lawn a wash of green. To Melinda's right was a gothic fireplace, ablaze with a log fire.

The table was decorated with fresh flowers and silver candalabras burning long white candles. In front of each guest were coffee cups and brandy or dessert wine glasses in leaded crystal. Brandy and port decanters were dotted around the table. Four silver platters were piled with a mountain of every conceivable fruit, and some of the guests still munched on grapes or slices of mango.

Melinda was brought to stand between the fire and the table. All the guests had turned to look at her. She saw Marion sitting two or three seats away from the Master. She also recognised another face. It was the young brunette she had talked to at the country house party who had told her about the X-list. Suddenly, of course, she realised what she had meant. The twenty people at the table, the twenty pairs of eyes trained avidly on her naked body, were on the X-list.

'Good evening, my dear. So glad you could join us,' the Master said, as if addressing a newly arrived guest, and not a naked and enfettered slave.

Melinda did not reply. It was not a question.

'Well, ladies and gentlemen. I think you'll agree, a very beautiful addition to our collection.'

There were murmurs of agreement. Those with their backs to Melinda had pulled their chairs out from the table, and half-turned them so as to get a better view.

'Please walk around the table, my dear, so my guests may examine you more closely.' The Master's eyes gazed into hers for the first time. Immediately, Melinda felt their power. She could not suppress a shiver. Was it excitement or a sudden chill? His eyes were cold, touching her body with ice. She felt her already puckered nipples harden more. She felt her sex throb.

The butler dropped the leash. The chain fell between her breasts, its lower links brushing her thighs.

Slowly she began to walk around the table. There was a mirror to one side of the fireplace and she caught sight of herself in it. She hardly recognised what she saw. The make-up she wore was completely different from anything she had ever done for herself, thick, dark eyes, dark red lipstick. Her hair was brushed differently too. Only her naked body was familiar, her round breasts quivering as she walked, her dark nipples erect, the downy pubic hair hiding little of what lay below it.

'Closer in, my dear,' the Master chided.

Melinda moved towards the table where the guests had turned their chairs. As soon as she was close to them, she walked slowly towards the Master again.

'Not so fast.' A woman caught her by the arm. Melinda stopped. The woman's eyes roamed over her body. She was young, her hair an auburn red. Her shoulders and the tops of her ample breasts were revealed by her tight, strapless white dress. Her hand pinched Melinda's flesh. There was cruelty in her eyes. 'She's very nice,' she said.

The man sitting next to her stroked Melinda's buttocks. 'Nice arse,' he commented.

'Come on,' the Master commanded.

The woman released the arm immediately. Melinda continued up the table. A man, who, like all the others, was dressed in black tie and dinner suit,

74

groped out to feel her tit. His hand grazed her nipple. Another hand felt for her thigh, pinching the long muscle at the front. She did not stop walking. She passed Marion, who did not touch her.

She arrived at the head of the table, wanting to look into the Master's eyes again, but he was not looking at her. He was watching his guests, looking at their reactions. A look passed between him and Marion. A look of desire, Melinda thought enviously.

Melinda walked around the back of the Master's chair and down the other side of the table. More hands groped at her body. She arrived at the young brunette she had talked to at the party.

'So now you know,' she said, smiling broadly. 'I told you you were his type.'

'Is she wet?' a man shouted.

'I can see it,' a woman said.

'Yes, look at her. It's on her thighs. It's running down her thighs.'

'That's sweat,' a woman claimed.

'See if she's wet.' The voice belonged to the Master. His eyes were back on her again.

The man she was passing caught the leash in his hand and brought her to a halt. He jerked the leash down hard so she was forced to bend over, her face inches below his. He was bald, short and fat, with little piggy eyes that danced with his excitement.

'See if she's wet, Sybil,' he said to the woman sitting beside him. She was wearing a bright, lime-green evening dress covered in little glass beads, her ginger hair cut short and brushed with a parting like a man.

Melinda felt Sybil's hand working up between her thighs. She knew what she would find there. Two fingers penetrated roughly into her labia.

'She's soaking,' the woman in green declared triumphantly. She thrust her fingers deep. Involuntarily, Melinda pulled at the leash, but the man held her tight. The fingers left her body. The man released the leash.

'Continue,' the Master ordered calmly.

Melinda circumnavigated the table and arrived back at her starting point next to the butler, who had not moved.

'Well, ladies, gentlemen, the climax of this evening's festivities seems to have arrived. Edward, would you be so kind?'

'Certainly, sir,' the butler said, bowing slightly.

It was his turn to walk around the table. In front of each guest, Melinda saw two small black balls, each inscribed with an identical number in red. The butler took, or was handed, one of these balls from each of the guests and dropped them into a large silver fruit bowl. As he progressed, conversations developed. Melinda heard snatches of comments that were clearly about her. ('Good long legs', 'no, but I like bigger tits', 'what about that tight little arse', 'not much hair on her', 'she's very submissive'.) She noticed that neither Marion nor the Master was talking, but they exchanged glances. There were no black balls in front of the Master.

Finally, all the black balls were collected.

'Marion . . .' the Master said.

Marion got up from the table. Melinda saw that she had a long strip of black satin in her hand. She came up behind Melinda, the velvet of her dress brushing her naked back, and slipped the silk over Melinda's eyes, plunging her into darkness. Melinda felt a surge of passion, transported back instantly to another time, another darkness, when all she could do was see and feel. She managed not to moan, but she swayed slightly and felt Marion's hands on her shoulders, steadying her. The silk was tied tight. She could feel it pressing against her eyelids, cold and slippery.

'Now, my dear,' she heard the Master say. She heard him get up from his chair and take the silver bowl from the butler's hand. Melinda did not need to see to know who came to stand beside her. It was as though his whole body radiated an aura of power. It made her feel weak. He raised his hand to the back of her neck. In the blackness it felt as though he were touching her most intimate parts. His hand seemed to be charged with sexual electricity. She swayed back against Marion again. This time she could not suppress a moan.

'Now, my dear, as is our custom, you must choose. Dip your head, and take one of the balls in your lips.' His hand pressed her neck down until she felt her face being thrust into the silver bowl he held in his other hand. She felt the balls against her face. They were hard and heavy. She opened her lips and groped around, trying to suck one into her mouth. It was not easy. The balls skidded away from her.

'Come on. Don't keep the guests waiting in suspense,' the Master chided, his hand firm at the back of her neck.

She managed to capture a ball with her lips, suck it into her mouth and hold her head up.

'Well, we have a winner,' the Master announced.

Marion's fingers extracted the ball from Melinda's mouth and handed it to the Master.

'Ladies and gentlemen, the winner is number sixteen.'

Melinda heard a whoop of victory and a loud burst of applause. She felt the Master and Marion return

77

to their seats, and heard the clink of glasses and words of congratulations and envy. She heard the walnut doors open, and the smell of fresh coffee being poured. She smelt the sulphur of matches and the rare tobacco of cigars as they were cut and lit.

Conversation turned to other things. For a moment she was forgotten. She had ceased to exist, inanimate again. She wondered if anyone was still looking at her, if eyes were glancing her way, roaming her naked body. It had been an elaborate way to draw a winning number and the assembled company seemed to have enjoyed it greatly. But what was going to happen to her now?

'I'm going,' a man's voice said above the din of conversation. His announcement was greeted with a cheer.

'You know the way?' the Master asked.

'Yes.'

'Marion can – '

'No. I'll find it.'

'Ladies and gentlemen, a toast to our winner,' the Master said.

Glasses clinked. Applause broke out. Then the hand clapping turned to a regular beat measuring the winner's strides across the room. It was only then, as Melinda felt a hand pick up the chain leash from the top of her thighs, that she realised she had not been brought to the room merely to pick the winner. She was the prize.

She felt herself being pulled forward. She was sure she would stumble with the blindfold still on, but dared not ask for it to be removed. She concentrated hard on putting one foot in front of the other. She felt the coldness of the hallway outside, as the rhythmical clapping faded and the dining room doors were closed.

On the marble floor she could hear the man's shoes, but they were not alone. She could hear another pair of high heels, besides her own, clacking on the tiles. The man was leading her by the leash, but a woman was following. It was not Marion. Melinda could smell her perfume and it was different from the one Marion was wearing; much heavier, more flowery.

Melinda felt the marble floor give way to carpet. They turned a corner and she bumped her shoulder against the wall.

'Careful,' a woman's voice said.

They seemed to walk on forever, turning left and right until Melinda lost all sense of direction. In the blackness behind the satin blindfold, Melinda's heart was beating rapidly. Where were they taking her? What were they going to do to her? She tried to push aside the excitement that crowded her mind.

Finally, she felt the leash go slack and a hand on her shoulder brought her to a halt. She heard a door being opened in front of her.

'This is it,' the man said.

'Oh, this is definitely it,' the woman said. Melinda felt her brush past into the room. Then she was pulled forward. She heard the door close. The leash was dropped to hang between her breasts again.

The room was warm, much warmer than the corridors.

'Look at all this stuff,' the man said.

'All the toys you could ever want,' the woman added.

'This is the only toy I want.' Melinda felt a hand on her hip.

'I can't believe we won. We never have before. Not in all these years,' the woman said.

'So let's enjoy it.'

'You enjoy it. I'm only allowed to watch, remember? If I'd won, you'd have had to watch,' the woman said with obvious feeling.

'Thank God you didn't,' the man said with equally obvious relief.

'Why?'

'Because, Jesus, I'd never have been able to stand it. You and her together. I'd have had to do something.'

'And you know what would have happened if you had?'

'Don't remind me.'

'That poor guy. How long ago was that?'

'Alfie you mean?' the man asked.

'Yes.'

'Did you see him tonight. He looked petrified he might win again.'

'After what the Master had those girls do to him, I'm not surprised.'

'So behave yourself,' the man warned.

'Don't worry.'

Melinda heard a rustle of clothing and the noise of a zip. She heard shoes being kicked off.

'She's very controlled, isn't she?' the woman said.

'Very.'

'So passive . . .'

'Remember that one in the winter?'

'God yes. It took two men just to get her into the room, even with that body harness.'

'I'm glad I didn't win that night,' the man said. Melinda heard the sound of trousers being dropped to the floor.

'Well, look at you. Look at the size of you.'

'Don't touch it,' he warned.

'I know, I know the rules . . .'

Melinda felt him coming nearer. He came round behind her. She felt the tip of his penis brushing the cheeks of her arse as he reached up to the knot of the blindfold. His penis was hard and hot. Almost unconsciously she pushed her body back against it, desperate for the contact she had been deprived of for so long. She wanted to touch and be touched. Her body was liquid again, her mind filled with the image of his cock nudging its way down between her legs. Only now did she realise how she longed for sex.

She felt the blindfold loosen and fall away. She screwed up her eyes against the light. Gradually she opened them. She was in a small square room, its walls and floor, even the door, covered in the same thick, light biege carpeting. Immediately in front of her, sitting in an upright wooden chair, was the woman in the lime-green dress with the masculine hair style, who had penetrated her body at the dinner table. She was sitting with her legs crossed, her eyes locked on Melinda's body. Though she was plump, she was not unattractive. Her body looked Rodinesque: rich round curves; pillows of flesh; her complexion smooth and unwrinkled.

What they had said was true. The room was full of toys. Sex toys. Hanging from one of the carpeted walls was every description of dildo and vibrator, every type of whip or paddle. There were shelves of leather harnesses, handcuffs, chains and ropes. There were masks and hoods in rubber and leather. At one end of the room was a large wardrobe. Its door was partly open, and Melinda could see it was full of leather and rubber clothing. There was a rack of high-heeled shoes in unusually large sizes, and several wigs on wig blocks.

The room had no conventional furniture. In the middle of the floor was a slatted wooden frame the size of a double bed, covered with a thin mattress. Leather cuffs were chained to the frame at each of its corners, and there were metal rings, clearly intended to be used to fasten further bonds, all round the frame. To one side of the 'bed' was what looked like a small vaulting horse, its top padded and covered in suede, straps screwed to opposite sides of its box-like structure, just above the ground. Standing against one wall was a narrow cupboard, the width of a coffin, its door open. Inside, Melinda could see heavy leather straps. The door was provided with a hole at the level a penis would be situated if a man were strapped inside. In the furthest corner of the room was a metal cage no more than waist high.

Melinda shuddered. Presumably, she thought, the carpeting on the walls helped to muffle the sound from the hapless victims.

The woman had seen Melinda's reaction. 'Don't worry,' she said, 'my husband's not into any of this.'

'Oh, I don't know, Sybil,' the man said. He moved out from behind Melinda so she saw him for the first time. It was the bald, short fat man with piggy eyes. Naked now, his penis bobbed below his well-upholstered belly. It was out of all proportion to his size, a big sword of flesh, its uncircumcised glans still partly covered by his foreskin. 'We could put her over the whipping horse.'

'That's not what you want,' his wife said knowingly. 'Come on, Brian, get on with it.'

The man stood in front of Melinda. Delicately, he took one of her nipples between his fingers. 'Lovely tits,' he said, almost to himself. He pinched the nipple, but not hard. He did the same to the other nipple, then ran his hand down to her soft pubic hair, his forefinger just nudging into the runnel of her sex. 'Oh, feels soft. She's still wet.'

His finger, just the one finger, was buried between her legs now. He rotated his hand from side to side, making the finger turn against Melinda's soft labia. She felt it moisten with her juices. He pulled it away and sucked on it enthusiastically.

'Lay on your back on the bed,' he said, his voice husky with passion.

Melinda obeyed immediately, her body throbbing with excitement. She had not had sex for a week, because somehow the Master had prevented it. Though she had come twice today, it was not as the result of any human contact. That's what she yearned for, that was the pulsing urgent need that filled her body. She wanted cock; hard, hot cock. She hoped he wouldn't tease her. She didn't think she could stand that.

She sat on the edge of the bed and managed to squirm herself backward until she was lying in the middle of the mattress. With her hands still tied behind her she was forced to arch her back. She opened her legs wide without being told to do so.

'Look at her. She's begging for it,' Sybil said.

It was true. If she had been allowed to speak she would have begged. Brian stood by the edge of the bed, one hand circling his cock and wanking it lazily. Melinda could see its gnarled veins engorged with blood. A tear of fluid formed at the slit of the urethra. Using his finger, the man spread the fluid over the smooth pink flesh, pulling his foreskin right back. He moaned and his body shuddered.

'I should beat her,' he said.

'You'd never last,' Sybil replied. 'Look at you. If you're not careful you'll spunk before you get inside her.'

'Don't worry.'

Brian walked to the foot of the bed and removed Melinda's shoes. He looked up her long legs as he did so, then knelt on the bed beside her. Suddenly, Melinda heard a tiny but familiar noise. She looked up. In each corner of the room was a video camera. One of them had just refocused its lens, zooming in on the action. They were being watched. That was how the Master would know what went on in the room. He was watching now, Melinda could feel it. All the dinner guests. Watching the show. Marion, the young brunette. Looking at her sex, open and wet.

The man was stroking her thigh, his fingers running down to the knee then up until his fingernails just brushed against her labia. Melinda moaned at the touch. Any touch was welcome, precious.

'Suck it,' he ordered.

'You wouldn't be able to take it,' his wife chided.

Brian replied by putting his finger to his lips to indicate the need for her silence.

Melinda rolled on her side and slithered down the bed, moving her body like a snake until her face was alongside his cock. Eagerly she opened her mouth and sucked him in. He was big. He filled her mouth, her lips stretched to accommodate his width. She felt her body melting. She had never wanted cock more in her life. She pushed her head forward to impale herself on it, get it deep, deep into her throat. She knew she was going to come. She could not possibly stop herself. Too much provocation. Too much excitement.

Her clitoris throbbed, her body churned. She sucked on his great hard stem of flesh and revelled in the feeling; coming now, not on some strange irritant,

84

nor on a leather strap, but on the overwhelming feeling of having a real cock deep in her mouth. She got what she wanted.

'Ah . . . ah . . .' she moaned, gagged by the cock, her body trembling out of control. As the orgasm raked through her, she tried to free her hands, knowing she could not, knowing that the thick white rope biting into her wrists as she struggled would drive her higher, reminding her of the helplessness she craved. Her body was shaking, all control gone, except in her mouth where she sucked on the cock like a limpet.

With an audible plop, Brian pulled his cock away. Immediately, he took her by the shoulder and threw her back on the bed, then fell on top of her. His belly flopped down on her and, as his cock slipped between her thighs, his hands found her tits, squeezing them tight. He arched his back and his cock slid into her liquid, smouldering cunt, pumping instantly up and down on the river of her juices.

She was coming again. Or was it just the same orgasm driven so high that it felt like another? She didn't know or care. She used all her strength to force her sex down onto his cock. She wanted every inch, every fraction. His considerable weight pressed down on her body and on her arms still bound behind her back. She felt the chain of the leash, trapped between their bodies, digging into their flesh. She raised her legs in the air and felt his balls banging into her arse.

He was coming. She could feel his cock tensing, pulsing out of control. But he did not stop pumping it into her. She felt it jerking as spunk spat out, but he pumped on and on regardless, until all his spunk was out, until it too formed a river inside her, until she felt wetness running out of her and over her thighs and his balls. With one final effort he shook his entire body – like a dog out of water – as if to rid himself of any last remaining spunk. That was the moment her orgasm broke again, flooding her nerves with sensation just as her sex was flooded with spunk, making her muscles lock, her legs wrapped around his thighs, clinging to him, her arms unable to do the same.

It was feeling his dead weight rolling off her that made her open her eyes. She found herself looking straight into the eyes of his wife. She was staring at them both with a crazy, wild expression on her face. She had extracted one of her breasts from the lime green dress and was tweaking its nipple between her thumb and forefinger. Her other hand was up her skirt, awkwardly trying to gain access to her sex.

Melinda saw one of the video cameras move onto Sybil, its lens turning to get a close-up.

Sybil had never seen her husband so aroused. She would have loved to have joined them on the bed, sucked all the juices from that delicious wet sex, so open and exposed. But she dared not. She knew the rules. She knew what the Master would do to her if she broke them.

It was not against the rules to touch herself. It was not against the rules to strip off the lime-green dress covered with little glass beads. It was not against the rules to turn her back to the camera, bend over the chair she had been sitting on and let the Master – and all his guests – see her. She wore flesh-coloured stockings held up by thin white suspenders. Her lacy French knickers were white too. She wanted to give him a show. Her body was not lithe and slim but her ample, round plumpness was nothing to be ashamed of. Many men found it attractive, liked the fullness of her figure.

She caressed her big fleshy buttocks, smoothing the

white silk of the knickers against the curves, before pulling them slowly down. Her pubis was hairy, with tight ginger curls. She let her fingers fall to her labia, intending to tease them gently, let the Master see her playing with herself. But she couldn't. Her need was too urgent. At the first touch of her fingers her body demanded more. She had no control. What she had witnessed had aroused her too much for subtle games.

Bending over further she drove two fingers into her sex, while a third slid up to her clitoris. Her clitoris was hard and swollen and tender. She moaned. She knew she would come. It was as though she was swimming in a sea of provocation. All around her was sex, and images of sex. The beautiful blonde lying on the bed – the woman she yearned to ravish – her hands still bound. The images in her mind of how they had looked, fucking for all they were worth. Sybil had seen the look on the blonde's face, the ecstasy and the joy. That's what Sybil wanted. As she felt her orgasm begin, as it started to take over her body, as its rhythm dictated her every movement, controlled her, led her, she looked into Melinda's eyes and they stared back at her. *She wants me too*, Sybil thought. Her fingers pressed hard, one final time, deep into her body, hard against her clitoris, and felt her nerves convulse as her orgasm broke and her eyes rolled back into exploding blackness. She groaned, a long deep animal voice, her whole body locked as the waves of sensation engulfed it.

'Stand up.'

Melinda must have fallen asleep. The voice started her awake. She was alone in the room, still lying on the thin mattress.

87

'Stand up,' the voice repeated.

Melinda struggled to consciousness. She squirmed to the edge of the bed and managed to get to her feet, focusing on the woman who stood before her.

The woman was young, a tall blonde, though her hair was a different shade from Melinda's; not as light and flaxen. She was dressed in black leather; a tight fitting V-necked leather leotard under a short, equally tight leather skirt. She wore knee-length black boots with a high spiked heel, but otherwise her legs were bare, though they were, like the rest of her, well tanned. Around her waist a wide belt was fitted, with two or three stiff leather pouches buttoned at the front, and, hanging from a loop, what could only be a whip. But it was not like any whip Melinda had ever seen. Its thick handle was made of braided black leather, suspended from which were a dozen or more thin leather thongs no more than twelve inches long. Each thong was knotted in several places along its length.

On the left-hand side of the leotard, just above the breast, was a small silver brooch, upon which had been etched the name 'HERA'.

Hera did not look at Melinda. Her expression was one of indifference, bordering on contempt.

'Turn around,' she ordered.

Melinda obeyed, her sleepiness gone. As soon as her back was turned, Hera began unlacing the white silk rope that had held her hands. Melinda felt the blood surge back as she dropped her arms to her sides.

'Follow me,' Hera said, not making any attempt to pick up the leash that still hung between Melinda's naked breasts and brushed against her pubic hair.

As Melinda had been blindfolded on her way in,

she had no idea what to expect outside the bizarrely furnished room. She found herself in a short corridor with several doors on each side. Each door was of a different design. The walls of the corridor were stone, like the dungeon of a castle.

Hera led the way down the passageway. Melinda could hear a voice coming from one of the other rooms, and Hera stopped outside its door. A loud thwack was immediately followed by a muffled moan. Melinda saw Hera smile. It was a strange smile, a crooked smile, one side of her mouth creased higher than the other. Another thwack rent the air.

They continued to the end of the corridor and out into the main house. Soon, they were crossing the covered courtyard. Hera punched the numbers into the computer lock and the door of the stable block sprung open.

This time they did not go right to the end of the passageway, but stopped about halfway down. Hera punched numbers into the computer lock of a door bearing the number 8 in white script. She stood aside for Melinda to enter first.

The room was identical to the one in which Melinda had first been bound. There was one inner door and no windows. The only difference was that this room had a mattress lying in one corner, and the floor was covered in a thick cream linoleum.

Hera opened the door to the bathroom, which was identical to the one Melinda had used before, with exactly the same furnishings. Quickly, she removed the velvet choker and leash, the leather of the leotard brushing against Melinda's breasts. Melinda felt a surge of passion. Any contact was precious.

Melinda was permitted to shower and use the toilet. A toothbrush and toothpaste had been provided. As soon as she had dried herself, Hera led her back into the outer room and locked the bathroom door. Melinda had not noticed the object lying on the mattress. Hera stooped to pick it up. Hanging from a thin leather belt, two metal chains were attached to a thick metal block. Two further chains hung from the other end of the block.

Hera strapped the leather belt securely around Melinda's waist.

'Open your legs,' she ordered.

Standing in front of her, she reached between Melinda's thighs and caught the chains, pulling them forward. Melinda felt the coldness of the metal on either side of her buttocks. The metal block fitted neatly between her thighs. It was at least an inch thick and concave on two sides. The concavity fitted it against Melinda's thigh, its length covering the whole of her sex from her anus to her clitoris, the metal being curved to follow the contours of her body. On its inner surfaces, the metal had been raised in little sharp peaks like the metal of a rasp. The chains were welded to the front and back. Hera pulled the two chains hanging from the front and clipped them into the leather belt. The chains followed the crease of Melinda's pelvis, where her thighs joined her belly.

It was uncomfortable. At its narrowest point, where the two concave sides met, it was at least two inches wide. It prevented Melinda from closing her legs. If she tried, the metal cut into her tender flesh. She knew at once why she was made to wear it.

'Take off the shoes. Lie on the bed with your hands above your head.' Hera's voice betrayed not a hint of sympathy.

Melinda obeyed. The metal block bit into her thigh as she manoeuvred herself into position.

Kneeling by the mattress, Hera took a pair of handcuffs from one of the pouches at her waist. She clipped them around Melinda's wrists. Set into the wall an inch or two above the level of the bedding was a large metal ring. Using a small padlock, Hera secured the handcuffs to the ring.

'To stop you playing with yourself,' Hera stated with obvious pleasure, her mouth curling into that peculiar crooked smile. She stood up and went to the door, taking the velvet choker and high heels with her. 'Sleep well,' she said sardonically as she swung the cell door closed.

The lights went out as Melinda heard the dead-lock turn. The room was plunged into total darkness.

Melinda lay uncomfortably. She tried to lie on her side so she could rest her head against her forearm but in this position her legs were forced together and the unyielding metal dug into the soft flesh of her thighs. The only way she could lie with any comfort was on her back with her legs open and her head between her outstretched arms. This put a strain on her shoulders but was the least uncomfortable of any of the positions she tried.

Remarkably perhaps, she was not tired. Her mind raced with thoughts, feelings and images. Walter Hammerton had taken her at her word. She had told him her fantasy and he had accepted it, had taken her submission for granted. She had been bound, as she was now, but only symbolically. The real bonds had been of her own making. She had wanted to show him, and herself, that she would not flinch, that she would do and say exactly what she was told. That was what would give her the greatest pleasure. And it had. Beyond her wildest imaginings. And now she was committed, now she was enslaved. There was no turning back. This was the first night of 365 nights in which where, how and when she slept – like everything else in her life – was to be determined by someone else. By the Master or one of his delegates. Her will had been taken away, surgically amputated, the moment she had walked through the front door.

The response of her body had not surprised her. Over the years, she had introduced Mark to her ways, got him to be her master, to bind her and use her. But that was not like this. To Mark it had been a game, a sex game. And she, ultimately, had still been in control; she still had to guide him as to what he should do. He had no natural talent for it. But this, this was reality, and not a game; and a reality she did not control at all. Now she was only an object. The door could open now, in an hour, in a week, in a month, whenever they chose. The choice had nothing to do with her. She had no idea what to expect, except they would demand her total obedience.

She had not realised how much she would miss being touched, held, embraced. She had been touched of course, but only as an object, only to be examined, as when she walked around the dining room table; or to be used, as Brian had on that bare mattress. To them she was not a person, just a thing. She needed more than that, she wanted to be caressed and held. Human contact.

She knew why, of course. Now she had been deprived of her will; now she was an object to be moved around at someone else's will; now her thoughts, her opinions, her desires, counted for nothing, for less than nothing; now there was not the slightest question of what she wanted; there was only her body. All she could do was feel. It had started in the taxi. Whatever they had used to irritate her body had worked perfectly. Instead of sitting thinking of what she was about to do, her last act of will, they had even taken that away from her. All she had been allowed was to think of her body, its discomfort, and then, rapidly, its pleasure.

She wanted to be touched, because that was the only contact she was permitted now. No conversation. No meeting of minds. No discussion or argument. Human contact was narrowed to flesh on flesh.

No wonder her appetite for sex seemed insatiable. It was all she had.

Was that why she so badly wanted to touch herself? Had the Master known that was how she would feel, and acted to prevent it? If the cold metal – it seemed to absorb no heat from her body at all – would have allowed it she would have used her thighs to squeeze her clitoris. That would have been enough in her current state. She wouldn't need fingers. But the metal kept her thighs apart. She tried to push herself down on the metal itself, but the surface was so pitted and sharp it brought not the slightest hint of pleasure.

The more she realised there was nothing she could do to touch her throbbing, swollen clitoris, the more she wanted to. She tried to relax, tried to forget her need, the hot pulses that swam up from between her legs, but she could not. She could not ignore the images that continued to crowd into her mind. Most of all she saw herself walking naked around the dining table, the hands pawing at her, the Master's eyes watching his guests' reaction to her body. Everything excited her, everything that had happened. It played over and over in her head like a video loop. It was torture.

And, she knew, it was a torture the Master had specifically arranged.

Six

The fluorescent light panel hummed and flickered hesitantly before it lit the room consistently with its bright white light. Melinda woke with a start. The computer lock on the door sprung open, and almost before she knew what was happening, a woman, dressed identically to the woman who had brought her to the cell last night, was kneeling by the mattress.

'Very nice,' she said, looking at Melinda's naked body. 'I'm surprised they didn't whip you.'

Melinda blinked the sleep from her eyes, and read the name on the silver brooch pinned to the leather leotard: 'CYBELE'. She was a big woman, with strong, powerful thighs and well-muscled arms that looked as though they were exercised regularly and hard. Her hair, a mousy brown, was cut very short, revealing a neck that was also thick with well-trained muscle. She was a picture of health, her fitness making her skin glow and her blue eyes bright.

She was unhooking the chains from the leather belt that held the metal block. It fell onto the mattress between Melinda's open legs.

'Roll over,' Cybele ordered.

Relieved at last to be able to close her legs, Melinda rolled onto her stomach, the handcuffs twisting against the metal ring.

Cybele unbuckled the leather belt. 'That's better, isn't it?'

'Yes, mistress,' Melinda said with relief.

Cybele's hand stroked the roundness of Melinda's pert apple-shaped arse.

'You're new, aren't you?'

'Yes, mistress.'

'Very beautiful.' Her hand delved down into the cleft of Melinda's buttocks. Her fingers were not gentle. She levered Melinda's thighs apart until she could feel her labia. She handled them roughly, but did not attempt to penetrate beyond.

'Get up.'

'I can't, mistress,' Melinda said in alarm. Her hands were still locked to the ring in the wall.

'Get up,' Cybele repeated, her fingers pinching and nipping at Melinda's sex.

'I can't, mistress,' Melinda said.

'You dare to contradict me?' Cybele got to her feet.

'No, mistress, but I ...' Melinda struggled. She managed to get her knees up under her body.

'I don't want to hear your excuses.' Cybele had unhooked the whip from her belt. It was identical to the one Hera had carried, a braid handle with numerous short knotted lashes. 'Weren't you told to obey without question?'

'Yes, mistress.' Melinda had managed to struggle to her feet but, with her wrists still bound at the level of her ankles, she was bent over double.

'You see. You can get up. How dare you contradict me!'

The tight curves of Melinda's arse pointed at her tormentor. Melinda know what the woman intended. Cybele raised her whip and lashed it down on Melinda's unprotected rump. A blaze of heat and pain exploded across the creamy white flesh. Another stroke followed immediately, then a third and fourth in quick succession. The little thongs of the whip curled into all the nooks and crannies of Melinda's body, down into the cleft of her arse, even lashing the top of her labia and the puckered corona of her anus.

Melinda hardly felt the pain. The heat the whipping produced spread through her so rapidly it overwhelmed any other feeling. It excited her. But what excited her most was not the physical feeling, but the mental image. This was what she wanted. She wanted to be whipped. She welcomed it. She wanted her arse marked with welts. She would wear them proudly. The symbols of her status, her obedience, her submission. She hoped the marks would be deep so the Master would see them. She hoped the Master had ordered her punishment. She wanted to cry out for Cybele to whip her harder, longer, but she knew she could not.

On the sixth stroke, Cybele stopped. Her hand caressed the reddened flesh she had created. The touch was more painful than the whip had been. Melinda winced.

'Sensitive little thing, aren't we?' Cybele mocked.

Melinda said nothing, realising too late that it was a question, lost in the unaccustomed sensations that were flowing through her body.

'Aren't we?' Cybele repeated, reinforcing the question by slapping her hand down hard on Melinda's left buttock.

'Yes, mistress,' Melinda managed to intone, the slap generating another wave of feeling that threatened to overwhelm her.

Cybele sensed her reaction. She rubbed her hand over the reddened arse again, harder this time, making Melinda rock from side to side. Then she pushed herself against Melinda's body, her hands slipping around to hold her at the top of her hips. She pressed against her rhythmically as if fucking her like a man, the little leather skirt bouncing against Melinda's rump.

Suddenly, Cybele stopped herself. What had started as a game was getting too difficult to control. And she had to remain in control.

Taking the key of the handcuffs from one of the pouches on her belt, Cybele knelt to release Melinda's wrists. There would be more time later. Perhaps the Master would allow her to indulge herself with his new helot. She sincerely hoped so.

Cybele unlocked the bathroom door. But she could not resist one final command, a precursor of what was to come, if not with her, then with one of the other women in the Master's employ.

'Kiss me,' she said.

Melinda had never kissed a woman before, not on the mouth. A momentary rebellion flared. She hesitated. Why didn't Cybele just take what she wanted, pull her into an embrace, force her mouth down on hers? Instead, she stood in the bathroom doorway, a knowing smile playing on her lips.

'If I have to repeat myself it will be bad for you,' she said quietly.

Melinda took the two steps towards her. Pushing aside any feeling but the desire to obey, she angled her head to one side, raised herself on her toes and pressed her lips against Cybele's mouth. Cybele's arms, those strong powerful arms, wound around her back and up to her neck, holding Melinda's head firmly to allow no escape. But Melinda wanted none. Not now. As her tongue probed Cybele's mouth, as their lips squirmed against each other, her reluctance disappeared. Her arms encircled Cybele, her naked body writhed against the leather uniform, suddenly relishing the contact. It felt so different from kissing a man, excitingly different. The mouth was softer, more open, more receptive somehow. She felt Cybele's tongue pushing into her mouth, and experienced a flood of passion.

Cybele broke away. She smiled that knowing smile again. 'That's enough,' she said. 'Use the bathroom now.'

She had sensed Melinda's feelings, knew she had created a need in her. It would be torture for her to have to stop what had been so easily started. But Melinda was not there to be pleasured, not yet at least.

Melinda hesitated for a second time, rebellion growing again. The kiss had left her breathless; hot and wet and aching; aching for more contact; more of being held tight in those strong arms. She wanted to throw herself on Cybele; devour her; taste the pleasures the kiss had hinted at; the pleasures she had never experienced, never chosen, but now, so suddenly craved. But something stopped her. Something profound. Something that held her back as tightly as if she had been bound. Her indenture was sealed. There was only one precept: obedience. What she wanted, she reminded herself firmly, was no longer to be considered.

She walked past Cybele into the bathroom, hoping she would reach out and pull her back into her arms, but knowing she would not. In the shower cubicle, she managed to slip a finger between her legs and feel her sex. It was wet, as she knew it would be. She ran the water cold to try to distract herself from her body's evident needs.

As she cleaned her teeth, she heard the outer door open. The make-up woman exchanged pleasantries with Cybele, before putting her black plastic box down on the dressing table. She was wearing Lycra leggings and a leotard again, this time in a shiny dark blue.

Melinda sat in the dressing-room chair without being told. The woman began her work, cleaning off the make-up Melinda had not washed away last night, then replacing it. She looked at Melinda only as was required for her work, focusing only on the areas she worked on. Melinda's body had not been stilled by the cold water. It was still throbbing with the taste and shape and feel of Cybele's mouth. It fluttered with expectation, like some young girl on her first date not knowing what was going to happen next. Something was definitely going to happen. They would not go to the trouble of making her up unless something was planned. Or would they?

Cybele had disappeared. Just as the make-up woman was finishing, she returned with a breakfast tray containing a croissant, orange juice and coffee.

The make-up woman packed up her box and left. Though she had no way of knowing, Melinda had the impression the make-up was less heavy than it had been last night.

'Eat,' Cybele ordered. Melinda needed no further encouragement. She had eaten nothing since yesterday lunchtime. She demolished the contents of the tray.

'Put these on,' Cybele said the moment she was finished, dropping a cellophane packet of stockings into Melinda's lap.

Melinda opened the flap of the packet. She had undone thousands of packets like this in her life but,

100

even after such a short period in the house, it felt strange to be doing this. It was mundane. It belonged to her other life, the life where she was free, the life she had left behind.

As she extracted the sheer, gauzy nylon from the packet, she realised her hand was shaking. The stockings were black hold-ups, with a wide lacy welt.

Holding her leg out in front of her, she pointed her toe and fitted it into the nylon she had bunched up in her hand. The nylon had been woven with Lycra to give the stockings a slippery, shiny feel, but it also made them feel tight as she unravelled them over her legs. She pulled them to midway up her thigh until the band of elastic under the lacy welt gripped her. She pulled it higher, until the welt almost touched the crease of her sex, the nylon below stretched taut. Raising her other leg she repeated the process, the sheer material transforming her legs, moulding and shaping them, holding them tightly, its sheen like a coat of translucent paint.

Cybele led her out of the bathroom and locked the door behind them. The nylon of the stockings rasped against each other as Melinda moved.

'Now put those on,' Cybele ordered. A red satin dress with long matching gloves and a pair of red high heels lay on the mattress. She picked up the dress and handed it to Melinda. It was tight-fitting, strapless and knee length. Its zip was already undone. Melinda stepped into it. The bodice was tight and boned. It fitted her breasts perfectly, forcing them upward and together to form a deep cleft of cleavage as Cybele pulled the long zip up. The skirt too shaped itself to the rich curves of Melinda's hips and the pertness of her arse.

'And the gloves,' Cybele said, not picking them up this time.

101

The gloves were in the same red satin. Melinda pulled them on over her fingers, smoothing them up her arms with a great deal of tugging and effort. Like the stockings, they seemed to have an elasticated band under the top edge that held them tightly in the middle of her upper arm. With her arms at her sides the gloves were at the same level as the top of the dress. It made the total bareness of the flesh above seem, by contrast to the shiny red satin, that much more naked.

Cybele indicated the shoes. Though their heels were high they were not as high as the shoes she had worn last night. Melinda slipped her feet into the red leather.

'Very pretty,' Cybele commented. 'Follow me.'

Melinda was expecting bondage, expecting to be bound in some way. Clearly now, they expected her to be bound by her obedience.

They set off down the corridor and through the covered courtyard into the main house. Marion was waiting in the vestibule under the double staircase. She wore a grey business suit and a white blouse. Melinda could see the lacy white bra holding Marion's ample bosom. For the first time in her life she experienced a sensation of desire. She was looking at Marion with new eyes. She wanted her.

Without a word, Marion brought her to a halt and inspected her, walking around her as if she were an animal in a farm show. Cybele was dismissed with a wave of her hand.

Marion opened the front door. Outside, a Jaguar saloon waited, its engine running, its nearside passenger door held open by a uniformed chauffeur.

'Get in,' Marion ordered.

Melinda walked out into the open air, just as she

had walked into the house last night. She was ostensibly just as free, unbound, unfettered. But as she walked out into the bright sunny morning she could not have felt more totally enslaved.

Stooping, she climbed into the car and sat on the leather seat. It was not an ordinary saloon, she realised. The car had been stretched. The passenger compartment was double the usual size, with jump seats folded away in front and a glass divider isolating the driver from the passengers. A deep pile wool rug carpeted the floor.

Marion got into the car. Melinda's eyes caught a flash of stocking-top under the skirt. Marion's stockings were a slate grey.

The chauffeur closed the door and got behind the wheel. The car pulled off down the driveway, the electric gates opening magically as they approached.

Marion's attitude to Melinda seemed to have changed again. Now it was simply as though Melinda did not exist. She made no attempt to speak to her or look at her. She gazed out of the window. In twenty minutes they were in the city. The Jaguar pulled up outside a modern, attractively designed block, four or five storeys high. A discreet logo over the main door, in Art Deco lettering, announced it as the 'HAMMERTON CORPORATION'. The chauffeur opened the nearside door.

'Out,' Marion snapped.

Melinda climbed out and stood by the car. Marion followed her. Passers-by stared. A woman as beautiful as Melinda in a tight strapless satin dress would draw attention at any time, but in the middle of the morning it was positively bizarre.

'Follow me,' Marion said. Melinda was used to the words now, denying her even the tiniest of independent thought. Marion led the way, not through the main doors, but to the side of the building where a long narrow passage separated one building from the next. Halfway down the alleyway, she took a key from the pocket of the suit and unlocked a single door set in the yellow brick walls.

She took Melinda's arm and led her through the door, locking it again behind them. They were in a small hallway, at the end of which was a lift. Marion pressed the lift button and its metal door opened immediately. Inside, the control panel indicated only two floors. Marion pressed the top button. The lift ascended rapidly to what Melinda judged to be the top of the building.

Marion led her out into a large and expensively decorated anteroom done in modernised Art Deco. Ash panelled walls were inlaid with shallow S-shapes. Electric lights set in wedges of opaque glass were regularly spaced around the room, and gave it a warm glow. The thick carpet was patterned in the same style, pastel shapes contrasting an angular black design.

There were three doors. Marion led Melinda over to the largest of the three and knocked on it twice.

'Come,' a voice pronounced immediately.

Marion opened the door and indicated that Melinda should go first. The larger room beyond was also designed in Art Deco, displaying the same extravagant use of wood. At its centre was an enormous oval conference table, built from the finest ash and inlaid with delicate marquetry in a pattern mirroring that on the walls. High-backed chairs in a design that looked as if they might be Bauhaus originals, surrounded the table.

Twelve men sat in the chairs. Walter Hammerton sat at its head. He was smiling at Melinda.

104

'Charming, charming. Gentlemen, may I present the woman in red . . .'

The assembled company laughed politely.

'Come over here, my dear.'

Melinda walked over the thick carpet, its pattern a continuation of the one in the anteroom. The men's eyes watched her walk.

Taking her wrist, the Master pulled her around to stand next to his chair, facing down the table.

'My latest acquisition,' he announced. Like a painting. An object, a chattel. He released her wrist. For a moment he stroked her iron-flat satin-covered navel. Then both his hands returned to the papers in front of him. 'Now we have to make a decision in relation to the proposed rights issue. Could you let us have the latest estimates of the brokerage costs, Gordon?'

A man at the far end of the table started reading from his notes. Other people spoke. Melinda stood stock-still. Marion had sat on a chair by the door through which they had entered, her legs crossed, her hands resting in her lap. She watched the Master, her eyes never leaving his face.

Melinda saw the men at the table gazing at her, sly glimpses, open stares, assessing her, appraising her, in more or less the same way the guests at dinner had done, except they did not have the advantage of seeing her nude. Were they used to this? Were the Master's helots, his new 'acquisitions', regularly made to stand here?

On the wall facing Melinda was a large clock. It had no numbers and no dial; just two hands and two marks immediately above and below the fulcrum of the hands. Melinda watched the hands describe ten minutes, then twenty, then forty. The conversation continued. Her back ached but she remained still. The

Master leant back in his chair, apparently listening intently to what one of the men was saying, but Melinda suddenly felt his hand running up her spine to the top of the dress. His fingers found the little metal tongue of the zip and pulled it down, right down to the small of her back. The zip sung. The boned bodice remained in place, only slipping down slightly. The Master's hand slipped under the open zip onto her bare flesh. His hand was warm and noticeably damp. He wormed his fingers down, over her buttocks. As the dress was still tight on her hips the action tugged the dress down a little. More of her breasts were exposed though not her nipples. The eyes of the room were centred on her. The man who was speaking tried to concentrate.

The Master must have signalled to Marion. She got up and came over to stand behind Melinda, her hands on her bare shoulders. Melinda felt herself being guided back and then over to one side of the room. Marion held the dress in place.

On the far side of the room, set against the wall, was a long table in the same style as the main conference table, but smaller. At one end it was set with a tray carrying glasses and bottles of Evian water. The rest of the table was clear, its polished surface reflecting the wall lamp hung above it.

Marion brought Melinda to a halt in front of the table. The six men on one side of the room had a clear view; the six with their backs to the wall could not see unless they turned their chairs. None of them did. The meeting continued uninterrupted.

Pulling at the red satin, Marion tugged it down Melinda's hips. It was tight and only moved an inch or two at a time. The first tug revealed Melinda's nipples, the second and third the whole melons of her breasts. Soon, the dress was at her ankles, its tight bodice still standing upright like the armour of a breastplate. Melinda stepped out of it only when Marion indicated that was what was required.

Six pairs of eyes locked on her nakedness. The black stockings cut her body in two. Below they were dark and sheer and sleek; above, her skin was white and smooth and naked. The little triangle of fluffy pubic hair seemed to point at the thick, black lacy welts of the stockings, so high up on her thighs.

Marion did not speak. She indicated that Melinda should sit on the table. Melinda did so, the movement rattling the glasses on the tray. Then, with her hand, Marion pulled Melinda's shoulders down so she was lying on her back in the middle of the table, staring up at the ceiling.

Like an artist arranging a model, Marion posed Melinda's body. She swivelled her around so she lay along the length of the table. She rested her arms by her side and pulled the leg nearest the wall up, its knee bent, the red high-heeled shoe flat against the table top. The other leg she left flat, only opening it slightly so that Melinda's labia were exposed. She took the shoe off on this foot and placed it on the table. She moved Melinda's head to one side so she was looking into the room and facing the Master. She had no need to tell Melinda she must be still; Melinda understood. Finally Marion squeezed both Melinda's nipples hard, though she had no need. They were already both fully erect.

The work completed, Marion returned to her seat, the red dress over her lap.

Melinda could see the men's eyes on her body. Occasionally, one of the men with their backs to her would sneak a surreptitious look over his shoulder.

Melinda's body was burning with excitement. She could feel Marion's fingers on her nipples. Her sex was throbbing. It was difficult to keep herself still. She wanted to squirm against the table top. She wanted to cram her fingers into her sex. She wanted to perform for all the sets of greedy eyes that looked at her with such secret longing.

Instead, she did nothing. Just as surely as if she had been set in stone she lay as Marion had arranged her. That became her performance. She tried to channel her energy, her incredible sexual energy, into that stillness.

She knew she was wet. She suspected her labia glistened with her juices. She had no control of that function of her body. She could not stop her excitation, cool her ardour, no more than she could get up from the table. The two were inextricably linked, of course. She had wondered why she had not been bound this morning. Now she knew. This was a test, a test of her ability to obey. The more she remained passive and inert, the greater her submission.

She felt so turned on that she began to wonder if it were possible to come without moving. She wanted to moan so badly, she had to clamp her lips together. Her whole body ached for a double release. Release from the invisible bonds that held her so tight, so she could roll and writhe and squirm and abandon herself to pleasure; and release from the sexual tension that stretched every nerve and sinew of her body as tight as piano wire.

'Well gentlemen, that seems to conclude our business for today. Thank you for your time . . .' There was a hum of conversation, a scraping of chairs, the sound of papers being tidied away into briefcases. 'Please feel free, gentlemen . . .' the Master said, indicating Melinda.

108

One of the men who had had his back to her sauntered over to her, as though she were some curiosity in a museum. He stood by the edge of the table, looking down at her. Two more men soon joined him.

'Beautiful body . . .' the first man said.

'Great . . .'

A younger man approached. 'Can we touch?' he asked, obviously new to the proceedings.

'I wouldn't,' the first man advised, looking back at the Master who still sat at the head of the conference table.

Melinda held her head to one side, not moving to look up at them. In her eyeline now were the flies of their trousers. She would have given anything to be touched. She would have given anything to have been able to reach out, unzip one of those flies and delve inside.

Eventually, all twelve men stood around looking at her.

'So what is your opinion, gentlemen?' the Master's voice boomed out.

Various comments filled the air. 'Beautiful,' 'Exceptional', 'Such lovely legs', 'Odd pubic hair, so fine', 'She's wet, you know', 'Those nipples are hard too, really hard'.

'Yes, I think she is exceptional. And what is more remarkable is that she is quite untrained.' The Master had risen. Two men made way for him to stand by Melinda's head. 'Aren't you, child?'

It was a question. Melinda was slow to realise that she had to answer. 'Yes, Master.'

'Quite untrained. A natural talent.' He extended his hand to the fine fleece of her pubic hair. He teased out individual strands, pulling it up until the flesh from which it grew was stretched into tiny pyramids. It felt like being stung by a nettle.

His hand made no firm contact. How she yearned for him to slip it down between her legs. Couldn't he feel her heat? Couldn't he feel her body throbbing, the engine of her sex turning over like a car idling, but stationary? Didn't he want to propel her forward? But all he did was tease out her hair, like a spinner teasing out the wool, rolling it between his fingers now, forming little clumps of twisted hair.

'Well, lunch I think,' he said firmly. His hand left her. He walked away. The men followed, talking among themselves. The young man was the last. Checking they all had their backs to him, he leant over and cupped her breast in his hand, squeezing it hard. The action was so sudden and so unexpected, Melinda only just managed to suppress a moan.

Quickly the man caught up with the others at the door. As they filed out, Melinda could see Marion had gone too. She was alone in the vast room.

Another test she knew. There would be a camera somewhere. Someone would be watching. She had to remain as she was. No one had told her to move. The performance must continue.

Her body ached. The table top was hard. Her weight rested on her buttocks and her shoulders. There was an ache in her neck from holding her head to one side, and the leg Marion had raised was cramped and painful. Even the welts of the stockings seemed tight and uncomfortable on her thighs. But Melinda did not move. The engine of her sex continued to throb, her mind and body full of anticipation. Was this like the raffle at the house last night? Would one of the men be allowed to come and use her after lunch? Perhaps while they all watched?

Or, better still, perhaps the Master would walk through that door. Perhaps that was why she had been brought down here. To satisfy the Master. He had seen her last night, seen her body and her attitude. He had, she was sure, watched as she was being fucked. It must have aroused him. Surely he wanted her, his latest acquisition?

As she lay prone on the table, she was convinced that was the explanation, that all she had been asked to do was a prelude. She was here to satisfy the Master, to satisfy the craving she had created in him.

Out of the corner of her eye she could see the clock. An hour passed. She waited.

She heard the door open. Her whole body tensed. Ready. Only too ready.

But it was not the Master. It was Marion.

'Get up,' she ordered. Melinda obeyed instantly though her limbs needed some coaxing to resume activity. Marion picked up the shoe that stood on the table and dropped it on the floor, indicating that Melinda should put it back on. 'This way.'

Melinda was unsteady on her feet, the blood rushing back into the leg that had been raised. But she was not downhearted. Marion was taking her to the Master. She had to be. She even stopped her to brush out the hair that had been flattened by the table top.

'Poor cow,' Marion said. She could see what was written on Melinda's face, her excitement, her anticipation. The back of her hand caressed Melinda's cheek. She trailed her finger over her lips. 'You wanted it so badly, didn't you?'

The disappointment registered immediately. Melinda's heart sank. She was not being taken to the Master.

'Follow me,' Marion said.

It was another crisis point. Melinda stopped by the door as Marion walked through it.

'Do it,' Marion snapped.

Melinda looked at her. She felt strange, ill almost, as though all her sexual frustration had turned to poison in her body. Mechanically, she walked forward. Once again she seemed to be seeing herself from on high, watching this near-naked woman trudge through the door, her unsupported tits quivering from the movement of walking, her nylons rasping against each other as her thighs met.

She saw herself standing by the lift in the ante-room. She could not form thoughts. She could do nothing but tell herself to obey.

It had been deliberate, of course. Another lesson. It was as though the Master had reached inside her, found all the levers and pulleys that operated her psyche, and used them to reduce her to nothing, to what she felt now: bereft, empty, totally alone and undesired. Untouched. Unwanted. It was all part of the plan.

It was only in the lift that she realised she had not been given her dress back. Was that part of the plan too? Were they going to make her walk through the streets naked? Or did they think she would rebel at that? Another test.

The lift doors opened. Marion led the way out, but did not head back in the direction of the door out into the passageway. Instead, she headed through another door and down a long corridor, at the end of which a half-glass door opened onto a loading area. The Jaguar waited, the chauffeur standing by the open rear door.

Marion took Melinda's hand as they crossed to the car. Two men were loading a truck. They stopped and stared, open-mouthed.

'You have been very good, the Master will be pleased,' Marion said comfortingly.

Why doesn't he want me then? Why doesn't he take me? Melinda wanted to scream out. She said nothing.

They got into the car. The chauffeur looked at Melinda's nakedness, his eyes lingering on her breasts and loins. The leather seat was cold against her flesh.

'Get on the floor,' Marion commanded. 'Lie on the floor.'

Melinda slid off the leather and onto the thick pile rugs. They felt soft and warm.

Marion had taken a silk blindfold from her bag. She leant over and fitted it around Melinda's head, pulling it down over her eyes.

'That is your reward,' she said.

And it was true. The blackness behind the mask was welcome, anonymous, healing. Melinda lay on her side and curled herself into a foetal position. In the darkness she faced no further humiliation, no more eyes that devoured her but did nothing. No more disappointments, no more torments. For the moment at least, she was, like the darkness, featureless.

Her thigh had come to rest against Marion's foot. She could feel the leather toe and the nylon on top of her foot. She had thought Marion would draw her foot away, but she did not. Instead she seemed to press it forward. Or was that just the movement of the car? It didn't matter. To Melinda it felt good, almost too good to be true. Contact. Touch. Human touch.

Seven

Melinda had been taken straight back to her cell. Without removing the blindfold, she had been told to lie on the mattress while her hands were cuffed to the wall and the cold metal block chained between her legs. The stockings and shoes had been stripped away.

Whereas before she had welcomed the blindfold, now it was a curse. It turned her mind inward, allowing her to do nothing but listen to the pulses and rhythms of her body, allowing her to see only mental images. There was nothing to distract her. Had she not been prevented physically, she would have been unable to stop herself from masturbating. Her sex throbbed almost painfully for some attention, some relief. But, of course, they knew that. That was the point of this morning's exercise. And why she had been so effectively prevented from even the slightest contact with the part of her body that would bring her release. The metal block chained between her thighs allowed no contact. No amount of squirming and writhing of her body could bring anything to bear on her swollen clitoris but the unpleasant rasping harshness of the upper surface of the metal. And with her hands cuffed above her head any sexual fulfilment was simply impossible.

The greater the need they created in her, the more

they denied her the means to satisfy it. Or so it seemed.

Time passed. She tried to think of anything but sex, but that was impossible too. She thought of last night, of that big hard cock buried deep in her throat, and immediately wished she hadn't. Involuntarily, she'd pushed her sex down on the metal block and been rewarded by a cold stinging pain for her trouble. But her mind was not deterred. Image after image filled the darkness behind the blindfold, like pictures on a cinema screen. Graphic, inescapable. The hands reaching out to feel her body at the dinner table; being whipped by Cybele; lying naked in front of all those men; their eyes looking down at her, the younger man cupping her breast . . .

Eventually she must have drifted off to sleep. She had no idea for how long.

The lock on the cell door springing open woke her. Hera walked in, carrying a tray of food. Without a word she uncuffed Melinda's hands, and peeled away the blindfold. She leant against the wall and watched as Melinda ate. As soon as she had finished, she made her lie down again and cuffed her hands back to the wall. She did not replace the blindfold however and, after she'd gone, the lights in the room remained on.

Melinda looked up at the video camera, wondering if she was being watched, but though the camera was pointed at her there was no way of telling whether it was operating.

Hours passed, or perhaps they were only minutes.

The cell door opened again. This time Marion entered. She was wearing a high-cut white silk teddy under a matching white negligée which was undone at the front. The teddy's lace panels were cut in a deep V-shape over Marion's breasts, revealing

115

glimpses of their ample proportions. Its cut at the top of her legs was so high, it almost reached her waist, making her long sculptured thighs seem even longer. A dark growth of pubic hair nestled under the translucent white silk.

Marion unlocked the bathroom, the handcuffs and the metal block.

'Use the toilet if you need to,' she said, and stood watching as Melinda peed.

'The Master wants you,' she said.

Melinda's heart leapt. *Wants me! Wants me!* She could hardly believe she had heard correctly. But she stopped herself short. This was probably another game, another exercise in disappointment. The Master might merely want to see her, as he'd seen her this morning. She must not allow herself to get excited. Her needs, she reminded herself, no longer counted for anything.

Marion stood with the handcuffs still in her hand. Without another word she clipped Melinda's wrists into one cuff, then walked behind her, pulled her other wrist round into her back and locked them together. Coming back to face her again, she took a loop of fine gold chain from around her neck, spread it between her fingers and lifted it over Melinda's head. In the middle of the chain was a small key, the key to the handcuffs. It rested between Melinda's breasts.

The red high heels Melinda had worn this morning had been left in the cell. Marion told her to put them on. There was something different about Marion's manner. Before, she had been cold, and then almost sympathetic. But this time she was surly, almost angry, as though full of resentment.

They walked through the house. Marion mounted

the sweeping double staircase and Melinda followed. At the far end of the landing was a set of double doors, panelled and painted white. Marion knocked once.

'Come . . .' It was the Master's voice, but it sounded distant, only just audible.

Marion opened the door and pushed Melinda forward. She did not cross the threshold herself, but closed the door as soon as Melinda was inside.

Melinda found herself in a small hallway. There were two doors, one facing the double doors and one at the far end. She did not know what to do. If she turned her back she could probably turn the handle of the door with her cuffed hands. But is that what she was required to do? Without orders she was lost.

She heard the distinct thwack of a whip, and a responding but heavily stifled moan.

The inner door opened. Melinda recognised the leather uniform and boots, but not the face. This woman was short and plump, but like Cybele, looked powerful and strong. Her hair was a reddish auburn, and her large eyes, too large for her rather small face, were green. The silver brooch pinned to the black leather leotard was inscribed: 'SELENE'.

She gripped Melinda by the arm, her strong fingers whitening the skin, and led her through the door. The Master's bedroom was massive. Large windows were covered by heavy white curtains. The floor was carpeted in a rich oatmeal long pile, the walls lined with a creamy silk fabric. Everything in the room was a shade of white or cream: the counterpane of the large double bed, the upholstery of the large sofa and the two soft comfortable armchairs. Only an occasional table, in front of the sofa, and the television mounted on the wall opposite the bed, were not. Both these items were black.

The Master was sitting in one of the armchairs. In front of him, on his knees, was a naked man. As Melinda entered the man was lowering his head to the floor and the Master was wrapping his white cotton robe around his body.

'Get your forehead down.' Cybele stood alongside the naked man. She raised her booted foot and rested it on his neck to ensure her order was obeyed.

The man's buttocks protruded obscenely in the air. From the red welts that criss-crossed his backside, and the whip in Cybele's hand, it was obvious that the man had been subjected to a severe lashing. What else he had been made to do Melinda could only guess.

'Get him out of here,' the Master said in a tone of voice Melinda had never heard him use before. Apart from the cotton robe, he was naked.

Cybele and Selene literally dragged him to his feet. Melinda recognised his face immediately. It was the young man in the conference room who had squeezed her breast. Was this his punishment for that? Had the Master seen it on a video camera as Melinda had suspected?

They dragged him out of the room. His cock was erect. From the marks across his belly and thighs it looked as though his front had been subjected to the same treatment as his backside.

The Master turned the full force of his gaze on Melinda. He beckoned her over to his chair. She stood in front of him, her hands locked behind her back, her body exposed to his stare. His eyes roamed. She felt them as surely as if they were hands, on her breasts, on her navel, delving into the apex of her thighs. Then up again, up to look into her eyes. She felt all their power, hypnotic, impossible to resist, just as she had felt them that first evening as he had greeted her at his front door.

'Kneel,' he said, his tone altogether different from the one he had used before.

Melinda obeyed, but slowly. It was not easy to kneel without using her arms for balance.

'Closer,' he said when she was down.

She scrambled forward on her knees until she was inches from the Master's naked legs. Her heart was in her mouth, her excitement coarsing through her nerves.

The Master leant forward, looking into her eyes. It was the closest she had ever been to him. The power of his eyes was overwhelming. She felt as though she could drown in them, drown in oceans of steely blue. He stretched out his hand and stroked her cheek lightly. Melinda had to resist the temptation to turn her head and kiss his fingers. His touch was intoxicating. Her heart was beating faster and faster. She begged with her eyes and her body. 'Take me,' she tried to express without words. 'Please.'

She dare not look into his lap. She looked only into his eyes.

He relaxed back into the chair. 'You pleased me today, Melinda.' It was the first time anyone had used her name in the house. 'You excited me a great deal. You are an extraordinary woman. Your obedience ... your ...' he searched for the right word, 'passivity. Perfect. So perfect. I don't think I have ever come across such a perfect example. You want it very much, don't you?'

It was a question. She was allowed to respond. She tried to cram all her emotions into the two words, 'Yes, master.'

'Good, good.'

He got up. As he did, the front of his white robe brushed Melinda's face. He walked behind her. She dared not turn around without being ordered to.

'I want you to do something for me, Melinda.' He did not have to ask. He only had to command. 'Get up now, come over here.'

She got to her feet with difficulty and turned round. He was standing by an open door. She could see a bathroom beyond. He beckoned her forward as he'd done before.

The bathroom was walled in white marble. It was lit brightly, much more brightly than the bedroom. One whole wall was a mirror. Melinda had only glimpsed herself briefly in the mirror in the dining room since she had entered the house. The sight of herself now, naked but for the red high heels, her breasts thrust forward by the position of her arms, was a shock. It did not look like her. It looked like someone else, a stranger. She even seemed to move differently. Her hair and make-up were different. It was another person.

The Master came up behind her, wrapped his arms around her and embraced her, looking over her shoulder into the mirror in front of them. Contact. Real contact. At last. Melinda felt herself melting around him. With her arms cuffed behind her, her hands were pressed into his groin. She thought she could feel his cock.

'Child,' he said quietly, then released her. The moment passed.

She swayed back, almost losing her balance without his support.

He took the key from around her neck and quickly sprung the handcuffs open.

'Do they hurt you?' he asked solicitously.

'No, master,' she lied.

'But they must do. I can see the marks on your wrists.'

She wanted to say that it wasn't important, that she'd do anything for him, anything. She knew she must say nothing.

'So good,' he said.

Her hands hung by her sides. He sat in a white Lloyd-loom chair by the bathtub.

'Run a bath,' he said, his hands pressed together in an attitude of prayer, the tips of his fingers touching his lips.

Melinda reached over to the mixer taps. She felt his eyes on her buttocks as the water gushed into the tub. He said nothing else until the bath was full.

'Get in now,' he said as she closed the taps.

She obeyed.

'Does that feel nice?'

It felt wonderful. She hadn't had a bath for three days. Her body was flushed pink with the heat of the water.

'Yes, Master.'

'Good. Wash yourself.'

Uncertainly she reached out for the soap. There was a shelf alongside the bath. She took the soap and a large natural sponge. She soaped herself quickly and rinsed the lather away with the sponge.

'Do you know what I want you to do for me, my dear?'

'No, Master.'

'Your hair. I want you to shave your hair.'

Despite the hot water Melinda went cold. He wanted her to shave her head. She went cold not because she was horrified at the request, but because she knew she would do it instantly, without question.

The Master went to a small bathroom cabinet. He extracted a shaving bowl and brush and a tiny razor, its blade no more than an inch wide. He set them down at the side of the bath. It was only then that she realised he meant her pubic hair.

'Use these,' he said.

She hesitated. She hadn't the slightest idea what to do next.

'Stand up.' A note of irritation had crept into his voice at her hesitation. He took it for disobedience. 'Don't disappoint me now.'

She picked up the shaving brush and bowl of shaving soap and stood up. The water cascaded off her body. Dipping the brush in the soap she worked up a lather. She transferred the lather from the brush to her triangle of pubic hair, painting on a thick foam.

'Good.' He sat down again, pulling the chair nearly to the edge of the bath and leaning forward.

Melinda picked up the tiny razor. She had no qualms about what she was doing. Her body did not belong to her any more. She was only concerned to do a good job. This was what he wanted. All she wanted was to please him, to earn more praise, to be perfect. She wished he had asked one of the women to shave her, someone who knew how to do it well. She had never done this before.

The razor cut a swathe through the white lather. After several passes most of the lather had gone, and with it her downy fleece of blonde hair. She looked in the mirror, not to see herself, but to check on the job she had done. There was still hair down at the apex of her thighs. Soaping the brush again she put one leg up on the side of the bath and painted more soap down between her legs.

The Master's eyes were rooted to her sex. She

122

looked into his lap, but could not tell whether he was erect. The folds of the cotton robe hid any tumescence. She hoped this was the prelude for him, the ritual that would incite him to take her, the first man to enter her slick, hairless cunt.

Carefully, she stroked the razor over the crease of her sex. She had to bend double to see what she was doing, her leg up, her crotch open. She scraped away at the lather.

The Master let out a tiny, almost inaudible moan.

Melinda reached for the sponge and rinsed away the rest of the lather. She was hairless. It was only now, now it had gone, that she realised how much her pubic hair had covered. Without it, the lips of her sex were clearly defined. Even standing with her legs together, the crease of her sex, at least the first delicate folds of it, was clearly visible. She stared at her sex in the mirror. Now she looked as she had looked as a child.

The Master got up. Melinda could see a clear bulge in the robe. But she could sense too that his mood had changed.

'Dry yourself. Then come into the bedroom. Quickly.' The kindness had gone from his voice. He walked out of the bathroom.

Melinda hastened to obey, taking one of the large bath towels and hoping his mood change was not the result of something she had done. She towelled between her legs, feeling, for the first time, the lack of hair. Her big, puffy labia felt different. She did not look at herself again in the mirror. She slipped back into the red shoes.

In the bedroom, the Master was pacing the thick carpet. The bulge in his robe had disappeared.

'Get over here.' He indicated the bed. What had

she done wrong? His eyes looked at her with anger. 'Lie down on your back.'

She obeyed. The counterpane had been turned back, and the cream-coloured sheets were silk. He came and stood beside the bed, looking down at her naked body. She felt more naked now, the final cloak of modesty shaven away. Her body pulsed. It was a pulse she recognised. Her sex was moistening.

The Master sat on the edge of the bed. *Please touch me, kiss me, take me. Do anything to me*, she wanted to scream. Every nerve in her body ached for contact, wanted her to wrap herself around him, plunge her head on his cock. Make him want her. Every nerve ached for release. The more his eyes looked at her, the more she wanted to touch, to hold, to have.

'I should have had you shaved. You shouldn't have shaved yourself,' he said almost to himself. 'You must do it every morning,' he said to her, 'every morning without fail. Is that clear?'

'Yes, Master.'

Involuntarily, she felt her body inch towards him. It was as though he were a giant magnet pulling her to one side.

'Use this,' he said. From the drawer of the bedside table he took a black dildo. It was a perfect replica of a cock, complete with balls, every detail moulded in hard black plastic. He tossed it onto the bed between her legs.

Oh no, no, she wanted to scream. *Not that. Of all things don't make me wank. Do it to me. Have me tied and bound and spread. Let Marion do it. Or Cybele. Cruel and hard. But not by my own hand, don't give me freedom again. Please, please.* Her eyes begged. This time her hesitation *was* rebellion.

'Melinda. You will obey,' he said.

She saw not anger in his eyes, but sadness. She had displeased him. Immediately, she took the dildo in her hand and scissored her legs open, bending her knees. She had made a mistake. She was thinking of herself, of what she wanted. She wanted not to masturbate, she wanted not to do it for herself. That was wrong, that was her mistake, because it no longer mattered what she wanted in this world. She no longer existed. It was as simple as that. That was what she had forgotten.

Brutally she jammed the dildo up into her cunt. There was no resistance. Her sex was wet. She pushed it up using both her hands, right up until she could feel it at the neck of her womb and the balls were hard against her arse.

This was what he wanted. That was all there was. She would do it because he wanted it, do it as well as she could.

She pulled it back again and felt her body gush with juices. With no subtlety or gentleness, cross with herself for her stupidity, she rammed the dildo to and fro, on the river of her excitement. She had to be excited, she had to excite herself because he wanted that. He wanted to see that.

Using one hand to manipulate the dildo she ran the other up to her breast. With all her might she squeezed each breast in turn, then used the long nails of her thumb and finger on her nipples, pinching them hard, so each had a crescent-shaped impression etched into the tender flesh. She wanted to feel the pain, wanted to punish herself.

She repeated the punishment as the dildo reamed into her cunt. But her eyes never left the Master, never stopped watching him as she saw his eyes roaming her body. This was what he wanted.

There was no longer any inhibition. What she was doing suddenly felt like nothing she had ever done before. It was different. It was not an act of freedom, but of submission.

She was coming. All the frustrations of the day were concentrated in her sex. The hard, big dildo filled her cunt. Her breasts and tortured nipples, her clitoris, every nerve in her body, strained for release. The Master's eyes, cool, detached, unblinking, watched the dildo as it sawed in and out of her labia, its shaft glistening with her juices. The first kick of orgasm jerked her body, rolling her eyes closed. Then, instantly, she was falling; falling into a deep black, endless abyss where she could feel only sensation and all conscious thought was gone. Her body was tossed from side to side as the dildo pressed, for the last time, deep inside her.

She lay, eventually, completely still, her hands at her sides, her legs still open. Slowly, inevitably, the dildo slid out of her cunt. The motion jerked her body in an involuntary spasm. She opened her eyes.

Marion stood by the bed. She was taking off her negligée, her long, very black hair flowing over her shoulders. Under the white silk teddy, her body looked exquisite, soft and rich and ripe.

'Leave us,' the Master said, not looking at Melinda. His eyes were fixed on Marion.

Melinda struggled to sit up, her body still lost in the feelings of orgasm, her nerves not co-ordinated with her muscles yet. Marion was kneeling on the carpet between the Master's knees, her hands caressing his calves.

'Now,' Marion snapped at Melinda. She smiled. It looked like a smile of triumph.

Melinda scrambled off the bed. She headed for the

door. She tried not to look, because she knew what she would see, but out of the corner of her eye she saw Marion unwrapping the robe, and her head descending into the Master's lap.

She ran through the bedroom door. Cybele and Selene were waiting. Cybele closed the inner door while Selene cuffed Melinda's hands behind her back. Melinda felt the tears welling in her eyes, but tried to blink them back. The cold metal cuffs were welcome. She strained her wrists against them, wanting to feel them bite into her flesh. She was an object. She should have no feelings. She was there to be used, and she had been. What else did she expect?

Melinda counted the days. Since the evening with the Master, five days had passed. Each day had become routine. She would be woken in the morning by one of the three leather-uniformed chatelaines who would bring her breakfast and supervise her shower and toilet. A razor, shaving bowl and brush had been put in the bathroom, and each morning she shaved. It was necessary. Her pubis sprouted bristles with surprising regularity. They felt different from the fluffy softness Melinda was used to; harsh and wiry. She had become more adept at shaving as the days passed and now her sex was completely smooth, all the little crevices shaved clean too.

After breakfast, Melinda was given a cotton bra to wear to support her breasts and taken to exercise. The regimen was strict. Each exercise was timed, and she was not allowed to stop until the chatelaine announced her time was up.

Another shower followed. In the afternoon, she would be taken to a solarium. As she was not taken outside, its tanning effect was necessary to maintain her summer colour. Clearly the Master did not want her developing a prison pallor.

The rest of the time she was given a menial task to perform – scrubbing the floor of her cell, or cleaning the bathroom – or left alone, her hands cuffed to the wall, the metal block between her legs.

After five days, Melinda was beginning to lose hope. In some way she had offended the Master. From considering her his favourite, from seeing her as 'perfect' he had, for some reason, lost interest in her. Even the camera in the cell wall seemed to bear testament to his displeasure. Not once had Melinda seen it move. The Master was not watching her anymore.

Neither was Marion. She did not see Marion either, in the days since being summoned to the Master's bedroom.

The only parts of her day that were not predictable were the beatings. They were never done at any set time, nor in any set pattern except that it was always two of the chatelaines together. They were never alone. Some days they would chain her to the wall, her breasts against the plaster, her hands chained so high above her head that she was forced onto the very tips of her toes. In this position they would whip her, alternating their strokes, one standing on one side of her body, the other opposite; her arse assailed from both directions. They never counted the strokes. Sometimes when it was over, they would twist her round to face them, then kiss her, bite at her nipples, penetrate her sex, pinch and maul her.

Then they would leave her. They knew the pain created a need in her body. They would leave her chained to the wall, the metal block placed between her legs, her body stretched, her nerves aching for the relief it would never be allowed to have. Having created the need they left her unable to fulfil it.

Once, after they'd turned her round, Hera and Cybele had lain on the mattress and made love. They had not stripped off their uniforms, just pulled up their skirts and unfastened the studs of the leotards between their legs. With no preliminaries, Cybele had climbed onto Hera's body and positioned her sex above Hera's face, while her mouth had plunged onto Hera's sex. They had lapped eagerly at each other's bodies, squirming and writhing with the pleasure they created, glancing occasionally at the helpless Melinda, smiling tauntingly at her as if to say, 'Don't you wish you could join in?' She did, of course. They knew that. They knew she would have done anything to feel what they were feeling. To be touched. To be had. Instead, all she could do was hang by her hands and watch and listen. Listen to their screams of joy as their bodies exploded in each other's mouths, trembling out of control.

At night, her body ached most. Not from discomfort. Not from the chains that held her or the marks of the whips. It ached for sex. Here in this cell, naked most of the time, waiting for the door to open, there was nothing to do but think of sex. For the first two days they had filled her mind with sexual images she could not forget. But then they had allowed her some release. Now she was allowed nothing. Five days of frustration reinforced by constant attention to, and provocation of, her body and her mind.

It was deliberate. She knew that. All part of a plan. She hoped it was the Master's plan for her. Not just routine. That it was all designed by the Master to make her feel, to make her what he wanted her to be. Not routine. Not what they did to all the women he

129

had trained. Just the same old routine because he could no longer be bothered with her, because he no longer cared. Not that. Please, she prayed at night, when such thoughts plagued her most, please not that.

Eight

The light woke Melinda. Though she had no way of telling, it felt earlier than she was usually woken. But the door, which usually opened as soon as the light was switched on, remained closed. Instead, the little whir of the electric motors that controlled the video camera attracted Melinda's attention. She was being watched again. The lens zoomed in on her body.

As usual she was lying on her back, her hands cuffed above her head, her legs forced open by the metal block. The thought of being watched made her nipples harden. She stared back at the camera.

It must have been half an hour before the computer lock sprung open and Marion entered, followed by the make-up woman, who carried clothing as well as her make-up box.

Marion looked stunning. Her long hair was pinned in a neat chignon at the back of her head, revealing her neck and the delicate whorls of her ears. Her slim body and heavy bosom were complimented by a simple yellow dress that clung to her bust and waist and the strong contours of her hips. Melinda had thought a lot about Marion. She could remember the details of her body under the white silk teddy, the richness of her breasts, the long stretch of her flank from waist to thigh. Now, as Marion knelt by the mattress, she felt a surge of desire. Whether she desired Marion for herself, or because she knew that Marion meant something special to the Master, she did not know.

With deliberate slowness, Marion ran her hand down over Melinda's neck, between the channel of her breasts, to the leather belt that girded her waist. Melinda shuddered at the touch.

'Special day,' Marion said quietly.

Her hand trailed down over Melinda's belly until her fingers caressed the shaven flesh of her pubis. She rubbed it with her fingertips as if testing to see how much stubble there was.

Quickly, she freed Melinda's hands and removed the metal block. She unlocked the bathroom door and ordered Melinda to shower and shave.

As soon as Melinda was dry, the make-up woman came in to begin her work. She applied the usual make-up. This time she paid more attention to Melinda's hair, styling it with a spray and combing it, as far as Melinda could tell, into a different shape. When she'd finished, she asked for Marion's opinion.

'Yes, that's fine,' Marion said.

Lastly, she applied lipstick with a brush. She held a tissue between Melinda's lips when she'd finished. Melinda pressed her lips together on it to remove any excess. She did not tell her to do it; just expecting her to act like a well-trained dog.

Back in the cell, the clothes had been laid out on the mattress. That was not the only thing that had been placed there. Marion picked up a stout leather belt, much thicker than the one used to hold the metal block in place.

'Stand still.' It was an unnecessary command. Melinda only moved when she was told to. Marion wrapped the belt tightly around her waist and buckled it in the small of her back. From each side of the belt hung a leather strap, attached to the end of which were two loops of leather. One was smaller than the other and they were firmly fixed together. Marion quickly opened the large loops, wrapped them round the very tops of Melinda's thighs, and buckled them tight, positioning them so that the smaller loops were on the outside of the thigh. As soon as this was done she picked up a pair of trousers and a light pink shirt from the bedding.

Melinda saw the lens of the camera move. Was the Master watching her bondage?

'Put these on.'

Melinda donned the shirt. It was a man's shirt, buttoning on the opposite side from a woman's blouse. She pulled the trousers up over the strange arrangement of leather straps. They bulged unnaturally. Marion held the jacket. Like the trousers it was a man's jacket, in a subtle pinstripe. Melinda was being dressed as a man. She slid her arms into the sleeves.

'Put your hands in the trouser pockets.'

Melinda obeyed. To her surprise there were no pockets and her fingers encountered her own flesh and the leather straps. Marion quickly wrapped one of the smaller leather loops around Melinda's left wrist and buckled it tight inside the opening of the pocket. She repeated the process on the right, effectively binding Melinda's hands to her thighs. But the bondage was completely concealed. To a casual observer it would look as if Melinda merely had both her hands in her pockets.

The make-up woman pulled up the collar of the shirt and fed a blue silk tie around Melinda's neck. She knotted it in place. She was made to lean against the wall while her feet were clad in pink wool socks, and men's black brogue shoes.

133

'Follow me,' Marion said after she'd minutely examined the finished article, carefully brushing something off the lapel of the jacket and patting down a stray wisp of hair.

They walked through the stable block and out into the covered courtyard. Melinda found it was best to hold her hands open and flat against her thighs. She could feel her muscles moving in her legs as she walked. In the marble vestibule at the front of the house the front door was open, and Melinda could see the stretched Jaguar waiting.

Marion led her outside and told her to get into the car. But all its doors were closed and the chauffeur was nowhere to be seen. Melinda tried to reach out of the pocket with her fingers to clutch the door handle, but it was impossible. Marion looked around to see why she hadn't obeyed the order, a glare on her face. Seeing the problem, she opened the door for her, but caught her by the arm as she was about to get in.

'When you get back, it's my turn,' she said, smiling. 'My turn with you. Do you understand?'

'Yes, mistress.' Melinda did not understand. Marion's hand released her and she climbed into the back of the car. With her hands bound at her sides, it was not an easy manoeuvre. Marion closed the car door behind her and walked back into the house.

The car was hot. Melinda shifted uncomfortably. How long it would be before she got back she did not know, nor what Marion's 'turn' would involve. She sensed Marion's attitude to her was complex; changing from moment to moment, just as her relationship with the Master seemed to change. Presumably, she was the Master's overseer in charge of the stables. But what that meant, Melinda did not know. With the three chatelaines and the number of cells in the stable block, there must be other slaves – perhaps men as well as women – but, apart from the man in the Master's bedroom, she had seen only the staff.

In the rear-view mirror of the car, Melinda suddenly caught a glimpse of herself. She looked like a man with rather long blonde hair. Her hair had been slicked back and parted like a man's; her make-up was minimal. Even the lipstick was a natural shade, not the flame red they had used before. Standing up, the line of her bust would have shown more, but while sitting down, her unsupported breasts were not much in evidence. At a casual glance she would appear masculine.

The front door opened. The chauffeur emerged, opened the rear passenger door of the car and stood aside as the Master left the house and climbed in beside Melinda on the back seat. He wore a pin-striped suit identical to hers. His shoes were the same too, and his shirt. The car door slammed shut.

'Charming.' The Master looked her up and down. 'Really charming.'

The car set off down the gravel driveway and through the gates.

'You make such a pretty man, my dear. Such a pretty boy.' The Master seemed totally enchanted with Melinda's appearance, smiling broadly like a young child with a new toy. 'And of course, you're in bondage. Marion's so clever.' He said the word 'bondage' with a special emphasis. 'All tied up and helpless. Do you feel uncomfortable?'

'Yes, master.'

'Poor thing. Where does it hurt most?'

'My wrists, Master.' These were the first words she had said to him that were not 'yes' or 'no'.

He felt down by her side until his hand was hooked

under her forearm. He pulled, pulling it against the binding. 'Here,' he said.

'Yes, Master.' He was hurting her, but she tried not to cry out.

He took his hand away. 'I have always found the idea of bondage exciting. Well, you've seen my sculpture room. The idea is immensely appealing to me. I wonder why? There is something about having another human being giving you control I suppose. Gifting you their . . . will. Allowing you carte blanche to do whatever you wish with them. I think that's what it is. Whatever I want, whenever I want it . . .' He slipped his hand inside the jacket of the suit and rested it on her breast as if to demonstrate. 'Quite lovely breasts. Quite lovely.' He found her nipple and teased it out until it was hard. 'You see,' he continued intensely, 'the limbs are the symbols of freedom. Without them it is impossible to express our will. Don't you agree?'

'Yes, Master.' His touch was making her body ache again. She had not had human contact for five days, other than the harsh probings of the chatelaines. His hand rested against her breast so tenderly, the side of his body pressed against hers.

The car stopped at traffic lights. Pedestrians stared into the impressively large car to see who might be inside. Two men. Two business-suited men, one with his hand inside the jacket of the other. A woman peered through the window, trying to see more. The car sped away.

'Can you move your hands?'

'No, Master.'

'Try. Try hard.'

Melinda struggled against the leather straps. She could not wriggle her arms more than an inch or so upward. The pressure pinched the larger straps into her thighs.

'Helpless,' the Master said with obvious delight. He dropped his other hand into his lap and eased his erection out of the creases of his trousers until it was flat against his belly.

'You see,' he said. 'You excite me. Your bondage excites me. The gift you have given me.'

She wanted to speak. She had never felt the constraint of silence weigh so heavily as now. Why had he left her alone for so long, if she excited him so much? Had she offended him that night? Why had he let Marion touch him, and not her? She was his to command. Didn't he know she would do anything for him, would do anything to have him inside her? A thousand questions that had to be bitten back. She remained silent.

The car sped on. The Master's hand rested on her thigh now. He would be able to feel the leather strap under the trouser.

'Have you shaved this morning?'

He must have known she had. The chatelaines had been given instructions. 'Yes, Master.'

'So good.'

He lapsed into silence, but did not take his hand away. The air-conditioning had rapidly cooled the car's interior but Melinda felt hot. His hand was making her hot.

They were out of the city streets now and on a dual carriageway. The car turned left and swung through the gates of a private airfield. The uniformed guard on the gate saluted.

The car swept up to a Gulfstream Jet, its engines already running and its boarding steps extended. The Master got out of the car and mounted the steps of the plane. For a moment, Melinda thought she was going to be left in the car. Then the chauffeur opened the door on her side of the car. Clearly he expected her to get out. It was a struggle, bound as she was.

A man, dressed in the uniform of a flight attendant, took her arm and guided her up the steps of the plane. The interior was luxurious: leather armchairs; a bar; hand-crafted cabinets; thick carpeting; telephones; videos; and even a large television. The Master sat in one of the armchairs, already talking on the telephone. He looked up as she was brought in.

'Put her in the back, Charles,' he said, covering the mouthpiece of the phone, 'I have some calls to make. I may have time later.'

'Yes, sir,' the man said, leading Melinda through the cabin to a bulkhead door in the back of the plane. The rear cabin was less well appointed. A space was cleared for cargo. Two normal airline seats were bolted to the aluminium floor. The steward pushed her callously into one and cinched her safety belt around her waist. As she had no way of undoing it herself, she was effectively bound to the chair.

The steward smiled lecherously. He was thirtyish, with thinning ginger hair, crooked teeth and the first signs of what would later become a pronounced belly. Closing the bulkhead door behind him, he returned to the main cabin.

A few minutes later the plane began to move. As Melinda heard the engine noise increasing as it turned onto the runway, the steward returned, slumping into the seat next to her and doing up his safety belt.

The plane soared into the air.

'So you're the latest,' he said, as the plane's ascent began to flatten out.

Melinda said nothing.

Charles stood up and bent over her, his face inches from hers. He pulled the jacket of her suit apart and looked at her chest.

'Very nice. Pity it's such a short flight. Otherwise we could have had some fun.' With that he turned and disappeared.

From the position of the sun in the little oval windows, Melinda guessed they were heading north. Despite the steward, she felt happier than she had for days. The Master had not forgotten her. The intimacy they had shared in the car was real. She could still feel the touch of his hand on her breast and thigh. Whatever he intended for her, she was obviously still included in his plan of things. As long as that was the case, she didn't care in the least what he did. As he'd said in the car, she had gifted her will to him. And from what he said he regarded it as a precious gift at that.

Ten minutes later, Charles returned. He snapped open her seat belt and pulled her out of the seat.

'He wants you,' he said.

The words thrilled her. He led her back into the main cabin and pushed her hard, so she overbalanced into a big brown leather armchair opposite the Master, who was still on the telephone.

'Charles . . .' the Master remonstrated, putting his hand over the mouthpiece. 'That is no way to treat a lady.'

Charles did not apologise and went to the galley situated at the front of the plane. The Master finished his conversation and put the phone back in its mounting. He got up and came to sit on the arm of Melinda's chair.

'Would you like a drink, my dear? The heat must have made you thirsty?'

'Yes, Master.'

'Charles . . .'

But Charles was already on his way back with a tray. Two large tumblers were filled with mineral water, ice and a slice of lime.

The Master took one of the glasses and brought it up to Melinda's lips. She drank eagerly. A little water spilt onto the shirt and tie. She strained with her hands as if to grasp the glass herself, then felt the leather holding her back. It was a reflex action; her body had not accustomed itself to its bondage. Deliberately, she tried to make her hands relax. The Master took the glass away in order to let her have time to breathe, then put it back to her lips, tilting it right up until the ice slid down onto her lips.

Charles watched this peculiar performance, a grown man feeding a grown woman. Melinda could see the lust in his eyes, the lust at her helplessness.

The Master left the empty glass against her mouth. The ice numbed her lips. He was looking into her eyes. He brought his face closer and took the glass away. For a second, she thought he was going to kiss her. Instead he touched her lips with his finger.

'Cold,' he said. 'I've made your lips all cold.'

She looked deep into those hypnotic eyes. She tried to see what he wanted from her, what he intended to do with her, what she meant to him. But she could see nothing. His eyes were like mirrors. They seemed to reflect and amplify her own feelings – at that moment, joy mixed with bewilderment and longing – but betrayed none of his own.

Abruptly he stood up, took the other glass from Charles's tray and sipped at the cool water.

'We have landing permission, sir. If you could fasten your seat belts, we will be making our descent . . .'

140

the voice came over the Tannoy system almost at the same moment that Melinda felt the plane decelerating.

The Master leant over her, wrapped the seat belt around her waist and snapped it shut. He pulled the loose end of the strap, tightening it unnecessarily hard around her hips.

He sat down opposite her. Charles walked back into the rear cabin.

'Perfect,' the Master said. 'You make a very convincing man. If your hair was cut short, your breasts strapped down properly . . .' he mused, moving his head from side to side like a painter assessing a canvas.

The telephone interrupted his reverie.

Ten minutes later the plane was on the ground. As it taxied off the runway, Melinda could see two cars waiting on the tarmac, a silver Rolls-Royce and a blue Ford Granada.

As soon as the plane was stationary, the Master unfastened his seat belt and got up. He did not look at Melinda or say anything to her, his mind on other things. Charles came through the cabin and unlatched the exterior cabin doors. Hydraulic motors deployed the boarding steps from the fuselage of the plane, and the Master walked out. From the window, Melinda could see him getting into the Rolls, which drove off immediately.

Of course, he had no need to smile at her, say goodbye to her, no need even to so much as gaze in her direction, or make any of the little social gestures that people observe on parting. He was the Master. Effectively he owned her, just as he owned the plane or the car. She was not a person, not even an employee or a servant. Whatever the intimacy he chose

141

to share with her, it did not change the fact that she was simply *his*.

For a while, no one paid any attention to her. Strapped tightly into the seat, there was nothing she could do but wait. The pilot and co-pilot came out from the flight deck, glancing briefly at her before leaving the plane. She could see Charles out on the tarmac, talking to a woman who appeared to be the driver of the Ford. Occasionally, she would glance up at the plane, then back at Charles as if trying to confirm what he said. No one seemed in any hurry to release her.

Eventually, the chauffeuse and Charles mounted the steps back into the plane. The woman wore a black suit, its short tight skirt displaying her long shapely bare legs. Her hair was tucked up into the cap she wore, but from the wisps that escaped and from her dark eyebrows Melinda could see she was a brunette.

'He won't be back at the house before three . . .' Charles was saying as they walked into the cabin.

The chauffeur came over to Melinda's seat and looked down at her. 'I love blondes,' she said.

'We've got all the time in the world,' he said, working the mechanism that closed the exterior door.

The chauffeur took her jacket off. She wore a white blouse underneath, through which Melinda could see a black bra straining to contain a voluptuous bosom.

Charles came to stand beside her. He put his hand on her back, then ran it down over the tight skirt that covered her buttocks.

'Too good an opportunity to miss,' he whispered.

'She'll tell him.'

'She won't say a word.'

'Really?' There was excitement in her voice.

'Trust me.' He pinched her bum hard and she

squealed. His hand pushed on up under her skirt. As it reached its objective, she grabbed the lapels of his jacket and kissed him. Melinda watched as their tongues vied for position, their mouths open, their lips wet, squirming and nipping at each other. Charles's hand had rucked up her skirt at the back and Melinda could see his fingers worming their way under a pair of white panties. Pushing the silky material aside he managed to get first one finger, then two, into the folds of her sex.

The chauffeur reacted to his intrusion by violently writhing against his body. Though she was still kissing him, she moaned, the sound muffled in their mouths. Her navel pressed hard against his thighs, touching his growing erection.

Melinda felt her body throbbing. The frustration that had been forced on her over the last five days became suddenly acute, like a sharp pain emanating from her groin. She would have done anything to be in the chauffeur's shoes; to feel, touch, be kissed. It was too much to bear, watching them, so close, their bodies full of feeling she had been denied.

'No,' the chauffeuse said, breaking the kiss, 'I want her.' She bent over Melinda's chair and raised her hand to caress Melinda's cheek, a caress so soft, so tender it made her want to cry. For the first time, Melinda broke the rules. Spontaneously, she turned her head and kissed the hand that stroked her. The chauffeuse's response was immediate. She squeezed Melinda's cheeks in one hand and kissed her full on the mouth, her tongue thrusting between her lips. Melinda sucked on it like a vampire. She *was* a vampire; a vampire for sensation, for contact, for sex. Her body ached for it. She knew none of this was allowed; that neither Charles, nor the woman should be doing anything like this. She should have fought them, put up a struggle. That was what the Master would expect her to do. But she did nothing. They were not in a position to report her disobedience just as she could say nothing of theirs.

Disobedience. What was she doing? For a moment she fought to control her feelings. She lost.

The kiss was long and deep and rich. Melinda closed her eyes. She wallowed in the sensation, the warmth and touch. The chauffeuse ran her hand over her breast, feeling its weight, then teasing the nipple. It explored further, examining the leather straps at her wrists and thighs under the trousers. Suddenly, she plunged her hand down into Melinda's lap and Melinda moaned as she felt the material of the trousers forced against her sex.

'You want it so badly, don't you?'

Melinda did not reply. The chauffeuse dropped to her knees, her hand fumbling with the zip of the trousers. As soon as it was free she pulled them down, not realising that the way Melinda was bound through the pockets prevented the trousers being removed until her wrists were freed.

Melinda wanted to tell her. But she could not. She could pretend to herself – and it was true, at least in part – that what was happening to her was not her fault. She was, after all, at their mercy. But if she told them what to do, how to free her, it became an act of will, direct disobedience, and she could not pretend she had merely been used.

It did not take long for the chauffeur to work it out for herself. She unbuckled the strap on Melinda's left wrist. Charles bent to undo the right. As soon as they were free they both tugged down the trousers. This time, the seat belt prevented the trousers' progress;

Melinda needed to raise her hips but the seat belt was too tight to allow it.

It would have taken a second for Melinda to snap off the seat belt with her hand. She did nothing.

Charles opened the belt. They pulled the trousers off her bare legs.

'Oh, look at that,' the woman said as Melinda's hairless pubis came into view. 'They've shaved her.'

Melinda's thighs were banded by the thick black leather straps. The chauffeuse pulled off her cap, letting her long hair tumble over her shoulders, then hooked her arms under Melinda's legs. She pulled them open and up around her neck and dropped her head to Melinda's sex. Suddenly, Melinda felt the tip of her hot, wet tongue probing under the hood of her clitoris.

The chauffeuse's tongue was deliciously expert, wily and practised. It tapped, circled and stroked the hard bud of nerves, tasting Melinda's juices, feeling her response. The first time. The first time with a woman. Melinda squirmed, the leather under her buttocks instantly wet. She knew she was going to come, and quickly too. Days of frustration, days of being able to do nothing to relieve the feelings forced on her, concentrated in her mind. She knew this was not allowed, was wrong, was breaking her indenture. But she could not resist, she could not fight it. The chauffeuse's tongue lapped hungrily at her sex and she felt her orgasm begin to rise, the first hot throbbing pulse that would lead, inevitably, to her climax.

The brunette felt it too. Instantly, she plunged her mouth down onto the whole of Melinda's sex, enveloping it, sucking it all in. And that was it. Melinda moaned and melted; melted over the mouth that greedily devoured her body. Her orgasm rolled up

145

and over her, almost painful in intensity, almost too much, taking her so high and so fast she thought she would never come down. Forbidden. The word echoed in her mind. Forbidden.

'Christ!' It was Charles's voice.

Melinda opened her eyes. Charles was kneeling behind the brunette. He had pulled her skirt up around her waist and had taken her from behind, pulling the crotch of her panties aside, fucking her while he watched her tonguing at Melinda. At least he had been. Now he was pulling his cock out of her and trying to stuff the wet, glistening shaft back into his trousers.

Melinda followed his eyes out of the window. The silver Rolls Royce was speeding across the tarmac towards the plane.

The chauffeuse saw it too. In panic she found the pinstriped trousers and pulled them up over Melinda's ankles. As she still had the brogues on it was not easy.

Charles started to rebuckle her wrists to the leather straps.

'No. Not until the trousers are on.'

They both struggled to get the trousers back up. They pulled Melinda to her feet. This made it easier. The chauffeuse zipped up her fly. Charles stuffed her left hand into her pocket.

'I'll do it. You'd better open the door.' The woman wiped her mouth. It was wet from Melinda's juices.

Melinda could have put her own hands back in her pockets, but she did nothing. Now her orgasm had subsided, the excitement passed, she felt uncomfortable. She felt guilty. Though she had done nothing to encourage them, she had done nothing to stop them either. She was filled with a flood of remorse. The

Master had been so good to her today, so kind, so intimate. He had given her water. He had touched her. And this was how she'd repaid him.

The leather was buckled to her wrists and the chauffeuse pushed her back into the seat.

Just as she wrapped the seat belt around Melinda's waist, the Master mounted the steps into the aircraft. The chauffeuse's skirt was still around her waist. She pulled it down just as he entered the cabin.

'What's been going on here?' he demanded, his voice like steel, his eyes looking from Charles to the brunette, with a gaze of pure ice.

'We were just taking her out, sir,' the chauffeuse volunteered. 'As instructed.'

'Charles, I want the truth.'

'Just obeying your instructions, sir,' Charles said disingenuously.

There was a silence. 'Do you think I am a fool?'

'No sir, we were – '

'Stand up.' The command was addressed to Melinda. She struggled to obey but without the use of her hands the angle of the seat was too steep to lever herself out. 'Help her.'

The chauffeuse pulled Melinda into a standing position. The Master raised the back of the suit jacket. The shirt hung down over the back of the trousers where they had not had time to tuck it in. It was not the only testament to their behaviour. The air in the cabin was thick with the musky aroma of sex.

'Now I want the truth.' The Master's voice was like thunder.

'We were just having some fun, sir,' Charles said, not looking directly into the Master's eyes. 'We thought . . .'

'You were both involved?' He was looking at the chauffeuse.

147

'Yes,' she said, a spark of defiance in her eyes.

The Master took two steps towards her. He took her cheeks in his hand, exactly, had he but known it, as she had Melinda's a few minutes earlier. 'You do realise what you have done, don't you?'

'So fire me,' she said.

His fingers wiped her lips. He brought them to his nose and inhaled. 'Oh my dear woman, I'm afraid it is not quite as simple as that.' He smiled and licked his fingers. He closed his eyes momentarily to savour the taste.

'I forgot my briefcase you see,' he said to Melinda, tucking the shirt neatly back into the trousers. He picked up the briefcase from the side of the seat he had used. For a long moment, he looked from Charles to the chauffeuse as if deciding what he was going to do with them. Then, without another word, he took Melinda by the arm and led her along the cabin, out through the main door and down the steps of the plane. He guided her across the tarmac towards the waiting Rolls-Royce. Another chauffeur opened the rear passenger door as they approached.

'Excuse me a moment, my dear,' the Master said, indicating that she should get into the car.

From the back seat Melinda watched the Master talking to two men by the Ford. It was not a long conversation.

The Master got into the luxurious leather and walnut interior of the Rolls. As it pulled away, Melinda saw the two men mount the steps into the plane.

Nine

The big car rolled effortlessly through narrow and winding country lanes. Melinda had no idea where they were, except that the plane had headed north all the way from London, and from the style of some of the small cottages along the car's route she suspected they had landed in Scotland.

The area was very hilly, and the car wound its way up to the top of a large escarpment from which the view of the valley below, complete with a lake sparkling in the sun, was simply breathtaking.

They drove for almost an hour, according to the clock set in the walnut dashboard of the Rolls. In that time, the Master said not a single word to her, reading a set of papers from his briefcase. But he gave no impression of anger; she did not have the feeling he was blaming her for what had happened. That did not stop her blaming herself.

Eventually, the car slowed and turned into a long gravel track through a gap in a tall beech hedge. After at least two miles, the track led to a large Victorian house perched at the very top of the valley, with sumptuous views of the countryside on every side.

'Beautiful, isn't it?' the Master said, looking around.

'Yes, Master,' Melinda said.

The Master got out of the car. An elderly housekeeper, thin but with a ramrod-straight back and white hair, had opened the front door, and two Irish wolfhounds had bounded out to greet him. Behind her followed a man dressed for all the world like a Victorian gillie, a shotgun broken over the crook of his arm, a belt of ammunition thrown over his shoulder.

The housekeeper looked into the rear of the car and, seeing it occupied, helped Melinda out. The Master had walked off with the gillie, the two dogs bounding about after them. Melinda watched as they walked around the back of the house. The housekeeper's boney hand, covered with skin like parchment, clasped her shoulder like a claw digging into her soft flesh. She led her into the house.

Compared to the warmth outside, the house felt cold. The old woman led Melinda through a labyrinth of dark corridors. It appeared that no attempt had been made to modernise the house, as it still retained its air of gloomy Victorian splendour. A great deal of money had obviously been spent in restoring the house to make it resemble as closely as possible what it had once been: the manor house for some landowning Victorian gentry.

They arrived in a large dining room. Wooden shutters were closed over the box-type bay windows, so that light filtered into the room in bright golden shafts through the gaps in the wood. This gave the room a misty, gauzy appearance. A large oak dining table stood in the middle of the room, surrounded by spoon-backed chairs. The floor was old oak, polished to a sparkling shine.

Along the back wall, near a long sideboard used to serve food and the double doors leading to the kitchen, two columns had been set on either side of the

room to support a decorative vault in the ceiling, sep-
arating the dining area from the serving area. The
housekeeper took Melinda over to the nearest column
and placed her against it, facing the smooth stone. Set
on the opposite side of the column, at neck and waist
height, were two metal rings through which were
threaded thin but strong steel chains. With apparently practised ease, the housekeeper pulled the chains
around the stone and then around Melinda, the neck
first and then the waist, until she was held tightly, her
stomach pressed against the convex stone. The chains
were secured by two small padlocks.

The whole operation was performed so quickly,
Melinda barely realised what had happened to her. It
was only as she heard the housekeeper's footsteps
fading into the distance and she tried to move, that
she discovered how securely she was bound. The
chain at her neck held her cheek against the column.
She could not move her head back far enough to see
the other side of the room. With her hands still bound
to her thighs, Melinda was utterly helpless, her bondage total. True, she could move her ankles and legs a
little, but the chain at her wrist was too tight to allow
even this to be more than the smallest of movements.

The house was silent, apart from the ticking of a
clock; heavy metallic ticks that echoed through the
rooms. She remembered they had passed a grand-
father clock in the passage outside. The ticks marked
the passage of time. Every quarter hour the clock
chimed a delicate arrangement of tiny bells and every
hour a larger tone sounded. She could count the
hours. It was the first time she had known the time
for over a week. Being able to keep track of it made
time seem to pass infinitely more slowly.

The discomfort of her bondage did not take long

to establish itself in her body. The chain around her neck was the worst. The small links dug into her neck. She could ease it slightly by moving her head forward and pressing her cheek against the stone, but this too was a strain and she could only do it for short periods of time. The chain around her waist was tighter and permitted no movement, but at least it was padded by the material of the jacket and shirt.

Melinda tried to think. The episode on the plane had disturbed her. It had spoilt her concentration, her intent. Up until that moment she had been entirely focused on her submission, on being the pawn in the Master's game, a piece on the board he could play, to be moved and sacrificed as he desired. But, however briefly, she had escaped his control. Her orgasm had been spontaneous, unplanned, not part of his careful calculation. Everything else that had happened to her, been done to her, was as a result of his wishes and his will. Her orgasm had not been.

As much as she had craved for it, as much as she had not been able to control herself or her orgasm, she wished it hadn't happened. She wished she could wipe the whole thing from her mind.

But she couldn't. She couldn't forget the touch of those lips on her sex, or the wicked sensuality of that tongue. Did it feel so different because it had been a woman, or was it just the result of her incredible frustration? The more she wallowed in the memory, the more guilty she felt.

And what would happen to the chauffeur and Charles? The Master's imagination seemed to know no bounds. She would probably never know what fate befell them.

After the little quarter chimes had rung nine times, and the hour chimes rang out four sonorous notes, the blinds on the windows were concertined back into their frames and the room was flooded with light.

Melinda could not see who had done this until they came round to the side of the column on which her cheek rested. It turned out to be a maid, stout and middle-aged. Almost at once, a stream of servants walked in and out of the room, preparing the table for the evening meal. As the table was behind her back she could not see how many people it was being set for.

None of the servants looked at her, spoke to her or acknowledged her presence in any way. She could have been a sculpture carved into the stone of the column.

The bustle of activity subsided and the room returned to the silence she had become used to, punctuated only by the monotonous ticking of the clock.

Slowly, Melinda's mood changed. The incident on the plane began to fade. Once again, the demands that her bondage made on her body made it impossible to think about anything but her physical being. She could no longer think of guilt and consequence, of what she should have done or might have done. Hour after hour of standing, of desperately trying to ease the aches and pains in her neck and back and wrists, of designing little movements that gave her relief, however temporary, from one area of discomfort, left her mind blank, erased like a cassette tape. She could only think of her body. She had no decisions to make, no choices. She had no will. She did not want to have a will.

As the big clock in the hall struck seven, another burst of activity erupted. Melinda could smell and hear food being prepared behind the double doors to the kitchen. At precisely seven-thirty, the Master

153

walked into the dining room and sat at the head of the big dining table. Though Melinda could not see him and he said nothing, she knew it was him. She could feel the power of his eyes. She knew he was looking at her.

A waiter came out of the kitchen, carrying a tureen of soup on a silver tray lined with white linen. By straining around against the chains, Melinda could glimpse the soup being served to the Master. He was eating alone.

The Master ate but said nothing. Grilled fish, white wine, mineral water and bread were all ferried in past Melinda. She could hear the sound of knife and fork striking the plates, of wine being poured and bread broken.

After each course, the waiter returned to clear the table. He did not look at Melinda once.

'No dessert,' the Master said, as the fish was cleared away.

'Yes, sir. Coffee?'

'Yes.'

The waiter went back into the kitchen. Melinda heard the Master's chair scrape back on the wooden floor and his footsteps approaching her, but he still remained silent. The waiter returned almost immediately, his silver tray this time containing a Georgian silver coffee pot, and a single cup and saucer in delicate white china.

'Shall I pour, sir?'

'No, just leave it on the table.'

The waiter did as he was instructed and then left the room. The Master's words hung in the air. His footsteps approached the stone column until Melinda could feel his breath on her neck. He did nothing for what seemed like hours; nothing but look. Then his hand brushed her short blonde hair. His touch made her start.

'Well, my dear,' he said. 'You must be very uncomfortable.' It was not a question. She knew better than to reply. 'Are you?'

Now she could speak, 'Yes, Master.'

'I'm sure. But you know it pleases me. It excites me. I explained that, didn't I?'

'Yes, Master.' *As long as it pleases you, Master*, she wanted to say.

He walked around the column until she could see him. In his hand he held a pair of scissors, big commercial tailoring scissors, their chrome blades catching the light. He came up to her, so close their faces were only inches apart. She thought he was going to kiss her. She looked into his eyes and immediately felt herself overwhelmed; it was a sensation like looking directly into the sun. He moved behind her, but his eyes still burnt on her retina.

She felt his hand on the back of the jacket. She heard the scissors slicing through material, and in a second he had cut the jacket in two from waist to neck. He pulled the shirt from her trousers. This time, she could feel the cold blade of the scissors as he cut the shirt in two along her spine.

He pulled the waistband of the trousers out from the small of her back, extracting it from the chain that bound her to the column, and cut along the crease of the trouser leg right down to her ankle. A second cut destroyed the other leg. He cut round the pockets and along the sleeves of jacket and shirt until the clothes hung in tatters from her naked body. He pulled the remnants away. The stone column felt cold against her naked breasts and belly.

He was kneeling at her feet, taking off her shoes, stripping off the men's socks.

'Beautiful,' he said. He was clearly excited; his voice sounded husky.

He ran the tip of the scissors up the back of her legs, from ankle to thigh, then up over the roundness of her arse and along her spine to the nape of her neck. Their coldness made her shiver. Then she felt his hand, warm by contrast, caressing her buttocks, moulding itself to her curves, feeling the weight of the rump overhanging her thigh. His fingers pulled the cheeks of her arse apart; she could feel his eyes on the puckered corona of her anus. His finger examined it, probing but not penetrating.

Suddenly, quite unexpectedly, he pressed himself into her, wrapping his arms around the stone column and squeezing her body between it and him, with all his strength. She could feel his erection thrust against her arse. Every muscle in his body seemed hard and tense, his face resting against her naked shoulder.

He had knocked the breath out of her. She gasped to regain it, as she wallowed in this sudden human contact, so total, so all-consuming, unlike anything she had experienced under the Master's control.

'I knew you were a woman,' he whispered, his breath hot against her ear. 'Under those clothes. I knew.' He was not talking to her. It was his own private fantasy playing in his head. His cock moved against her rear, but only the smallest of movements. She heard him moan, a peculiar sound, a cross between a cough and a yelp of pain.

As suddenly as he'd started, he stopped. As she panted for breath, she heard him walk back to his chair at the table. He poured a cup of coffee, and she heard him sipping it. There was a long silence. The clock ticked away the minutes.

Had the Master come? Had his elaborate private

fantasy – her bondage, the men's clothes – made him come so quickly? Melinda would never know.

'Tell me what happened on the plane?' His voice rang out across the room.

Melinda hesitated. She had not said more than a few words to anybody for a week. What should she say? She had to tell the truth but she had lost the art of forming sentences.

'The woman ... I was ... They unstrapped ...' She couldn't think of the words.

'They unstrapped you?' the Master prompted.

'Yes, Master.'

'The man fucked you?'

'No, Master. The woman ...' She came to a grinding halt again.

'The woman. What did she do?'

'Sucked me, Master. Licked me.'

'And what did you do?'

'I couldn't help it, Master.'

'Answer my question.'

'She made me come, Master.'

'You had an orgasm?'

'Yes, Master.'

'While the woman licked you. You had an orgasm.' She could feel his eyes on her naked back.

'Yes, Master.'

'And what did the man do?'

'Nothing, Master, not to me.'

'He touched you?'

'Yes, Master.'

'But that was all?'

'Yes, Master.'

'Did he do anything to the woman?'

'He was ...' She was just about to say 'fucking' and hesitated.

'Fucking her?' the Master prompted again.

'Yes, Master.'

'I see,' he said, lapsing into silence.

After another cup of coffee, Melinda heard the chair scraping back on the floor, and footsteps leave the room.

Almost instantly, the housekeeper appeared. She bustled over to Melinda, and quickly unlocked the padlocks that chained her to the column. Her long thin fingers unbuckled all four leather straps at her wrists and thighs. Finally, she released the thick leather belt at her waist.

Standing without the support of the column, Melinda felt weak. The housekeeper took her by the arm and helped her over to the dining table. A tray of food was brought out from the kitchen by the same waiter who had served the Master. He took considerably more interest in her naked body this time. The housekeeper indicated that she should eat.

'This way,' the old woman said as soon as the food was finished. She set off across the room. Melinda got up from the table and followed, not at all sure her limbs would obey her commands. Unsteadily, she walked out into the corridor.

They mounted the stairs. Melinda found she was out of breath at this sudden exercise. She put her hand out to steady herself against the bannisters. It was the first time she had been able to move her hands all day.

The old woman opened the first door on the landing. It was a small bathroom. Everything was Victorian in design, but with modern plumbing.

'Use the facilities,' she said, a Scottish accent now evident.

There was no shower, so Melinda ran herself a

bath. She used the toilet while the bath filled. The old woman's eyes never left her but Melinda was used to performing the most intimate of activities in public now. She eased herself into the bath, but was not allowed to luxuriate in the warm water.

'Hurry up,' the housekeeper snapped.

As soon as Melinda was dry, the housekeeper led the way up a second flight of stairs. At the top, she walked down a small corridor and opened one of the doors. Indicating that Melinda should enter, and without another word, she locked the door the moment Melinda was inside.

Melinda stood in the room alone. She felt totally lost. No bonds, no cuffs, no metal block between her legs; no camera either as far as she could see. Within the confines of the small room, furnished with only a single bed, she was free. She could even switch the overhead light on and off herself.

She stood unmoving on the room's bare wooden floorboards. Just as she had found it difficult to form sentences earlier, now her sudden freedom made it difficult to think of what she should do. Within the room she could do anything. The choice was suddenly overwhelming. She could touch herself, she could spend all night in endless masturbation. She could torture her nipples, invade her cunt, stroke her clitoris. Do everything she had so desperately wanted to do all the nights she had been chained and helpless. There was no constraint.

Except she knew what the Master intended. This was her punishment. He knew what had happened on the plane. He knew she had not resisted, that she had come in the chauffeur's mouth. This was her punishment. Freedom was her punishment.

She lay on the bed. The room was warm and she

159

did not need to cover her body with the blanket that lay across the bed. She looked down at her body. The marks left by the leather straps had faded slightly but were still evident on her waist and thighs. She rubbed her thigh then stopped herself. Mechanically she raised her hands above her head, her wrists together. She would show him. She would show herself. She would take her punishment. She opened her legs so her thighs were not pressing against her sex. She would show him. She would not touch herself. She would lie all night and take her punishment. She would show him she did not want to be free.

The punishment continued in the morning. Her breakfast arrived with the housekeeper, who stood over her while she ate it. Then she was led down to the bathroom. A razor and shaving brush had appeared, and she used them to shave off the daily growth of pubic hair while the old woman watched impassively. At any moment she was expecting to be cuffed and bound. But she was not. As soon as she was dry the housekeeper led her downstairs, through the dining room where she had been chained last night to the back of the house.

'In here,' the woman said, opening a glass-panelled door. Melinda stepped into what looked like a vast Victorian conservatory. In fact, the curved glass roof housed a large rectangular swimming pool, bordered by lush tropical plants on three sides, with a small gym area on the other complete with various exercise machines and a jacuzzi.

'You will not be required until seven,' the house-keeper said. It was the first time Melinda had known from one minute to the next what she would be doing.

The door was closed but not locked. Melinda was left alone. Alone and free. All part of her punishment. She was sure of that now. She could see the Master's eyes, calculating, making the punishment fit the crime. She had come, allowed her body to escape his control, and this was the result.

It hurt. It hurt more than any of the bonds had done, more than the chains yesterday, more than being whipped. She no longer wanted freedom.

She swam without enthusiasm and used the exercise machines, half-imagining one of the chatelaines standing over her, telling her what to do. She lay uneasily on one of the many sun-loungers, and felt the heat of the sun through the glass roof beating down on her naked body. The housekeeper brought a meal at lunchtime, but did not watch her while she ate it.

Without the constriction of her bondage to distract her, her mind roamed freely. She yearned to be back in the house in London, back where her life was controlled, her movements decided. What made the punishment worse was that she knew she deserved it. She should have controlled herself, she should have fought the couple, fought her orgasm. She went cold when the thought occurred to her that the Master might not take her back, that this was the prelude to her release, that she might never see the London house again.

Such thoughts were torture, more painful than anything she had endured so far.

At six, the housekeeper opened the conservatory door again. Without a word she indicated that Melinda should follow her. They retraced the morning's journey through the house and up to the bedroom, having first used the bathroom. Melinda was locked in.

Sitting on the bed, she comforted herself with the thought that at least she hadn't been told what the next hours would bring. She was back with not knowing. Such crumbs of solace were important to her, her mind still full of unwelcome thoughts.

It was only a few minutes before the door was unlocked again. The housekeeper entered. She dropped several items on the bed next to Melinda.

'Play time,' she said, a slight smile flickering on her face; a cruel smile rather than one of pleasure. 'Put these on,' she ordered, holding up a pair of what looked like full-length black leather gloves, with the addition of a flap about an inch wide, perforated from top to bottom with holes reinforced by metal edges.

Melinda pulled the first glove over her arm. The soft leather was tight, and it took a great deal of effort before her fingers slid into the carefully tailored stalls, and she could smooth the glove flat. The leather extended right up to her armpit. Here, sown to the top of the glove was a leather strap which the housekeeper buckled over Melinda's shoulder. The second glove followed with equal difficulty, once again secured by a strap fastened tightly over the shoulder.

'Hands behind your back,' the old woman ordered. She grasped Melinda's arms in her hands. Despite her frailty, her grip was strong, her hands pinching like the claw of a bird. She pressed Melinda's hands together, fingertip to fingertip in an attitude of prayer, except that her hands were pointed to her feet. 'Now don't move,' she instructed.

From the bed, she picked up a long leather lace and threaded it through the holes in the flap attached to the gloves, as if lacing the eyes of a shoe. She worked quickly, pulling the laces tight after every two or three eyelets, effectively binding Melinda's arms together, tighter and tighter, from wrist to shoulder. At the very top, the laces forced Melinda's upper arms together, her shoulder blades almost meeting, her breasts pushed out prominently in response to the position of her arms.

The old woman took a black satin basque off the bed. She made Melinda step into it, then drew it up around her body. The basque was laced too. Once satisfied that it was correctly positioned the housekeeper drew these laces tight, until Melinda felt its constriction encasing her body. It had her breathless.

The basque had no bra. It was topped by two half-crescents which tucked under the breasts, but did not hide or support them.

Melinda was pushed into a sitting position on the bed. Sheer black stockings were rolled over her legs and clipped to the long satin suspenders of the basque.

The woman brushed Melinda's hair, and applied make-up, blusher, eye liner, eye shadow and lipstick. Finally, she dropped a pair of black high heels on the floor and indicated that Melinda should put them on. Then she left the room, locking the door behind her.

Melinda's breathing had not returned to normal. She was breathing in rapid, shallow pants. Her heart was beating fast. There was no mirror in the room. Melinda could only look down at her own body, her naked tits hanging over the incredibly tight, black satin corset, the welts of the black stockings bisecting her thighs, her hairless pubis revealing the folds of her sex. She could not suppress a shudder of pleasure.

As her body had been bound, her excitement had increased, every pull of the laces of the gloves like a

163

notch on a gear that racked up her feelings. Once
again she was helpless, her body held and bound. Her
shoulders ached, her whole torso a tightly wrapped
package. And, in the centre of it, open, exposed and
available, was the melting wetness that throbbed
between her legs.

With every muscle in her body she fought the
bonds, wanting to feel their constraint. To her delight, she could move them not an inch. This bondage
was the tightest she had experienced. She gloried in it.
She welcomed it. She knew her punishment was over.

Darkness had fallen before the bedroom door was
unlocked again and Melinda had no means of reaching the light switch, now, to switch on the light. She
had sat on the edge of the bed, where she had been
left, relishing the feelings her body generated, her
doubts and fears, her ability to think, gradually sub-
merged in waves of discomfort. Once again, she had
no will. Once again, her body, bound and dressed and
made-up to someone else's design, did not belong to
her.

The door finally opened. The housekeeper turned
on the light and beckoned her forward.

Without being able to use her hands for balance,
she had to walk down the stairs with care, not wanting to pitch forward. On the first floor landing, the
old woman led her to the far door, rapped twice,
opened it, and pushed Melinda inside, closing the
door behind her.

'Come in, come in . . .' The Master's voice sounded
different, softer; even, Melinda thought, a little
drunk.

'Well, don't you look pretty.'

The bedroom was not as large as the one in the

London house, and contained little more than a large double bed with tables on each side supporting two bedside lamps, which were dimmed to give the room a deep rich glow. Hanging from the ceiling to one side of the bed was a thick white rope. It was wrapped around a pulley and trailed off to the side wall where it was tied off on a large brass cleat. The rope's silhouette was reflected on the opposite wall. It looked like the shadow of a gallows.

The Master lay on the bed in a white silk robe, his back propped up on pillows against the wall. He was not alone. Kneeling in a tight ball, his knees under his chest, was what from behind appeared to be a naked young boy. The boy's mouth was devouring the Master's cock; riding up and down on the shaft, licking and sucking as it went, covering the hard shaft with saliva.

'Come close, and watch,' the Master said.

Melinda obeyed. The robe had been pushed up to allow access to his cock. It was the first time she had seen it. It was big and handsome. From what she could see it was very smooth, almost polished-looking and neatly circumcised. She could see his balls were big too, and very hairy.

'Stop,' the Master ordered. The boy's mouth obeyed, immediately pressing into his crotch as it happened to be on the downward stroke when the order was issued. 'Put the clips on her.'

The boy raised his head. The cock slipped from his lips. It was only then that Melinda saw that the slight figure kneeling on the bed was not a 'boy' at all. The short-haired waif was, in fact, a girl, though the most masculine girl Melinda had ever seen. Like a man, her figure was angular: big shoulders and very little waist; her features large; her breasts non-existent; and even her nipples, though erect, no more than tiny buttons on her flat chest. Had it not been for the absence of a cock nestling between her legs, had it not been for the labia of a female clearly visible under a shaven pubis, there would have been nothing to point to her femininity.

The Master could see Melinda's surprise. 'Beautiful, isn't she? Entirely natural, I assure you. Not the result of a surgeon's knife. The most unique specimen in my collection. Her name is Harriet, but of course everyone calls her Harry.'

Harry was taking two small black metal rings from the drawer of the bedside table. She approached Melinda, looking her in the eyes. Even without the short hair, her face would have passed for a boy. Her chin was wide and firm, her eyes – like the rest of her face with not a trace of make-up – large, and her eyebrows bushy.

Without a word, she circled Melinda's exposed breast with one hand and guided the black ring over her nipple with the other. The ring neatly enclosed the nipple. Holding it securely in place, the girl released a strong spring set in the ring that clamped it firmly in place, reducing the inner radius like the shutter of a camera, except its edges were serrated to bite into the tender flesh. Melinda could not stifle a moan of pain. The girl placed the second ring with the same effect. Melinda moaned again, her body instantly charged with the pleasure this type of pain always generated in her.

The girl looked over to the Master, as if for reassurance that she should go on. The Master nodded. His hand had circled his erection, wanking it lazily up and down. His eyes darted from Harry's body to Melinda's. There could hardly have been a greater contrast.

'Do they hurt?'

'Yes, Master.'

'And you like that, don't you?'

'Yes, Master.'

Harry had unwound the end of the white rope from its cleat on the wall. She went to the end that hung in the middle of the room and pulled it down over the pulley. Quickly, she tied this end tightly around Melinda's wrists, manoeuvring her back until she stood directly under the pulley wheel.

Again, she looked for reassurance from the Master. Melinda saw him nod and smile. The smile was for Harry, not for her. Back at the cleat, Harry took the rope and pulled. Melinda's wrists were hoisted backward and upward forcing her to bend forward from the waist. Harry pulled until Melinda's arms were almost vertical and she was bent over at right angles. She had to spread her legs apart to keep her balance. Harry secured the rope to the cleat.

The position was agonising, but at the same time incredibly exciting. Melinda was bound and spread, her arse forced into the air, her whole sex, from the hood of her clitoris to the rose of her anus, open and exposed, every detail on view. The oval of her labia, the especially thick, puffy labia, looked like a strange vertical smile, lips ready to suck in whatever they might.

The Master beckoned Harry back to the bed. Melinda had to force her head up to watch, further increasing the pressure in her shoulder blades, but it was worth it. With an affection she had never seen or thought him capable of, the Master kissed Harry on the cheeks, one at a time, and then on the mouth. They kissed long and hard, the girl bent over the bed, just as Melinda was but with no constraint, her labia

167

too exposed by her hairlessness, though nothing like as fleshy as those of the woman in bondage.

The kiss went on for a long time. The girl's hand circled the Master's cock, squeezing it tightly. Melinda felt the moistness of her sex turn into a torrent. She was sure her juices had begun to run over her labia and down her thigh. She put herself in the girl's shoes, strained to imagine the Master was kissing her, that she was being allowed such intimate pleasures. Where did she fit into the scheme of things? The Master had implied she was one of his collection, but clearly she was not a slave. Nor was she a chatelaine. What, then, did she mean to the Master?

Harry straightened up. The Master patted her rump, half with affection, half as a gesture of encouragement. She padded across the room out of Melinda's line of vision, which was severely restricted. With her head down, in the position which brought her least pain, she could see little but her own legs, the sheer black stockings stretched taut by the suspenders, her hairless pubis, the crease of her sex, and beyond, a stretch of carpet. That was all.

Harry was back in front of the bed again. Melinda made the effort to look up. Around her hips, Harry had strapped a harness. It snaked around her waist, down between the cleft of her arse, around under the line of her buttocks, up between her legs. Jutting from the front, at the apex of her thighs, was a cream-coloured dildo. The Master stretched out his hand to encircle it. He wanked it as though it were a real cock.

'I wish it were real,' Harry said. Her voice was as masculine as her appearance, deep and gruff.

'Do you?'

'For you,' she said.

Harry picked up a bottle of oil from the bedside

table, a little stoppered bottle like they used to use in chemist's shops. She poured the oil over the head of the dildo and the Master's fingers. He spread it out until the whole dildo glistened.

Harry turned. Again the Master patted encouragement on her scrawny rump.

She walked towards Melinda, who rested her head. She had seen enough.

'You want it, don't you?' the Master asked. His hand had gone back to his cock. The residue of the oil coated his erection, making that shine too.

Melinda felt Harry's hands on her hips, the dildo pressing hard against her arse. Her breasts trembled, the nipple clips biting her tender flesh.

'Yes, Master, yes,' Melinda breathed, having difficulty with the words because her excitement was so intense. She felt Harry's hips buck and direct the dildo downward. Her whole body was trembling. This was almost too much to bear. Too much intimacy. She felt so close to the Master now. Part of him. He'd allowed her to see something private, something personal. What was happening in this room was different, not part of the system, not part of the public displays.

'Do it,' the Master said, his voice not relaxed any more. Instantly the dildo pushed into the lips of her sex. It was easy. Frictionless. Her cunt was soaking wet. But Harry flicked her hips back and withdrew immediatedly. That was not the target. Her hand directed the dildo more precisely, until it was centred on the puckered crater of Melinda's anus.

Melinda was coming. Her body churned, the tortured nerves of her bound muscles egging the rest of her body on. The first misdirected thrust of the dildo had fired the motor of her orgasm. Despite the difficulty, she strained her head up to watch the Master wank his big, elegant cock, his fist rising and falling over his length. The dildo nudging at her anus provoked the first wave, the first explosion, the one that released her, cleared the way, and then, as Harry's hips bucked it deep and effortlessly into her tight passage the rest of the explosions followed, like gunshots from an automatic; each shot recoiling in her body until the magazine was empty and she was limp and damp and helpless, hanging from the thick white rope like a discarded rag doll.

How long the orgasm had lasted she did not know, but she felt the dildo slip from her body. She opened her eyes and strained her head up, to see that the bed in front of her was empty. The Master had gone. She could not see him anywhere. She dropped her head and at that moment realised there were now two pairs of feet on the carpet behind her black high heels.

The heat and hardness of a cock nudged against her buttocks. The Master's cock. She wanted to scream with pleasure. He was going to take her, at last. The Master's hands held her hips, pulling her helpless body back onto his bone-hard cock. Harry's hand was guiding it, holding it into the bud of her anus, opened and oiled by the dildo.

The Master slid his cock effortlessly into her arse. She could not remember ever wanting anything so much in her life. It was as if her whole being was centred on his cock. Her bondage concentrated the feeling. There was nothing else to do, no movement she could make, nothing for her to think about but what was being done to her.

He bucked his hips again and his cock buried itself in her tight, hot rear. She could feel his balls against her labia, feel Harry's cunning little fingers snaking

170

down to catch his scrotum, playing with the Master's balls and her clitoris at the same time.

He moved now, in and out; full deep strokes, reaming into her. He could feel her coming. His whole body was trembling. He felt Harry's thin masculine body pressing into his back and her hands working at his balls until finally he could hold out no longer. He knew he should pull out, pull out of her and spunk over her buttocks, over the black satin that held her waist so tightly. But he couldn't. For once, he let himself go, let his cock settle in the hot, tight passage of his slave, and let her take control of him; her inner convulsions milking the spunk from his eager, excited balls.

Ten

It was a week since Melinda had seen the Master. She had been flown back to London on her own the next day. Cybele had returned her to her cell in the stables and the previous routine had been resumed, only exercise and solariums breaking the monotony of being bound to the wall of her cell with the metal block chained firmly between her legs. This time she was not beaten or abused by the chatelaines. She had no human contact whatsoever.

Nor had Marion appeared. Melinda had speculated as to what Marion's 'turn' would involve, but apparently, at the moment, she had other priorities to fulfil.

Not that Melinda minded that. After her experience with the Master in Scotland, her attitude had changed completely. He had punished her disobedience and rewarded her submission. He had, what is more, allowed himself to be seduced by her. She knew – at least she felt – what he had done with her was not something he allowed to happen often, not with the slaves. For the Master, the slaves were objects, things of beauty, part of his possessions, part of his collection. They were to be played with like toys. Whatever sexual acts he performed with them were public. What had happened in Scotland was reserved and private. Not for public consumption. Reserved, she suspected, for women like Marion, and Harry, and whoever else was not part of his three-ringed circus.

But Melinda had touched him and, more importantly, he had touched her. She was content. She could lie on the thin mattress for hour after hour without complaint. The metal block did not bother her. She had no desire to touch herself. It would wipe away the memory of him, the deep impression he had left in her body. She could still feel him, hear him, see him.

It was late in the evening of the seventh day after her return from Scotland that Marion appeared in her cell. Melinda had already been cuffed to the wall by Hera, and was expecting the lights to go out at any minute.

Marion was smiling, an odd, unfriendly smile. She knelt by the mattress, her nylons rasping against her skirt.

'Been having a good time, I hear.'

It was not a question. Melinda remained obediently silent.

'Haven't you?'

'Yes, mistress,' Melinda said. She inhaled Marion's strong perfume and felt her heartbeat increase.

'You little bitch,' Marion said with no real malice, just as a statement of fact. She ran her hand over Melinda's body, as if looking for evidence of what had gone on. 'You'd better tell me about it, hadn't you?'

'Yes, mistress.' The last thing she wanted to do was tell Marion the details of what had gone on in Scotland. Then it would no longer be private.

Fortunately Marion did not pursue the subject. She uncuffed Melinda's hands from the wall and pulled her to her feet. She was wearing a rich flame-red dress that clung tightly to her figure, its low neckline revealing her ample cleavage. Her long black hair was pinned up. She looked as though she had just come from dinner at some elegant restaurant.

The metal block was unchained and fell away.

'Do you remember what I said?' Marion asked.

'Yes, mistress.'

'I've been thinking about you.' Melinda could see her eyes were sparkling with excitement. 'Follow me.'

Melinda, naked and bare-footed, followed Marion's elegant court shoes, sheer hosiery and fine silk dress out of the cell and, in turn, out of the stable block. They took a new direction. Instead of crossing the covered courtyard, they turned left into a short corridor, at the end of which was a staircase leading down to the cellars. At the bottom of the stairs there was a door immediately in front of them, and a corridor to one side. Marion opened the door, closing it firmly when they were both inside.

The room was small, its walls and ceiling painted black, its floor a short-pile black carpet. A small double bed and a single bedside table were the only furniture. Across the centre of the ceiling a lighting bar carried an array of spotlights, but only one, the one aimed at the bed, was turned on, casting a pool of white light around the bed while leaving the rest of the room in comparative darkness. There was something odd about one of the black walls, Melinda thought, but in the dim light she could not make out what.

At each corner of the frame of the bed a stout post extended above the level of the sheets, like a four-poster that had been sawn off short. Each post was inset with a metal ring and chain, attached to which was a stout leather cuff.

'So here we are,' Marion announced. She came up behind Melinda, wrapped her arms around her body and pressed into her back. Melinda felt the silk sliding against her nakedness. 'Just the two of us,' she added, hugging Melinda to her and kissing her neck.

Her lips felt hot. They left a wet trail as they worked along Melinda's neck. Her hands cupped Melinda's breasts, squeezing them tightly. Then one hand dropped down to the flatness of her belly. 'You must obey me, you know that, don't you?'

'Yes, mistress.' Judging from the reaction of her body, obeying Marion was not going to be a problem. Melinda's heart was racing, the mainspring of her sexuality already beginning to tick.

Marion was kissing the nape of her neck now, their bodies separated. 'I know what happened on the plane. Did you enjoy it?'

'No, mistress.' Melinda's body arched back involuntarily as Marion's tongue, darting out between her lips, found some hidden nerve.

'I thought you did.'

'No, mistress . . .'

'Why not?'

'They forced me.'

'You've never been with a woman, have you? Not properly.'

'No, mistress.'

'Have you ever imagined what it would be like?' The hot, wet tongue still plied the furrows of Melinda's neck, sending electric shocks of sensation coarsing through her body.

'Yes, mistress. With you, mistress.' It was true.

'I've been waiting for you.' The nipping little kisses were running along Melinda's shoulders now. 'Patiently waiting my turn. Now you're mine. Aren't you?'

175

Yes, Melinda wanted to say. *If the Master says I am.* 'Yes, mistress, yes.'

Marion's fingertips had worked down to the apex of her belly, down over her shaven pubis, down between her thighs, her forefinger delving into the runnel of her sex.

'Such a pity. All that pretty blonde hair shaved away,' she said, punctuating every word with a kiss.

Melinda found herself being turned around to face Marion. Eye-to-eye Marion examined her, looking for emotion, looking to see what she felt. If she had expected discomfiture she would have been disappointed. Melinda's eyes sparkled with excitement.

'Kiss me,' Marion said. 'Hold me.'

The words sent a shiver of pleasure through Melinda. She obeyed immediately, pressing her mouth into Marion's, feeling, for only the second time, a woman's lips against her own. Her arms wrapped around the silk dress and she rubbed her breasts on the slippery material. She pressed her thigh up between Marion's legs, until she could feel the hard curve of her pubic bone.

Marion allowed herself to be passive, let Melinda's tongue probe her mouth, while her hands roamed her back. She had desired Melinda from the moment she had seen her. She'd had to wait. Now she let the pent up passion flow through her body, knowing that, at last, the moment had come.

They stood wrapped together, arms and legs, a curious Indian sculpture. One naked woman wrapped around the fully clothed body of another. The red of Marion's dress gave Melinda's skin a rose glow.

Marion broke the embrace.

'Unzip me,' she ordered. However much passion she felt for this beautiful blonde, she must not forget that Melinda was still the Master's slave. The Master would not be pleased if she forgot that. It was not easy.

Melinda walked behind Marion, her body still humming from the length of contact she had been allowed. For a week, the only human contact she had had was the occasional brush against one of the chatelaines as they chained her to the wall. No surprise then, that her heart was pounding and she had to keep reminding herself to breathe.

She pulled the long zip of Marion's dress down into the small of her back.

'Take it off,' Marion said, quietly trying to keep her passion in check.

Melinda pulled the thin shoulder straps from Marion's finely boned shoulders, then worked the red silk clear of her bust. The dress fell to the floor. Marion stepped out of it. Her lingerie was flame-red too: a red underwired strapless bra, its scalloped cups spilling her heavy breasts, bisected her tanned ribs. Another band of red wrapped around her waist: a silky suspender belt that fitted her slim waist tightly. Its thin suspenders snaked down her navel and flanks, under a pair of matching high-cut panties to her thighs, where they gathered up the welts of her sheer stockings. The panties were inset with lace at the front and sides. The lacy panel at the front revealed her tight black curls of pubic hair. Her full, rich, fleshy thighs stretched the welts of the stockings taut, a tiny sash of red satin on the suspenders hiding the metal hoop that gripped the nylon, as if to see it would offend the eye.

Marion turned to face Melinda. For a second, their eyes met. Melinda had been used by the woman on the plane. But this was different. This was the first time. As Marion sat on the bed, Melinda remained where she was. She had not been ordered to move. She could see Marion's eyes roaming her body, her prominent breasts, her long lithe legs, the folds of her sex no longer hidden by pubic hair.

'Come over here,' Marion said, not content to look any more; wanting to turn the anticipation that coarsed through her body like a drug, into a reality.

Melinda stood directly in front of her. Marion leant forward slightly, wrapping her hands around the backs of Melinda's thighs and stroking them. 'So many things to do. So many things to teach you. Do you want to learn?'

I want what the Master wants, Melinda thought. 'Yes, mistress.' But her body had needs too. Her excitement was intense.

Marion's hands pulled Melinda forward until her pubis was pressed against Marion's face. Immediately, Melinda felt her hot tongue licking the flesh she now shaved meticulously every morning. It was as though the shaving had made it more sensitive. Then the tongue dipped lower, finding the groove that led down between her thighs. The tongue curled round her clitoris, already hard and swollen, and stroked it lightly. Melinda felt her body shudder.

'Not yet,' Marion said, raising her head, a teasing smile on her lips.

Melinda tried to ignore the feelings her clitoris pumped into her nerves. It was difficult.

Marion lay back in the middle of the bed. She knew perfectly well what Melinda was going through.

'Kneel, here next to me. Take my panties off,' Marion ordered, trying to keep her voice flat and level and not being altogether successful.

Melinda climbed onto the bed, kneeling beside

Marion's hips. She leant over Marion's body and took the waistband of the panties in her hands, pulling them down. Marion arched her buttocks off the bed so she could pull them clear. As soon as they were off, Marion opened her legs. She opened them wide, stretching them out across the bed. Melinda looked into her sex. She had never seen a woman's sex like this, spread out in front of her, displayed for her benefit. The pubic hair was thick. It covered her labia as well as the triangle of her pubis. It would have covered her thighs too, but it had been neatly trimmed so as not to extend beyond the bikini line. On her sex, the hair was plastered down. It was as wet as Marion's labia, as the hole of her cunt that Melinda could see so clearly, an almost perfect circle, opened and inviting.

'Get your head down there,' Marion said, her voice now husky with passion. She could see what Melinda was looking at. 'Lick me out . . .'

Melinda did not hesitate. She plunged her mouth down onto Marion's sex immediately, using her tongue to probe the nether lips, anxious to please. She found the little bud of Marion's clitoris and heard Marion moan as her hot tongue explored it. She knew what to do, despite the fact that this was the first time she had ever done this to a woman: she did what she had loved men to do to her. She remembered what had driven her wild with passion on a man's mouth. Her tongue circled Marion's clitoris, then licked it; big full licks like licking an ice-cream cone. She then dipped down further, straining to penetrate her cunt itself, licking at the sensitive opening and its silky walls, pushing in as deep as she could go.

The first time Melinda felt her body throbbing, her own sex pulsing as much as if it, too, were being licked. She relished the taste of Marion's juices and the musky, delicious aroma of sex. Her mouth, her chin, her cheeks were wet. Marion was copious, like a river. She could hear her moan and feel her body trembling. She was bringing her off. She regulated her actions, began a rhythm, concentrating on her clitoris, circling it with the tip of her tongue, taking exactly the same time for each circumnavigation, then flicking the bud itself before starting the next round trip.

'Yes, yes,' Marion moaned. 'Use your fingers.'

Immediately, Melinda slipped her hand under Marion's thigh and plunged two fingers into her wet and open cunt. There was room for more. She pushed a third finger home. The juice from Marion's cunt had run into her anus and, as Melinda pushed three fingers deep, her fourth slid into her rear passage, effortlessly, on the flood of wetness. She felt Marion's whole body tense, waiting for its release. With all her strength Melinda pushed her fingers up into Marion's sex, and centred her mouth on her clitoris, sucking it between her lips.

'Oh, oh . . .' Marion cried, her body arching off the bed, her eyes rolled back, the explosion of orgasm raking through every nerve, breaking over Melinda's hand and mouth, convulsing her muscles in spasms out of all control.

It was a long time before she regained her senses. Melinda knelt by her side, patiently waiting. Not moving. She had not been ordered to move.

Marion took Melinda's wrist and pulled her fingers from her sex. The withdrawal produced a minor spasm, a miniature of what had gone before. She sat up, wrapped her arm around Melinda's body and kissed her lips. It was not a usual kiss. Marion

180

wanted to taste her own juices. She licked them eagerly from Melinda's mouth and face.

Finally she was satisfied.

'Now . . .' she said, letting the word hang in the air. Her hands pressed Melinda down onto the bed. She knelt by her side. 'You are not to come until you are told,' she said with that teasing smile again.

Melinda bit her lip. That was asking the impossible. She was on the brink of it now. She had nearly come as she'd felt Marion climax over her mouth. She couldn't be expected to hold back.

Marion read her thoughts. 'Or would you rather I stopped?'

Melinda said nothing. She did not know what to say.

'Answer,' Marion barked.

'No, no, mistress.'

Marion's hands were parting her legs, running along her thighs. Melinda could feel the nylon of Marion's stockings pressing against her side. 'Please, please . . .' she whispered, not being able to help herself.

'Shh . . .' Marion cautioned quietly.

Melinda felt fingers parting her labia. Marion leant over and kissed her again, this time lightly. She felt Marion's bra grazing her naked breasts. 'Don't make me punish you,' Marion whispered, forming the words with her lips still on Melinda's mouth.

The fingers probed Melinda's cunt; long fingers, going deep. Inside, Melinda felt them scissor apart, pushing against the wet slippery flesh. How was she going to hold back? It was impossible.

Marion's mouth descended to her breasts, licking and sucking at them, pinching at the nipples with her teeth. 'Undo my bra,' she commanded.

Melinda found the catch of the bra and managed to open it with one hand. The bra fell off and Marion threw it aside. Melinda felt the heat and weight of Marion's breasts crushing into her own, their nipples as hard as stone. She writhed and squirmed so that their tits, all that spongy soft flesh, rubbed together.

Marion trailed her mouth down across Melinda's belly, down to where it had been before, the shaven triangle. Her fingers were reaming in and out of Melinda's cunt like a cock. She too found room for three. She too rode a finger into Melinda's anus. She too felt the juices flooding out like a gushing tap.

'No, no, no . . .' Melinda moaned. They were not really words. She tossed her head from side to side and bit her lip, trying to get herself back under control, trying to remember her obedience. But it was impossible. Her body was on fire, quivering with sex. Worse, her mind was full of images and sensations. Full of thoughts, and new experiences. *The first time with a woman*, it kept telling her.

Marion's tongue found her clitoris. It was not difficult. It was swollen and throbbing like a tiny cock. Melinda's body went rigid at this new intrusion. How was she supposed to resist this too? How could she? The tongue circled and probed. It licked at the fingers buried in her cunt. It was not like a man. Different. More pliant. More telling. More able to find the secret places, the hidden nerves. Or was that just the product of her fevered imagination? Was that just because it was driving her wild? She was going to come and she knew Marion would feel it, feel her cunt tense, her clitoris spasm, her juices flood. She had to resist; she had to obey.

Suddenly, Marion swung her thigh over Melinda's body. She positioned herself to kneel above Melinda's face. Melinda looked up at her hairy wet sex, framed by the welts of the stockings, the suspenders at the sides still taut, but those at the front loose and looped down until they almost touched Melinda's breasts. Without breaking the rhythm of her movements on Melinda's cunt, Marion slowly and deliberately lowered her sex onto Melinda's mouth.

With relief, Melinda arched her head off the bed to meet it. Eagerly, she latched her mouth to Marion's labia. It was an escape. It was a way out. She could control her body now, now she had something else to concentrate on. She could distract herself by giving Marion pleasure.

Immediately, she matched her mouth to Marion's. What Marion did to her she did to Marion. She felt her crisis pass. She had obeyed. She was still intensely excited, she wanted her completion desperately, but it was under control. As Marion's tongue flicked at her clitoris, she, in turn, flicked at Marion's. As Marion's fingers pushed into her cunt, she reached up with her hand and penetrated Marion again. Tit for tat. Melinda could feel Marion's body respond, just as her body did. She could feel Marion's breasts, their nipples as hard as pebbles, pressed into her belly, just as hers were crushed into Marion's.

She could feel Marion coming too. She felt Marion's body trembling. She had learnt quickly. Learnt to provoke it, manipulate it. She felt Marion losing control, felt her strokes falter, her tongue slacken, unable to concentrate any more on anything but her own feelings.

'Yes, yes . . .' she moaned triumphantly, as though this second orgasm was a wonderful bonus.

Melinda pushed her mouth hard up against Marion's sex, all subtlety abandoned now. Her fingers were deep in the silky wet depths of Marion's cunt and she felt it contracting around them. More, she felt Marion's breath, the panting desperate breath of her orgasm, expelled against her own sex as Marion went rigid, her body locked.

Marion's orgasm cascaded through her, so soon after the first that it was as though the two were joined, to double the intensity of what she was feeling.

Melinda felt her recover. Marion's fingers began to move again, up and down Melinda's tight vagina and anus, in and out. Her mouth started to suck and lick and tease again too.

'I give you permission to come . . .' Marion said, taking her mouth away from Melinda just long enough to say the words.

The words released Melinda just as surely as bonds being unchained from her body, the feeling she had experienced so many times in the last weeks. She felt the motor of her orgasm change gear, no longer held back. She turned her head to the side. Something caught her eye. Something strange. Something she did not understand at first. A crack of light, like a door being opened in a darkened room. But the door was on the other side of a solid wall. How could she see it, a crack of light through a black wall?

The light vanished, the door closed. Suddenly her mind leaped. She had noticed something strange about that wall when they'd first come in. Now she realised what it was. It was not a wall at all. One whole side of the room was glass, glass that had been tinted black, like the windows of a limousine. This room was a theatre, a tiny stage, and behind the glass people were watching, watching everything that happened, every detail, every moan and cry, every kiss and caress. The Master was watching. Melinda knew at once he was there. She could feel his eyes.

Her body tensed. From that moment, Melinda's eyes never left the glass. This had not been for Marion's benefit at all, but for his. She had been performing for him. She could feel his eyes so strongly now that she could imagine where he was sitting. She stared at the spot. She wanted him to see her, legs spread, compliant, open. Coming. Coming as she had been ordered to do, coming on Marion's tongue and fingers. It was perfect. The Master had planned it. Using Marion's passion, using her needs, for himself.

Melinda's body pulsed out of control. She could not have stopped her orgasm now. Marion's tongue was relentless, her fingers wily. Melinda let herself go. She felt her nerves crying out for relief, felt her muscles lock and her eyes roll back and the wave of her orgasm build to an impossible height before, finally, it crashed down on her body, washing her away, carrying her down into its depths like a piece of helpless flotsam until, after an infinity of time, it washed her up on the shore.

She felt Marion climb off her, but she did not have the energy to open her eyes. When, finally, she managed to persuade her eyelids to lift, Marion was gone.

Melinda raised her head off the bed and looked down her naked, sweating body and through the black glass wall. Though she could see nothing, she knew the Master was gone.

Melinda was taken back to her cell by Selene, who had allowed her to shower before the metal block was chained between her legs and her hands were cuffed to the wall again.

Lying in the dark in her locked cell, Melinda had never felt the need to touch herself so badly. For the last week she had not minded the restraints one bit. But now her body had been brought to life. If she had been able, she would have played her body like an instrument until its tunes were exhausted, squeezing climax after climax out of it. She would have come easily, effortlessly, her mind full of images, of memories of feelings and feelings themselves. She ached for sex, and more sex, like a thirsty man given only a sip of water. She could still taste Marion's lips. She could still feel Marion on and in her cunt. Her whole body seemed to be alive with sexual feeling. She needed relief. Desperately. They had, she realised, done it to her again. After a week of contentment they had created a need more urgent than ever before. A need she had no means to fulfil.

But it was not only her body that was tense. Her mind was racing too. After the time in Scotland she had been convinced that she was something special to the Master, something unique. That is why she had been untouched since then. This belief had been reinforced by her shocked realisation that her initiation into lesbian love was not at Marion's behest, but at the Master's and he had watched it all.

But why had he not then had her brought to his room? Why hadn't she provoked him to want her again? There was only one answer: that her exhibition with Marion had been merely the precursor to the main event, and that event did not include her. Marion had disappeared quickly, leaving Selene to bring her back to the cell. Was that because the Master was ready for her, wanted her? Was watching Marion take Melinda only the foreplay to Marion taking the Master?

It was depressing. After the euphoria of last week, when she'd convinced herself their intimacy had meant something, why hadn't he wanted her?

With mind and body tortured in turn, sleep proved impossible. Melinda lay, feeling used in a way she had not felt before. Her physical bondage suddenly seemed intolerable. Briefly, hopelessly, she struggled against it, trying to wrench her wrists from the handcuffs, flexing her legs. But the cold steel of the cuffs hurt her wrists, and the inner surface of the metal block, like the roughest sandpaper against her softest skin, soon convinced her to stop. It was useless. She was a prisoner, a slave. What she wanted was not important. The only wish that mattered belonged, as she did, to the Master.

Perhaps, it occurred to her in a flash, what had happened in Scotland was as deliberate as everything else that had been done to her. The Master wanted her to feel special and unique precisely so he could dash her hopes and leave her feeling as she felt now, abject and deserted. He had allowed her to think, for a few days, that she was still a person in her own right, with feelings and thoughts and emotions, only to prove to her conclusively that she was not. She was an object, a piece of property. To be done to, not to do.

She felt this thought comforting. In the end, after all, it was submission that she craved.

As, finally, she drifted off to sleep, somewhere deep in the house, or outside in the grounds, she could not be sure, she heard a distant bell, like a burglar alarm going off. She thought she heard dogs too. But it was a long way off and it might have been the beginning of some complex dream where she had set the bells ringing herself, and the dogs running at her heels as she tried to sneak, uninvited, into the Master's bedroom.

Cybele brought her breakfast, watched her use the toilet and shower and shave. She washed her hair too. By the time it was dry and she had eaten her breakfast, the make-up woman had arrived. Her appearance, Melinda knew by now, meant that she was not to spend the day idly as she had over the last week.

Though she had no way of telling, the make-up applied to her face felt unusually heavy, especially around the eyes. Her fingers and toe nails were cleaned and revarnished. Her hair was brushed. A lipstick, last of all, was applied with a brush. No matter how long she was at the house, Melinda would never get used to someone else performing these basic tasks. It did not make her feel pampered. It made her feel, as she knew it was meant to, helpless.

As she was brought back into the cell she saw that, once again, clothes had been laid out on the bed.

'Get dressed,' Cybele ordered, locking the bathroom door.

The yellow dress on the mattress was made of some sort of Spandex material. Melinda stepped into it and pulled it up over her body. It was not easy. She had to wriggle and squirm before she could wheedle her arms into the shoulder straps. But the effort was worth it. The dress clung to every curve of Melinda's flowing figure, its low neckline revealing her cleavage, its slick, shiny material following the line of her waspy waist and the smooth curves of her pert, up-tilted arse. It hid little of her thighs.

A pair of matching yellow shoes had been laid out. Melinda slipped her feet into them after a prompting by Cybele. Naturally, there were no knickers.

Melinda realised she had not been allowed to wear knickers since her first day in the Master's house.

Cybele had taken two gold chains from one of the pouches on her belt.

'Hold your hands out in front of you,' she ordered.

Melinda did as she was told. The first chain was the width of her body with a loop at each end. Cybele slipped the two loops around Melinda's wrists, securing them with what was, in fact, a tiny padlock, though it looked more like a gold ornament of some kind. The second chain went around Melinda's neck again secured, similarly, by a tiny gold padlock. From this chain, another hung down between Melinda's breasts. Quickly, Cybele attached this to the middle of the wrist chain by means of a fourth golden lock.

The make-up woman had stood watching all this. As Cybele snapped the final lock into place, she picked up the last item on the mattress and handed it to her. It was a black leather hood fashioned in the softest of glove leather. The hood was laced at the back. Pulling the lacing open, Cybele guided the hood down over Melinda's head.

'Open your mouth,' she ordered.

As the hood descended Melinda caught a glimpse of a thick rubber tongue-shaped block sewn into the inside of the hood where the mouthpiece should be. Cybele adjusted the leather so the rubber slipped into Melinda's mouth. It was huge. It filled her mouth, making it completely impossible for her to move her tongue or speak.

At the front, the leather was cut away from the bottom of the forehead to the top of the upper lip, revealing eyes, nose and cheeks. Other than these features, the face and head was completely enclosed in clinging, tight leather. The make-up woman tucked stray wisps of hair under the leather as Cybele tightened the laces, and Melinda felt the hood gripping her head tighter and tighter until, finally, the laces were tied off.

'Oh I think that's so sexy,' the make-up woman said walking out of the room.

Cybele stood back to admire her work, her strong body straining against the short leather uniform. She ran her hand down Melinda's body, over her breasts. Melinda could see a flash of desire in her eyes, desire she had seen before. Then she turned on her heels to leave Melinda alone in the cell.

Melinda's body throbbed with excitement. The gag in her mouth was uncomfortable and impossible to forget. It was big. It felt like a cock, like the cock she had sucked on her first night in the house. That was what was making her pulse race. That, and the anticipation of what was to come. Some new experience. She hadn't been dressed and chained and hooded like this without a purpose. The Master had issued his orders. He had thought of her, wanted her used. This was his plan, and Melinda revelled in that thought.

It was half-an-hour later when Cybele opened the cell door again, beckoning Melinda forward.

'They're ready for you,' she announced, leading the way through the house and out under the double staircase to the front door, her leather boots clacking on the marble floor, and her big arse swinging as she walked. The front door was open and the Jaguar stood outside, its engine running, the chauffeur sitting behind the wheel.

Cybele opened the rear door and indicated that Melinda should get inside. With the chains restricting her movement only slightly, it was a far easier manoeuvre than the last time she had climbed into the car. Immediately she was seated, Cybele slammed the door shut and the chauffeur drove off down the long driveway. Today, Melinda was not to be escorted.

As the car headed into the city, Melinda could see the chauffeur's eyes looking at her in the rear-view mirror. After a few minutes, his hand adjusted the mirror. She knew why. Sitting down, the skirt of the dress was not long enough to cover much of her legs.

She could see herself in the mirror too. It was a strange sight. The tight leather hood emphasised the shape of her head, held high by her long neck. She looked unreal, like a sculpture: 'Woman With a Gag'. Her eyes burnt fiercely, neatly framed by black leather.

At traffic lights, people stared into the car, not believing what they saw: her long bare legs; the strangely laced hood covering her head and mouth; only her eyes and nose on view. Some new fashion they thought, perhaps. Leather hoods and gold chains. What will they think of next?

The reaction was the same when the car drew up outside the Master's office building and the chauffeur opened the door for Melinda to get out. People stopped and stared as he led her over to the side passage where Marion had taken her before. But Melinda was not embarrassed. It did not even occur to her to feel embarrassed. She was an object, a thing of beauty, a possession being moved from place to place. How she was dressed, what she looked like, was not up to her. If the Master had chosen to have her brought down here naked, it could not have mattered. Not now.

She returned the stares of passers-by with defiance, her eyes flaring. They did not know. Most looked away quickly.

191

The chauffeur took her down the passage, guiding her with his thickly gloved hand on her forearm. He unlocked the door into the building. She had never noticed him before. He was a young man, and under the grey uniform he looked well-developed. He moved with the confidence of someone who was fit and athletic. He exuded an air of strength and health. Inside, he directed her to the lift.

'You're quite a piece of work,' he said admiringly.

He pressed the call button for the lift. She heard it begin its descent. The chauffeur's eyes were still on her body. His gloved hand reached out and with one finger he traced a line down her cheek, over the area that was exposed and then over the leather. She could see what he was thinking, knew he was trying to imagine what it would be like to have her, use her.

The lift arrived.

'Be good,' he said, pushing her inside. He reached in to press the control button and retracted his arm quickly as the metal door slid shut. She saw him grinning before the door finally closed.

At the top, as the door opened, Melinda was surprised to see Hera standing waiting for her. Hera was undoubtedly the most beautiful of the chatelaines, her long elegant legs looked superb in the black boots and short leather skirt of the uniform, her blonde hair tied in a pony tail.

'Out,' she ordered.

She took Melinda's arm and marched her across the Art Deco anteroom to the wall immediately opposite the lift. She pushed Melinda roughly against the wood panelling, her back to the wall, took hold of the padlock that joined the neck chain to the one connecting her wrists, and snapped it open.

'Hands above your head.'

Melinda was used to orders. She obeyed immediately. The chain connecting her wrists hung down in a loop in front of her eyes. Hera had taken an upright chair and positioned it in front of Melinda. Standing on it, she caught the loop of chain in her hand. Melinda looked up. High above her head, set discreetly into the panelling, was a small but sturdy brass hook. Hera pulled the chain up to the hook.

'Higher,' she said irritably.

Melinda stretched higher. Hera snagged the chain over the hook, effectively binding Melinda's hands above her head. Immediately, Melinda felt the strain in her wrists and shoulders. She had stretched almost on tip-toe and now could hardly lower herself at all.

But it was not the pain that was Melinda's first concern. It was an entirely different reaction. As Hera had manipulated the chain above her head, her body had pressed into Melinda's face; her breasts, confined in the tight leather uniform, right in front of Melinda's eyes. The sight had provoked a feeling she had experienced before. She felt a surge of desire; hot, sexual desire.

She had never experienced desires for women before she had met Marion, but now her body vibrated with an almost tangible passion. Her mind imagined what it would be like to feel and do the things to Hera's long slender body that she had felt and done with Marion.

Hera stepped down from the chair and replaced it in the position she had found it. Melinda watched her lithe body move with new interest, the blonde hair bobbing, her long finely contoured legs disappearing under the skirt which hugged her neat, pouting arse. Melinda closed her eyes. She could almost feel what it would be like pressing down onto her face, while she worked up between those legs . . .

When she opened her eyes, Hera had gone.

Of course, Melinda knew the source of her new emotions. The experience with Marion had reached deep into her sexual psyche. It had touched nerves, and given her pleasures she had never even dreamt of. A woman's body was so different from a man's. Not that she wanted men any less. But now she wanted women too. Really wanted, ached for, as much as she had ached for cock.

As time passed, the pain of unrequited sexual desire was replaced by more physical discomfort. The pain in her shoulders and wrists, tightly clinched in the gold chains, began to wipe away any other concerns. The tight dress had ridden up her thighs as the result of her position, and now barely covered her sex.

By standing on tip-toe in the shoes, she could ease the chain cutting into her wrists, but only temporarily. Her calf muscles soon tired and she had to relax back into the shoes, causing the pain in her wrists to resume. Nothing she could do mitigated the strain in her shoulders.

There had been an occasional noise during the time she had been chained against the wall – a telephone ringing, a typewriter, the muffled staccato of a computer printer – but far off. Now, Melinda could hear voices. They seemed to be coming from the door to her left.

The voices got louder. The door opened. A tall, red-haired woman emerged, followed by the Master. The woman was the picture of elegance. Her hair was the reddest of red and combed out into long, soft waves. Her face was thin and sharp with high cheekbones and a delicate straight nose. Her body was slender, though her breasts were obviously full. She wore a black Valentino suit, with a vivid red silk blouse under its exquisitely tailored jacket. The skirt of the suit revealed half of her long thighs and all of her finely shaped calves. Her ankles were narrow, the Achilles heel perfectly formed, her feet shod in patent leather shoes, a tiny gold chain sewn across the leather of the toe.

She walked with grace and poise, like a model on a catwalk. Her long fingers were bejewelled, with two rings on one hand and one on the other. Beneath the hair, Melinda caught the glint of diamond studs set in her pierced ear lobes.

She was one of the most beautiful women Melinda had ever seen. She exuded style, and a feeling of being completely at ease with herself.

'So you see, it is just not possible at that price,' she said. Her English was perfect, but she spoke with a French accent.

The Master smiled indulgently. 'That is the lowest price I can offer.'

The woman had not even glanced at Melinda. 'Then I'm afraid my trip has been something of a waste of time.'

'Not entirely, I hope,' the Master said.

'Everything is a question of price.'

'And quality surely? Quality is important.'

'*Bien sur*. But I have to think of my customers.'

'But what about when you think of yourself?'

The woman smiled, her thin lips parting to reveal a set of perfectly regular and very white teeth. She turned her emerald green eyes to Melinda.

'When I think of myself? That is different, I think.' She walked up to Melinda, who immediately smelt her musky and expensive perfume. 'She has green eyes too,' she said, looking Melinda up and down as if examining a painting. 'This is what you wanted me to see?'

Melinda felt her body pulse with excitement.

'Yes,' the Master said quietly.

The Frenchwoman looked again more closely, examining the details, Melinda's eyes, the rise of her breasts, her waist, the contours of her thighs.

'Very,' she struggled to find the word, 'interesting.'

'I'd hoped you'd think so.'

'You know me, Walter.'

'It occurred to me this morning. Since you were coming in anyway. I thought we could combine business and . . .'

'The business of pleasure.'

The Master laughed. 'Neatly put.'

The woman stroked the soft leather hood. Her hand dropped to Melinda's shoulder.

'She has something special, doesn't she?'

The woman did not reply. Instead she took the hem of the dress in both her hands and wriggled it up over Melinda's hips to her waist. Melinda's belly was exposed, the shaven triangle of her pubis revealing the first fold of her sex. Taking her hips in her hands, the woman pulled Melinda round to face the wall. Her hands caressed her apple-round arse.

'She hasn't been whipped.' The woman's voice was surprised.

'Just the faintest of tastes.'

'Why is that?'

'She is very new. Her training hasn't begun.'

'I would have her whipped.'

'I know.'

'I would have her whipped every day. She has the arse for it. And the belly . . .' The woman pulled Melinda round again to face her. She reached into the

196

low neckline of the dress and extracted one of Melinda's breasts. 'And the breasts.'

'I knew you'd think so.'

The woman's long fingers delved between Melinda's legs. She fingered her labia, found her clitoris and pinched it, then, casually, crudely, pushed two fingers into her cunt, right up to the knuckle. Her other hand fingered the exposed breast, squeezing it like a lemon.

Despite her admiration for the woman, Melinda got no pleasure from the handling. It was curiously unsexual. If the Master had done exactly what this woman was doing to her, she would have been swooning with passion. But the Frenchwoman provoked no such response nor, clearly, intended to. It was as though she was examining an animal to make sure it was healthy, nothing more.

Apparently satisfied, the woman removed her hands. The fingers that had been inside Melinda's sex she licked tentatively.

'Very good quality.'

'Yes.'

'But not trained?'

'That is the attraction, isn't it?'

'*Mais oui.* A considerable attraction.'

'So we return to the question of price.'

The Frenchwoman laughed. 'Walter, Walter. You will never change.' It seemed so strange to hear the Master's name.

'I'm doing it as a favour. Otherwise you'll have to bid with the others.'

'I know. I know. I'm grateful.'

'Good. I want you to be grateful.'

The Frenchwoman turned to Melinda again, looking her up and down as though trying to make up her mind.

'I had her gagged,' the Master said.

'So I see. Why was that?'

'In case . . .'

'In case I couldn't control myself? Is that it?'

The Master smiled. 'I like to think of everything.'

The Frenchwoman laughed again. She went over to the door they had entered by and walked out. The Master followed, and closed the door behind them.

Melinda was confused. Listening to the conversation, she couldn't understand what on earth they were talking about. She imagined the price they were discussing was the price of some item the Master was supplying and that the favour he'd mentioned was allowing her to agree a price before some sort of general auction. Melinda had presumably been brought along as an added inducement to get the woman to agree.

But the more she thought about it the more she thought the conversation had been, at least in part, about her; that the Master was asking the Frenchwoman to agree a price for her.

As the thought gained credence, Melinda's mood darkened. The pain in her shoulders had got worse. Her breast stuck out of the tight material uncomfortably and there was no way she could wrest the material back from around her waist. She could still feel the woman's bony fingers exploring her sex. Her clitoris still throbbed from the pinch she'd delivered.

Melinda felt used. She had only herself to blame of course. It was what she wanted. The Master owned her. She was his chattel. He could do with her whatever he wished. Her feelings did not count. She had to keep reminding herself of that. She was there to be used and abused. If she found that depressing, that too, counted for nothing.

Angry voices came from behind the closed door. She heard the Frenchwoman's voice shouting angrily. What was being said she could not tell. She heard the Master too.

Suddenly the door crashed open and the Frenchwoman marched out and over to the lift. She pressed the call button and the lift door opened. Inside she turned to face the door, looking straight at Melinda's helpless form. The vision seemed to provoke her anger again and she stabbed at the control button in the lift until its metal door slid shut and she was hidden from view.

What had happened, Melinda did not know. Clearly whatever the Master had tried to do hadn't worked. Melinda could not help but think that somehow it was her fault.

For the first time since she had come to the house Melinda felt an impulse to scream. She wanted to tear herself from the wall, cover her body, rip off the gag and hood, and escape. Escape into oblivion. No more eyes and hands pawing her body. No more of anything.

It was her rebellion. It came and it passed. There was no one there to see it. She said and did nothing.

Eleven

It was night. Melinda lay on the thin mattress of her cell, her hands cuffed to the wall above her head, the heavy metal block chained from the leather belt around her waist, her body, as usual, naked. She would have liked to have slept, to have wiped the slate of the day clean, but her mind dwelt on everything that had happened. She thought about the strange Frenchwoman, and the cause of her row with the Master. There had been an air of cruelty about the woman as well as her air of elegance. Perhaps it was that which had provoked Melinda's rebellion. Whatever it was, she was glad she had not been consigned to the woman's perfectly manicured hands.

She was also relieved that she had managed to control her emotions, and contain the feelings that had so suddenly gripped her. What the consequences would have been if she had not, she had no way of knowing. She was pleased she did not have to find out.

Nor could she tell how long it finally took her to get to the brink of sleep, but as she was just falling over it, the bright fluorescent light blinked on again, and Hera strode into the room.

'You're required,' she said, kneeling by the mattress to release the cuffs and unchain the metal block.

With Melinda's eyes still adjusting to the light,

Hera led her naked and bare-footed out through the stables and into the house. It was obviously late and most of the rooms were dark. They mounted the stairs and headed for the Master's bedroom, but instead of going to the double doors, Hera opened a small door alongside them. Melinda found herself in a small, narrow, windowless room, with one inner door that clearly led to the Master's bedroom. The furniture reminded her of a doctor's surgery: a padded leatherette covered examination table and a metal chest of drawers on castors.

The make-up woman, looking as though she had been roused from her sleep, and wearing a towelling robe rather than her usual leggings and leotard, was waiting for them.

'Sit on the table,' Hera ordered.

Melinda obeyed. The make-up woman got to work. The make-up was not heavy. She brushed Melinda's hair and, as always, finished with the application of lipstick.

'Now, lie on your back,' Hera said. As soon as Melinda obeyed, the two women left the room, closing the outer door behind them.

The room was warm and dimly lit. Melinda found herself struggling to keep awake. The next thing she knew, she woke with a start as the inner door opened and the Master slipped into the room.

Without a word he stared at her naked body, standing with his hands in the pockets of a silk navy blue robe that seemed to deepen the colour of his blue eyes.

Melinda's mind filled with questions. There was so much she wanted to ask him. She wanted to ask him about Scotland and Harriet, about Marion and what had happened in the black room, and about the

201

Frenchwoman this afternoon. She wanted to tell him how she felt, how he made her feel. But she knew she must not say a word. It was another need he had created that she was forbidden to fulfil.

Silently, the Master wheeled the metal chest of drawers over to the examination table. He opened the top drawer. Neatly packed inside, each one coiled like a snake, were a mass of leather straps. He saw her eyes looking into the drawer and smiled at her indulgently.

'Sit up,' he said quietly.

She obeyed, her arms by her sides. She had seen the look in his eyes before. It was the look he'd had as he'd watched Harry using the dildo on her in Scotland.

'Perfect,' he said to himself.

He uncoiled a leather strap from the drawer, looping it round her back and arms just above the elbows. He fed the end of the strap into the buckle and jerked it tight, very tight, fastening the buckle at the side of her arm. He picked another identical strap from the drawer, and looped this around her shoulders and body at the point where her breasts rose from her chest. A third belt went around her lower body cinching her waist. All the buckles were fastened on the side of her arm, her breasts pinched slightly between two straps.

He worked slowly, uncoiling each belt carefully, treating them as if they were the sacraments of some arcane ritual, of which he was the high priest.

'Lie back,' he said, his voice barely audible.

Melinda obeyed. She could hardly contain her excitement. She was alone with the Master. Before, there had always been someone else in the room, someone else to obey his commands. But not now. He was binding her; he was using her. There was no one between them. Why he had suddenly granted her such intimacy she did not know or care. She wanted only to feel his touch as his fingers manipulated her body, as he gradually took away her ability to move. Her sex was already wet, her nipples corrugated and hard. All she could think about was what he was going to do to her next.

It occurred to her that this might be another test, that he would leave her suddenly and not finish what he had started. Another hope of intimacy dashed on the rocks of indifference. Another way of telling her that her desires and feelings had no importance.

It might be. But not from the look in his eyes . . .

His hand was on her belly. He had touched her before, but never like this. The expression on his face was glazed, almost vacant. A bulge had appeared in the front of his robe. It rested against the side of the padded table.

He opened another drawer in the metal chest. This, she saw, was full of dildos and vibrators. Every size and shape. Some stubby, wide but not long, others bigger than she'd ever seen. He selected a small dildo, its shape like an elongated oval. While one hand still pressed on her belly, gently stroking her shaved pubis, he pushed her thighs apart with the other and inserted the dildo between the lips of her cunt, pushing it home until it disappeared completely. It needed little encouragement. It went in rapidly as though sucked in by Melinda's eager sex.

Using both his hands he closed her legs, pressing her thighs together. A strap from the drawer was looped under her ankles, then pulled up until it was at the top of her thighs. He buckled it tight at the side, burying the dildo inside her. Another strap followed the same route, this time being fastened above her knees. He strapped her below the knees too. He strapped her ankles and even ran a strap around the soles of her feet. Each strap was jerked as tight as it would go.

She was completely helpless. She could not move a muscle; only her head was free. In all her fantasies, in all the times she had enacted her fantasies, she had never been bound like this. Though the dildo was not large, its effect on her body seemed to be out of all proportion to its size. It filled her cunt as effectively as it filled her mind. She half expected to be left now; that being left alone like this would be a new torture, a punishment for the secret rebellion that morning. She deserved it, after all.

But that was not what the Master had in mind. Slowly, he took off the silk robe and let it drop to the floor. She had never seen his upper body before. It was lean and well muscled, his chest covered with a thick mat of hair as white as that on his head. His big, smooth cock was fully erect, a tear of fluid forming at its tip.

'You see how you have excited me,' he said.

'Yes, master.'

With one hand wrapped around the stem of his cock he began to wank slowly, while his other hand touched the leather straps. They were buckled so tightly, Melinda's flesh bulged from either side of them, especially at her thighs and belly. But he touched only the leather, not her flesh.

From the drawer of the metal chest, he took a thin leather strap and looped it around the base of his cock and under his balls. He buckled it tight. Melinda saw veins swell on the long shaft, the blood trapped by the strap. He started to wank again, coming round to the head of the table until his cock brushed her blonde hair.

Melinda was so mesmerised by seeing his naked body for the first time, she had temporarily forgotten her own feelings. Or perhaps that was just a defence. Perhaps her mind was unconsciously telling her this was all a tease, and was trying to protect her from a massive disappointment. But now she knew it was not. She knew the Master was not going to leave her. He was too excited.

The bondage freed her, freed her to do nothing but feel. The straps that held her felt like a giant hand, squeezing and pressing her onto the dildo that was completely enveloped by her body. Her breasts throbbed; her nipples ached. Her whole body, every nerve, every muscle and tendon, sung with excitement. He was going to use her. Alone. Together. Almost like lovers . . .

She strained back to look at his body towering above her. His hand was wanking his cock with more purpose. Before it had been leisurely, its length slick with the fluid from his own secretions. Now the rhythm was more urgent. Every so often he moaned faintly. What was he going to do? Was he going to come on her face? She didn't care, as long as he came.

His eyes played up and down her body, taking in the shape the leather straps created. The bondage excited him as much as it did her. He'd said as much in the car, she remembered. His cock twitched with pleasure.

For a moment he stopped. Melinda sensed a hesitation in him that she did not understand. Whatever it was he resolved it. Reaching forward, he hooked his hands under the leather strap around Melinda's shoulders and used it to pull her up the table until the nape of her neck was right on the padded edge, and her head dropped below the level of the table.

She knew what he intended, and almost before her body could register its thrill of pleasure at the idea, she was proved right. As soon as her head was lowered he moved forward so the underside of his cock brushed Melinda's lips. She licked and sucked at it eagerly. He moaned.

He grasped the shaft of his cock again. While her mouth suckled at its base his hand wanked its whole length, brushing past her lips on the downward stroke. He pushed forward more, levering her head down further and making her arch off the table. Her mouth could reach his balls now, pushed out by the strap around his cock. It was easy to get them into her mouth, one by one. She felt him shudder with pleasure.

Her position was excruciating but at the same time exciting. Her bound body was churning. She knew she was coming, and coming like she had never come before. The leather straps constraining her so totally that reaction and counterreaction became the same thing, like the recoil of a gun recoiling only on itself. Her body was concentrated, distilled down to the lake of juices in her cunt, and the dildo drowning in them. She was just managing to hold back. If she came, she would not be able to concentrate on the Master and what he wanted. That was what mattered. His pleasure. Pleasing him.

She sucked and licked at his balls. She could see his hand draw back one last time, then squeeze and pull the sword of flesh until it jerked in his fingers. He cried out, as she felt great gobs of white hot spunk bursting from his cock and splattering down on her throat and collarbone, and on her bound and constricted tits.

That was all she needed. Her body spasmed and

the first wave of orgasm broke. But, as the convulsion shot through her it was held back by the bondage, doubling the sensation as she felt the tight leather holding her in. Like an echo trapped in a canyon, her feelings reverberated unable to escape just as, physically, there was no escape for her either.

When finally the feelings died, the ripples diminishing, though still not entirely gone, she opened her eyes. The Master had disappeared. Only his white spunk remained, spattered over her body.

With a huge effort, Melinda managed to wriggle herself down the table. She knew she shouldn't do anything she was not told to do, but the pain in her neck was acute and the effort of supporting her head level with the table was too much to bear. Resting her head against the leatherette at last gave her some relief. It even sparked a little aftershock of orgasm, her cunt contracting on the hard plastic still trapped inside her.

It was some time before the interior door opened again. Melinda's mind was so full of the residue of exquisite pleasure, that she had made no attempt to keep track of time.

The Master returned. He was dressed in a pair of slacks and a white shirt, open at the neck. Behind him Melinda saw Marion. Marion was dressed for seduction. A black silk and lacy teddy showed tantalising glimpses of her big breasts, and the curls of her pubis. Her legs were sheathed in black hold-ups, shiny and slippery with Lycra, the band of white flesh above them appearing so much more exposed in contrast. A black silk negligée was wrapped around her shoulders. On her face she wore an expression like thunder.

She had come to the Master's room unbidden,

Melinda thought, only to find his energy spent. To add insult to injury, she could see his spunk on Melinda's neck and was under instructions to clean it away. A cold wet flannel in Marion's hand removed every trace. She glared down at Melinda while she worked. With equally bad grace she unbuckled all the straps from Melinda's body. She did not need to extract the dildo. It slid out of its own accord.

'Stand up,' Marion said, her displeasure clear in her voice.

The Master walked back into his bedroom. Marion pushed Melinda through the door and followed her, closing it behind them. The Master had gone to sit in the armchair he had used last time Melinda was in this room. A silver tray on a small table next to it held a decanter and two crystal tumblers. The Master poured an inch of a light golden liquid into the glasses, and handed one to Marion who took it and drunk it down in one gulp. From the smell, Melinda knew it was whisky, and from the pale colour she guessed it was a rare single malt.

'Did you hear the alarms last night?' the Master asked, sipping his glass more delicately.

'Yes, master,' Melinda replied, remembering the bells she had heard. Clearly, she had not imagined them.

'It was your husband,' the Master said, his eyes staring into hers.

'What!' The exclamation escaped her lips before she could do anything about it. It earned a smart slap of rebuke from Marion, who lashed her hand down on Melinda's naked rump, no doubt glad of the excuse.

'He was trying to break in,' the Master continued. 'We have a very extensive security system. Naturally he did not succeed.' The Master sipped his scotch again. 'Apparently he has become convinced that you are being held in this house against your will. He was concerned for your welfare.'

Melinda's mind was spinning. If she was honest with herself, she had hardly given Mark a thought since she'd left their house, wearing the clothes the Master had provided. All her connections with, all her feelings for, the outside world had been severed. The Master's world had its own reality.

Her first reaction to Mark's intrusion was anger. He knew perfectly well she had chosen to come here. How could he be so stupid as to imagine she was being held against her will? She had no will. That was the point.

Her second reaction was fear, like a cold hand gripping her heart. Fear that the Master would think her in some way responsible; would blame her for what had happened. Fear that he would make her leave, throw her out, out through the electric gates, back into the real world. She could almost see them clanging shut with terrible finality, excluding her from the world she craved so desperately, excluding her forever.

What could she say to convince him she had no part of it, that her husband's actions were nothing to do with her?

Her anger rose again. All this after such intimacy with the Master. All this after what had just happened between them. It wasn't fair. Tears welled in her eyes. She fought them back, determined not to cry.

'He is downstairs now,' the Master said calmly, seeing her obvious distress. 'Presumably you do not wish to leave?'

'No, master, no please!' She tried to make the words express all her feelings.

'I was going to tell you all this tomorrow but as you are here . . .' He did not complete the sentence. 'I have decided to give him a little demonstration. To reassure him that, far from being held against your will you have fully embraced our little . . .' He searched for the right word. '. . . regimen.'

The relief that flooded through Melinda's body was almost as strong as her orgasm had been. He wasn't going to throw her out.

She expressed her gratitude by remaining absolutely still, resisting the temptation to throw herself at his feet. She would reward him with total passivity. That's what he wanted from her. That's what she wanted to give him. If he thought she was perfect before, from now on she would be faultless. He could do anything with her. She was his. His. Her relief knew no bounds.

'In order for this demonstration to be thoroughly convincing,' the Master was saying, 'we need to be, let us say, outrageous. You will then tell him you wish to fulfil the rest of your contract. Is that understood?'

'Yes, master.' Her response was crisp, unemotional. Perfect.

'Good. Very good.' He turned to Marion. 'And you will make all the arrangements. Tomorrow night.'

'Yes,' Marion replied.

'Take her away then,' the Master commanded.

Marion gripped her arm and led her to the bedroom door, the knuckles of her fingers turning white as they dug hard into Melinda's arm. Taking Melinda away meant taking herself away too.

* * *

There was time to invite a few guests. It was going to be amusing at least. There was a possibility that Melinda would baulk at what they had planned for her husband. But he could not imagine it. Her submission, her obedience had survived every test so far, and he had devised many. But this test had been forced on him.

It would be a pity if she failed. She was something special. He had known that from the first time he had set eyes on her. He'd sensed her proclivity. That's why he'd sent her down to the sculpture room. Most women would have been revolted or frightened or both. Not Melinda. Melinda had felt curiosity and passion.

And since she had come to the house, she had been perfection. Other women had to be trained for weeks before they even approached Melinda's standard of acquiescence. The Master had sometimes enjoyed the training but not as much as he enjoyed Melinda's instant automatic submission. He had watched her with Marion, watched her in Scotland, watched her in his office. She was perfect.

He had even broken his own rule for her. He had never taken any of the slaves alone, as he had her tonight. But his need had been too great. The image of her chained to the wall in the anteroom, her skirt up around her waist, one breast exposed, her little shaven pussy so soft and delicate, so alluring; the expression on her face, a mixture of the pain she must have been feeling and a profound and absolute acceptance, had stayed with him all afternoon, burning in his mind like a smouldering cigarette.

He had to have her. He had to have her alone. He did not want Marion there. Or one of the chatelaines. He wanted only Melinda.

Of course, he would have to send her away. That was the one rule he could not break. L'Organisation Internationale de Maîtres was very strict on such matters. He had hoped the French *maîtresse* would take her before the auction so at least he'd know where she was going, but the woman had wanted to take her for six months, not three. Three months without Melinda was bad enough, the way he felt at the moment, but six would be intolerable.

The problem with being rich was that it was possible to have almost anything, at any time. But there are some things money could not buy. Membership of the OIM was one of them. Of course you had to have a considerable fortune and considerable facilities to be eligible, but once a member it was not a question of money. No one was allowed to break the rules. If they did, their membership was revoked no matter how much money they offered in compensation. The rules were the rules.

The Master, therefore, had no intention of doing so, however much he would have liked to keep Melinda for his own. As he hadn't been able to arrange a private sale before the stated deadline, she would have to be auctioned.

He comforted himself with the thought that she would be back. And if her new *maître* was not too cruel, or demanding, it was possible she would be little changed. Possible.

The stage was prepared. Down in the cellar behind the black glass wall, guests had been seated after an excellent dinner. These were guests from the X-list. The seats were raked like a tiny auditorium, so everyone had a clear, unobscured view.

'This way,' Hera said. The chatelaines had all

drawn straws. Hera had won. It was a prize she coveted.

Melinda was naked and barefoot. She followed Hera into the black room. The overhead spotlights still illuminated the bed, but another part of the room was also basking in their bright white light. Spotlights had been trained on the wall opposite the door. In their light stood Mark Elliot. He had been stripped of his clothes and was spread-eagled against the wall, his wrists and ankles strapped into leather cuffs and chained to strong metal rings. A thick band of leather held a gag in his mouth, so big his cheeks bulged. A leather blindfold covered his eyes.

'Take off his blindfold,' Hera ordered, unnecessarily. Melinda knew what to do; she had been told what was expected of her. They had rehearsed the details.

Melinda went over to her helpless husband, pulled his head forward so she could get at the buckle of the blindfold, and stripped it away. As soon as he saw her, he struggled violently against his bonds, trying, at the same time, to shout something. Whatever abuse he no doubt had in mind, nothing more than an indistinguishable murmur escaped the gag. Melinda did not look into his eyes.

'Unzip me.' Hera stood by the bed. She undid her equipment belt and dropped it to the floor. The leather skirt of the chatelaine's uniform had a zip at the back. Melinda quickly pulled it down. The skirt fell away, revealing the rest of Hera's slender legs. She untied her long blonde hair and shook it out.

'The leotard,' she prompted, her voice tinged with an edge of excitement.

Melinda knelt by the black boots. She reached up to Hera's thighs as Hera opened her legs. The black leotard fastened in the crotch. It cut deeply into the lips of her sex. Melinda could see the wisps of pubic hair escaping its sides. Her fingers struggled with the studs, pressing them into the softness of Hera's labia before they sprung free.

Immediately, Hera pulled Melinda's head down onto her sex. Melinda kissed it enthusiastically. She made an exaggerated 'Mmm ...' noise as her tongue lapped out into the channel of the labia and she tasted Hera's juices. already flowing liberally from her sex. She wanted to let her husband know what she was feeling. She used the tip of her tongue on Hera's clitoris, teasing it out from the thick mat of pubic hair that surrounded it. She felt Hera's body tremble.

Hera stepped back. There were things to be done before she allowed herself the luxury of orgasm. She pulled the leotard from her body. Her breasts, freed of their constriction, trembled. They were not large, but were shapely, their nipples hard and puckered by her excitement.

Leaving Melinda on her knees, she walked over to Mark, who had stopped struggling and was staring in amazement at what he was seeing. She took his head in both her hands and kissed him, kissing the leather holding the gag in place on his mouth just as if it were his lips, squirming her mouth against it and licking at the leather with her tongue, just as she writhed her naked body against his, making sure her navel rubbed against his cock.

Despite himself, despite his anger, and bewilderment at his wife's behaviour, his erection sprung up against the belly that provoked it so.

As soon as she felt his hardness, Hera moved away. She went back to the bed and sat down.

'Boots,' she ordered.

Melinda gripped the black heels one by one, and pulled them off.

'Do you want to give me pleasure?' Hera asked, looking down into Melinda's eyes.

'Yes, mistress,' Melinda said with real feeling.

Her response started Mark struggling again.

'How much?'

'Very much, mistress.' Though this was all a performance for her husband's sake, Melinda felt her blood coarsing through her body with passion, as she looked from Mark, his eyes bulging, his muscles twitching, his erection waving out in front of him, to Hera, her sex nestling under her thick blonde pubic hair.

Hera lay back on the bed. She hooked one leg over Melinda's shoulder and then the other, digging her heels into Melinda's back to press her down onto her open sex.

Mark became still. He was torn between disgust and fascination. He could not look away.

'Mmm ...' Melinda murmured again, as her tongue burrowed into Hera's delicious sex. She felt a surge of raw passion and a flood of wetness between her own legs. Now it was not a performance. She knew the Master was watching her too.

'Oh ...' Hera moaned, as Melinda's tongue found her clitoris and worked on it. Her tongue felt hard and sharp and hot. It circled the tiny mountain of nerves, then flicked at the summit. Hera crossed her ankles on Melinda's back, trapping her head in a vice of thighs. Melinda's touch was perfect. Now Hera could let her passion flow.

Melinda's tongue dipped lower. It explored the opening of Hera's cunt, then plunged inside. Out again she moved it lower still, licked at the anus and penetrated there too. She could feel Hera's body trembling, and knew she was close to her orgasm.

Slowly, teasingly, she pulled her tongue back, letting Hera feel its roughness all the way along the length of her sex until it lighted on her clitoris again. This time she let her tongue stay there, making tiny little strokes, regular now, a rhythm established.

'Oh, oh . . .' Hera breathed, her body convulsing, as the tongue licked relentlessly. Her orgasm engulfed her, a great dark blanket of sensation throwing her backward, down and down and down, until she thought it would never stop. It did. Eventually.

Hera opened her eyes and pulled her legs away from Melinda's shoulders. She sat up and leant forward, unable to resist the temptation to kiss the wet mouth in front of her, and taste her own juices, lapping them from Melinda's mouth and chin greedily.

'Now it's your turn,' she said, standing up and walking over to Mark. He tried to say something. Idly Hera stood beside him taking his cock in her hand and squeezing it hard in her fist. 'What's the matter? Don't you want to see her fucked by me?'

Mark shook his head vigorously.

'That's not very nice. She loves it so. Don't you?'

'Yes, mistress.' Melinda had not moved from her knees.

'Or perhaps you'd rather I got a man in here to do it. She loves that too, don't you?'

'Anything, mistress.'

'So obedient. Show him. Lie on the bed. Wank for me.'

Melinda lay on the bed. Bending her knees and opening her legs, she ran her hand over the curve of her pubic bone into the crease of her sex. It already glistened with her juices. She prodded her clitoris, then pushed two fingers deep into her cunt.

216

'Come on . . .' Hera encouraged, her fingers still wrapped around Mark's cock.

Melinda pumped her fingers in and out, adding a third to join the other two, arching her hips off the bed. Would he see now that this was what she wanted? Would he realise how stupid he'd been? This was her choice. Her body throbbed. She felt the Master's eyes on her from the other side of the glass. She knew he was watching her, taking pleasure from her. Her anger with her husband resurfaced. She wanted the Master again. Wanted the intimacy again.

She was coming, calling on the memory of what the Master had done to her. Her mind was full of him, his body, his cock, his hot white spunk.

'Stop that,' Hera snapped.

Immediately Melinda's hands left her body. The surge of feeling subsided like a deflated balloon. But she had to obey. To show her obedience. That was the point.

They had planned one further demonstration.

Hera let go of Mark's cock and patted him on the cheek.

'A special treat,' she said, walking to the door and opening it. She beckoned with her finger and a naked man entered the room. He was tall and muscular, and his cock – since he had been watching from the other side of the glass – was already erect. He held a riding crop in his hand. His body glistened with oil.

Melinda lay on the bed, her legs still open. The sight of the crop made her quiver with expectation. The man did not say a word as he walked to the side of the bed. He had been told what to do.

Hera stooped, and picked up the tassled whip from her equipment belt. The man stood on one side of the bed and she on the other.

'Beg,' she said.

'Please, please whip me . . .' It was a performance carefully rehearsed, but Melinda wanted it so badly she had no need to act.

'Nnnn . . .' Mark tried to shout, writhing helplessly, tossing his body against the unyielding cuffs.

Melinda turned on her stomach. Bending her knees up under her, she stuck her apple-shaped arse, round and tender, into the air. 'Please whip me . . .'

The man did not hesitate. The crop whistled down onto her naked rump. Immediately, Hera's fell from the other side. Their strokes rained down alternately. Six from one side, six from the other. Melinda's buttocks reddened, long welts appearing. She had never been closer to orgasm without actually coming. Her whole body seemed to be on fire. The whipping heated her like a fever, her cunt throbbing. But it was not just the whip. It was what it meant. She was being used. They were reaching down into the deepest darkest pool of her sexual spring.

The man threw the whip to the floor. His cock was big, bigger than Mark's. Pulling Melinda's legs apart he knelt between them in one effortless thrust stabbed it into her cunt, riding up to the hilt on the river of her juices.

Melinda had never felt a cock so big. It filled her. Choked her. Made her body open, like a flower blossoming, so he could go deeper. She came instantly, the moment he drove into her, his hands on her hips pulling her back onto him. Her orgasm was so sharp it was almost painful, her body already overwhelmed with the feelings the whips had left on her arse.

She heard the thwack of leather on flesh. Hera was using the whip on the man's buttocks now, urging him on with it, deeper and deeper, every stroke reaching as deep as any man had ever been in her.

Melinda raised herself on her elbows so her back was straight. Her buttocks were on fire. As the man drove forward, his navel hit the tortured flesh. She was coming again. Harder. Higher. Everything out of control. Forced by his cock into another cycle of pleasure, as Hera's whip lashed his naked arse. She could feel his cock pulsing inside her, his body driven on by his own passion just as much as the whip.

As the tip of his cock broke new ground in her cunt, Melinda came again. She thought she heard herself scream in pleasure but was so high, so choked full of unbelievable sensation, she could not trust her senses.

Hera threw the whip aside. Lying on the bed she pushed her head between the man's and Melinda's open legs. Above her she saw his cock driving into Melinda's cunt, her labia sucking it in, stretched taut by its girth. Reaching up to hook her hands around his thighs, she levered herself up to plant her mouth on his balls, sucking them into her mouth.

He stopped pumping as Hera's tongue massaged the oval pods, and an electric shock of sensation ran through his nerves. She felt his spunk swelling his cock.

Melinda felt it too. Involuntary, Melinda's cunt contracted, squeezing on the bone-hard shaft embedded inside it.

Hera let go of his balls and slid herself out from under the bodies as she saw him moving again. She had her orders, she knew what she was supposed to do, and she had done it. But her body demanded more. She wanted to be part of this. Moving around the bed she lay down again, this time with her thigh against Melinda's left arm. She pushed against it, Melinda knew instantly what she wanted, and raised her arm off the bed so Hera could slide her body over until the top of her thighs came to rest under Melinda's head. This accomplished, Hera insinuated her head under Melinda's navel and down to where the man's cock pumped remorselessly into the puffy lips of Melinda's sex.

Hera opened her thighs wide. Melinda did not need to be told what to do. Eagerly, her mouth dropped to Hera's wet, glistening, hairy cunt. She licked and sucked and lapped at it. This was the perfect triangle: a hard, hot cock buried in her cunt, while her mouth played with all the recently discovered delights of a woman's sex. Perfect. And with the knowledge that the Master was watching; that all this, everything, was being done for her sake.

Melinda's passion erupted in her cunt, pulsing against the hardness of the man's cock as Hera's tongue licked at his balls again, then slipped down to lock on Melinda's swollen clitoris, exposed wantonly by the overstretched labia.

It was the beginning of a chain reaction. Hera felt Melinda's orgasm explode. As Melinda came she panted for breath, the hot air blowing on to Hera's clitoris and labia as her tongue lost its rhythm. That carried Hera over the edge, made her, in turn clutch desperately at the man's balls with her lips, as she lost control and pitched into the black abyss of infinite feeling.

And finally, he came. Thrusting one final time, no longer able to resist the temptation he had held back from for so long, he found his place in the silky wet depths of Melinda's body, then stopped, looking down at her gorgeous long back and her head buried between Hera's long slender thighs. He felt the two convulsing bodies underneath him taking him over

the precipice, until his cock jerked against the confines of her tight, clinging cunt and white hot spunk
spat out into the dark wet cavern that surrounded
him. He fought to keep his eyes open, to drink in the
erotic spectacle before him, but finally he was forced
to close them, and sink into the blackness of total
pleasure.

'Do you now think that your wife is here against her
will?'

The Master stood in front of Mark, with Melinda
at his side. Mark's gag had been removed, but he was
still tethered against the wall. Sweat ran down his
body from his efforts to free himself. His cock was as
hard as it had ever been in his entire life.

'No,' he replied, his voice strained by all the words
he had tried to force past the gag without success.

'Melinda,' the Master said. 'Do you wish to leave?'

'No, master. No.'

'Good. Then our business is almost concluded.
You do not, of course, expect me to overlook your
intrusion into my property.' The Master looked into
Mark's eyes. He did not wait for a reply. 'You will
have to be punished.'

'Punished,' Mark said.

'Yes. You broke our agreement. Unless you would
prefer to discontinue our association . . .'

'No,' Mark said quickly.

'No, I thought not. Then you will submit?'

Melinda could not suppress a shiver at the way the
Master said the last word. He made it sound holy,
like some ritual phrase.

Mark said nothing.

'Answer my question,' the Master snapped.

'Yes, yes.'

221

'Good.'

The other actors in the performance staged for Mark's benefit had already left the small black room. The Master took Melinda's arm and led her out too. Behind a thick velvet drape he guided her to the other side, behind the black glass where his guests, the privileged members of the X-list, sat watching in the miniature auditorium. He sat in one of the big, comfortable theatre-style seats, and indicated that Melinda should sit next to him. It was remarkable. Sitting here, the black room appeared exactly like the stage of a theatre. And as she watched, Melinda saw Marion enter the scene and stride over to Mark.

Marion was dressed in a short black slip, with thin spaghetti straps on her finely boned shoulders, its lacy bust struggling to contain her heavy breasts. Its hem bounced as she moved, revealing the dark triangle of her pubic hair. Her legs were sheathed in sheer black hold-ups, and her feet in black high heels. The powerful, muscled figure of Cybele followed her into the room.

Standing in front of Mark, Marion took his erect cock in her hand. She appeared to be examining it, much as if she were inspecting the penis of some stallion about to go to stud. She pulled it from side to side, then slapped it quite hard. Mark moaned. But his cock responded to this rough handling. It had never been so hard.

Marion sat on the edge of the bed. 'Bring him here.'

Cybele quickly freed the cuffs that tied Mark to the wall and, his limbs numb from their imprisonment, he collapsed to the floor. In his present condition he was in no position to resist anything. He felt Cybele's arms dragging him to his feet, frogmarching him over to the bed, allowing him to collapse onto his knees again in front of Marion.

'You have to be punished,' she said, smiling.

He said nothing.

'If you do not do exactly as I tell you, if you do not obey, you will never see the Master again.'

'I know.'

Marion pulled the black slip over her head. Her breasts quivered. She trailed the silk across Mark's face. It was redolent of her musky, heady perfume. She dropped the garment. It fluttered down to his knees brushing his cock before sliding to the floor.

'Kiss my feet,' she said, kicking off her shoes and crossing her legs so one foot dangled in front of his face.

He hesitated.

'Do it,' she snapped.

He leant forward and pressed his lips against the sheer nylon. He kissed around her toes, over her instep, down to the heel and up around the ankle. She recrossed her legs, presenting him with the other foot. He did not hesitate this time. He traced his lips around the nylon-covered toes, kissing with small sharp kisses.

Marion uncrossed her legs and put her feet to the floor, her knees together. He looked at her questioningly.

'I didn't tell you to stop, did I?'

He ducked his head down to the floor and resumed his task. The position raised his arse into the air. Marion nodded to Cybele who had already taken the whip from her belt. She slashed it powerfully across his naked rump.

'Ah . . .' Mark exclaimed, rearing upright, glaring at Marion.

'Continue,' she said calmly. 'My feet, then my legs; all the way up my legs . . .'

He bent down to obey. It was useless not to. He was committed to Walter Hammerton now. All he'd wanted to do was find out if his wife was all right. Over the weeks since the party at the country house, when Walter's explanation for needing Melinda had seemed so reasonable, its plausibility had worn off, like a drug. He had become more and more suspicious. Well, his suspicions had been confirmed in spades. But he didn't care. Not now. Not after what he'd seen. Hammerton's business was making him rich. He didn't want to lose that. He would do anything not to lose that. That was his only concern, he reminded himself, as the second stroke of Cybele's whip lashed his unprotected rump.

He kissed and licked the black nylon, working gradually higher, up the side of the slim calf, up over the thigh and the welt of the stocking until his lips felt the smoothness of her flesh, in stark contrast to the coarseness of the nylon. He felt the hardness of his erection digging into his belly.

'The other leg,' Marion said, as his lips lingered on her naked flesh.

He obeyed immediately, dipping down to her ankle and beginning the long climb all over again.

A third lash of the whip landed squarely on his buttocks. The first two had been a shock but he was expecting this. He had listened for the sound of Cybele's arm being raised, the leather of the uniform rustling and the sound of the air as the whip whistled down. It stung with pain, but to his amazement the pain turned to a strange heat almost immediately, a heat that seeped through his body, throbbing and pulsing, increasing the temperature of his sexual need, translating to excitement, making his cock harder, hotter, if that were possible.

He had never been whipped. He could feel each little mark where the thin lashes had landed, criss-crossing his buttocks. They felt like fingers; hot sensitive fingers probing at his body, and, more tellingly, into his mind. What was happening to him?

His mouth reached the welt of the stocking on the other leg, where the tight elastic held it firmly to Marion's thigh. He crossed the divide onto the glorious, smooth creamy flesh. He kissed and licked it enthusiastically.

Suddenly Cybele grabbed his head and yanked it back. Marion opened her legs. He stared down into her sex: the neatly trimmed but thick black curls; the wrinkled oval of her labia like an exotic orchid, open and moist.

Cybele pushed his head forward. He had no need to be told what to do. Eagerly, his tongue sought out the clitoris, probing through the thick hair until he found the crown of nerves.

Marion moaned. He was good at this, very good. His tongue was on exactly the right spot, its tempo perfect. Marion felt her body respond with a surge of pleasure, her thighs closing on his head to hold him tight. She tried to remember she was there to serve the Master.

Cybele picked up the other whip, the discarded riding crop that still lay on the floor. Buried between Marion's thighs he would not anticipate this blow. She lashed his arse, the single cut of the crop so much more cutting than the many lashes of the other whip. She saw him rear-up. She lashed again. Two long red welts appeared. She hit out again, a third stroke to form another welt.

Marion could not stop herself. His mouth had been turned to fire by his pain, each stroke provoking a cry of protest, gagged by her sex. She felt her body flooding, her juices running down her cunt, over his mouth and tongue, soaking him as if she had spunked. She could not muffle a gasp of pleasure.

She struggled to regain control. Still trembling, she caught Mark by the ears and pulled his head away. She knew the Master was watching, knew they were all watching.

'Give it to him,' she said to Cybele. 'Quickly.'

Cybele took a small white pill from her equipment belt. Marion squeezed Mark's cheek in her hand, forcing his mouth open. Cybele popped the pill inside.

'Swallow,' Marion ordered. He hesitated. 'Swallow, damn you.'

Marion saw his Adam's apple move. She relaxed. Now it was Cybele's turn. She was already stripping off her uniform. Cybele was tall, but her big body was beautifully proportioned. Naked, the leather uniform at her feet, her muscles glistening with the sweat the heat of the room had produced, she looked like an Amazon warrior queen, her pubis hairless, her breasts no more than crescents on her armour-like chest.

She lay on the bed next to Marion and opened her legs, her big powerful thighs ready to crush any man who dared to lie between them. Marion stroked her body. Cybele's nipples were huge, like cupboard knobs and, at the moment, just as hard. Marion pinched them both in turn, harder than she would have risked with any other woman. She ran her hand over the iron muscles of Cybele's belly, down to the hairless apex of her thighs. She stopped there suddenly, remembering where she was and why. The idea of taking this wonderful body was all too seductive.

'Get up here,' she snapped at Mark.

He needed no encouragement. If this was punishment he would like to be punished every day. The whip had left his body coursing with passion; visceral, unaccustomed, almost uncontainable passion. He knelt between the Amazon's thighs, his cock inches from her big, hairless cunt. He could see every inch of her sex, every crease. It seemed to be winking at him; inviting, open.

Marion's hand pulled him forward.

He lay on Cybele, his cock nudging against her sex. He bucked his hips and he was in her, swallowed right up to the hilt. His balls banged against her arse. He reamed into her. The movement made the muscles of his arse ripple. He felt the welts there react with a sting of pain. It turned to heat, sexual heat. It spurred him on. He was going to come. After all they had done to him, he couldn't possibly hold out.

Marion stood up. She took the riding crop in her hand. It whistled through the air and landed low, almost at the top of his thighs. Virgin territory. He moaned, hanging on to Cybele's body as though it were the cliff face of some mighty precipice.

He was going to come. He pumped faster and harder. His spunk filled his cock, ready to jet out of him. Another stroke of the whip would do it, provoke him beyond recall.

Marion's arm slashed down. He bucked in response to Cybele's wonderful cavernous sex. But nothing happened. He was at the brink of orgasm. But not over it.

He pumped harder still, and faster. The whip landed again, always finding new areas of flesh, where it had not been before, always provoking, its pain immediately translated to throbbing, hot pleasure.

Harder and faster. He was sweating too, their bodies sliding against each other as if they had been oiled. He could feel the sweat on their chests, against their bellies. He had never wanted to come more in his life. He pummeled into her, feeling her cunt squeezing him, milking him.

Cybele's fingernails reached for his nipples. She pinched them hard, sending an electric shock of pleasure straight to his cock. Marion threw the whip aside. She slid her hand between his legs and found his balls, playing with them as if they were some strange toy. They drove his need. He bucked and writhed and squirmed. But nothing he could do would make him come.

They played with him; they toyed with him. Marion's hand stroked his welted arse; Cybele tongued his ear. Every provocation.

'No, no, no,' he screamed. 'Stop it . . .'

Every nerve in his body cried for release. None came. The more they provoked him, excited him, massaged and kissed and fucked him, the more he ached, the more desperate he grew. It was worse than pain, much worse. It was agony. It was his punishment.

Eventually, Cybele rolled him off her body. They stretched his arms above his head and cuffed them to the posts of the bed, leaving him lying on his back. During the night, the other chatelaines would use him, and any of the staff. His erection would not go down. Like a dildo it would remain hard and available for use. Tomorrow he would be sent home.

Behind the black glass, Melinda watched impassively. She felt no emotion other than relief, relief that her husband had not been allowed to spoil her sojourn with the Master. Nothing else mattered.

The Master had slipped his hand into her lap. His fingers delved between her legs. She was wet, soaking wet.

'He will be released in the morning. You can go with him you know. You do know that?'

'Yes, master.'

He withdrew his fingers from her sex.

'And you wish to stay?'

'Forever, master,' she said, never having meant anything more in her life. Had she known what was to come, perhaps she would have felt differently.

Twelve

A week passed. Melinda's routine was relentless. The morning: shower and shave and toilet, a vigorous workout, the solarium. In the afternoon: various menial tasks. In the evening: cuffed to the bed, the metal block between her legs.

She had not seen the Master, but she had the strong impression that he had been watching her. The lights had been left on in the cell, and the video camera was operated, its lens zooming in and out, focusing on her naked body. She could see his eyes, cold and blue, and imagined him laying on his bed naked, his big smooth cock erect and excited.

She was not depressed that he did not call for her in person. In fact, she had reached the stage – a stage which she knew had been brought about by everything the Master had planned – where she thought of herself hardly at all. She did what she was told to do.

The only exception was her sexual feelings. Since the incident with her husband, her body and her mind found it difficult not to dwell on sexual imagery. At night especially, in the dark, the sexual experiences she had gone through under the Master's guidance danced through her mind. Her inability to relieve herself, after all the years when she had masturbated freely, and with such pleasure, made matters worse. The fact that she was bound and unable even to squeeze her thighs together to get relief, was a provocation in itself. It reminded her forcefully – painfully, even, if she tried – that everything she did was controlled by someone else. And that, after all, was for her the ultimate sexual image, sending currents of feeling coursing through her body at the very thought, further enhancing the need she had no means to fulfil.

The routine was broken on the eighth day. Melinda had only just been cuffed to the wall and left on her own by Selene, when the cell door opened again and Marion walked in, a black leather bag, like a doctor's bag, in her hand. She looked beautiful: her long very black hair pinned up to her head; a dark blue dress tight to her bust, but with a full, knee-length skirt. Her neat nylon-sheathed ankles and navy high heels came to rest only inches from Melinda's face.

Melinda felt a surge of desire. She remembered how Marion had felt, pressed against her body.

Marion was looking at her with an expression Melinda could not read. Desire was there, but mixed with something else. Pity? And sadness? She knelt, and stroked Melinda's cheek tenderly. With no human contact for seven days Melinda could not suppress a moan, as though Marion had touched her sex.

'Yes I know. This is the hardest part. But it's the rules.'

Rules? Melinda's mind filled with questions as it had so often in this house. What rules?

'You are very special. The Master was right. I was jealous when he took you instead of me. That was stupid. I see that now. You have such special qualities. I wish we could be together again.'

Her hand stroked Melinda's naked breasts, followed the curve of her waist, her eyes riveted to Melinda's nakedness.

231

Melinda was puzzled. Why couldn't they be together again? Why didn't she unchain her now, spread her legs and take her, suck and be sucked. Melinda yearned for that experience again. Why couldn't she? Had the Master forbidden it?

Marion was kneeling on her haunches. Melinda could see up under the loose skirt. She was wearing stockings. Melinda could see the suspender holding the stocking on the side of one thigh. It was white. She could see the crotch of Marion's white knickers too, containing her sex. It looked puffed up and soft, like a cushion, the tight curls of her pubic hair pushing against the white silk. The view disappeared as Marion rested her weight on her knees and opened the black bag.

'Do you know, you're making me wet. I can feel it,' she said quietly.

I'd like to make you very wet, Melinda thought. I'd like to lick and suck you till I could drink your juices. She said nothing, trying to make her eyes express her feelings.

Marion extracted a roll of Elastoplast from the bag, and a pair of scissors. She stretched out about a foot of the roll and cut it off. She then cut this in half. Stripping off the backing from one piece, she took Melinda's breast in her hand and pulled it up towards her chin so the underside, usually hidden by the weight of the breast, was exposed and stretched taut. Using the Elastoplast, Marion taped the breast in this position. The second piece held it firmer still.

Slicing another foot off the roll, Marion repeated the procedure with the other breast until it too was firmly held upside down.

She was not looking at Melinda now. She concentrated on her work. Putting the scissors and plaster

232

back into the bag, she extracted a shiny chinagraph pencil.

The position had to be right. She climbed over Melinda's body so her knees were either side of her hips. Her bottom rested on Melinda's thighs, the material of the skirt brushing her legs. Marion stared at the area of flesh she had exposed. With the pencil, she made a dot about an inch under the crescent of the upturned left breast, dead centre. She dotted the right breast in the same way but, on consideration, rubbed the mark away with her finger and did it again. Satisfied she had got it centred this time, she climbed off Melinda's prone body.

Melinda looked down. She could see nothing but her own breasts grotesquely plastered to her chest, their nipples pointing to her face.

Delving into the bag again, Marion brought out a small tin. Carefully she took the top off the tin and laid it on the floor next to the mattress. Another trip into the bag produced a leather strap, to which was attached a tongue-shaped gag of rubber.

'I have to gag you,' Marion said, with an apologetic tone Melinda found odd. To make it clear she did not mind, Melinda opened her mouth wide. The gag filled it as the one in the hood had done. A gag was a relief. It took away her ability to disobey, to voice the thousand questions filling her mind. Marion buckled it around her blonde hair.

From the tin, she produced two squares the size of large postage stamps. They were dark purple in colour, with white edges. Carefully, using her long fingernails, Marion tore the backing off one of the squares. Leaning over, she positioned it over the centre of the dot she had made on Melinda's flesh. The second square followed. Melinda could feel them sticking to her skin.

Marion put the tin tidily back in the bag. She extracted a little glass bottle, its cap attached to a long stem like the old-fashioned eye droppers, with a rubber bulb to produce the drops. Carefully she brought the tip of the dropper to the first square, and squeezed the rubber bulb. Two drops of liquid fell on the square. She squeezed two more onto the other patch and returned the bottle to the bag.

'Try not to struggle,' she said, solicitously. On previous occasions, some had struggled violently, thrashing and fighting their bonds. Others remained calm. It was a simple process. The liquid reacted with the chemical impregnating the paper to form an acid in the pattern with which the paper was stamped. The acid burnt away a thin layer of skin and allowed the ink in the paper to seep below the surface, exactly like a tattoo. It was painful, but only momentarily.

Marion saw Melinda's body tense. She did not struggle. Her body arched slightly off the bed, her chest rocking from side to side as if trying to shake the patches off. Melinda did not try to scream. Then, the tension in her body relaxed. Her eyes were looking at Marion like the eyes of an animal. *What have you done to me?* they said. The look filled Marion with desire. She felt her sex pulse. She wished there had been time. But there was not.

Marion got to her feet, looking down at Melinda's awkwardly taped breasts. They had to be left until the morning, the ink from the patches seeping in slowly. She should have taken the gag out, but she did not want to take the chance that Melinda might speak. She didn't want to hear Melinda's voice again. That would have been too much. She knew what Melinda was feeling. She'd felt it herself when she'd been marked. The pain soon turned to pleasure; squirming, heated pleasure. She didn't want to hear Melinda beg, beg for sex, for contact, for love. That would have been a temptation she could not resist.

'Goodbye,' she said. She would see her in the morning of course, but not alone. Tonight was the last time they would be alone together for a long time, perhaps forever.

She closed the cell door behind her, the noise of the lock clicking into place echoing down the long corridor with an air of finality.

Melinda could not sleep. She had seen something in Marion's eyes she did not understand. Nor had Marion ever said goodbye before. Something was going on, and though she had not the least idea what, her mind was full of a deep foreboding.

The pain from the patches under her breasts had been sharp and strong, but had not lasted long. What the patches were she couldn't imagine, but she had the feeling they had been used to mark her in some way. The purple colour had reminded her of indelible ink.

It was not only her mind that refused to go to sleep. The pain from her breasts had turned to an insistent inner throbbing, the familiar tempo of sex. Her whole body was consumed with it: the need she had no means to satisfy.

Eventually, she drifted off to sleep. She dreamt and woke with a start. She had dreamt of her husband. He had been in the Master's bedroom in Scotland. Instead of her tied in the laced gloves, suspended from the white rope, it had been him. She had strapped on the dildo, had approached, and fucked him with it. She had then been pulled away by the Master, who'd taken his cock and put it where her dildo had been . . .

She was drifting back to sleep when the cell door opened. A triangle of light from the corridor outside spilt into the room before the door closed again and a thin beam of torchlight played across the floor.

Melinda knew at once it was the Master. She pretended to be asleep. She knew that's what he expected her to be.

The torchlight lit her body. She could feel his eyes examining her.

'So lovely,' he whispered to himself.

He knelt beside the mattress and used the torch to scan her breasts, and the little patches under them. He shone the beam down onto her shaven pubis and her open legs. He shone the beam up onto her face.

'I shall miss you,' he said, getting up from his haunches. He unlatched the door and tip-toed out.

Now she knew she had been right. Why should the Master miss her? Something was going to happen tomorrow and whatever it was, it clearly involved her.

It was Cybele who strode into the cell in the morning. She knelt by the mattress and removed the gag, then the tiny patches and the tape holding Melinda's breasts so awkwardly, before she freed her from the cuffs and metal block. As soon as she sat up, her breasts resumed their normal position, completely covering whatever marks the patches had left.

Cybele unlocked the bathroom, and watched as she showered, shaved, used the toilet and ate breakfast. Melinda was convinced the make-up woman would arrive and, sure enough, as she finished her coffee the woman hurried in.

She worked with unusual haste.

'She's the second,' she said to Cybele.

'How many's going up?'

'Four. They've all got to be done by twelve.'

After twenty minutes, the woman appeared satisfied with Melinda's appearance.

'You'll do the hair?' she asked.

Cybele nodded and the woman hurried out.

Back in the cell, laid out on the mattress were a pair of thin white gloves, what looked like a nylon body stocking and a pair of very high-heeled shoes.

'Put the gloves on. They're to stop you laddering the nylon.'

Melinda obeyed. Cybele picked up the body stocking. In fact it was not only a body stocking, but a garment that covered the entire body from neck to toe; a catsuit made from the same sort of sheer nylon used for stockings.

Cybele showed Melinda how to get into it, stepping in through a large slit in the back of the bodice. It took minutes before the nylon, woven with Lycra so that it held and shaped the figure as well as covering it, was smoothed over the curves of Melinda's body. The material was so sheer, it hid nothing. Only the opening in the back appeared to have any sort of seam, where tiny studs had been sewn to fasten it together.

Cybele brushed Melinda's hair and ordered her into the shoes. She stripped off the thin gloves.

'Put your hands together in front of you,' she said.

Melinda obeyed, suddenly remembering how Cybele's big body had looked, naked and glistening with sweat. She felt a shiver of pleasure. Strangely the patches nestling under her breasts reacted too, like new erogenous zones. Her nipples puckered.

Cybele noticed. 'Getting excited, are we?' She was strapping a thick leather cuff around each of Melinda's wrists. The cuffs were heavily padded on

the inside and joined by a sturdy chrome chain of just
two links.

Once the cuffs were in place, the familiar command
was issued.

'Follow me,' Cybele said, setting off out of the cell.
Outside the stable block they took a new direction, to
a part of the house where Melinda had not been
before. A long corridor, carpeted in rich green Wilton
with wood-panelled walls, led to a sitting room from
which Melinda could see the beautifully tended
gardens and sweeping lawns. She could see two
gardeners working in a bed of shrubbery. A door
opened onto another more austere corridor, at the
end of which were a pair of panelled doors, one of
which was already open. As Cybele led her through
the door, Melinda realised her heart was beating
rapidly and her breathing coming in shallow pants.

The room was about the size of a tennis court.
Apart from the space for the doors, the walls were
completely covered in heavy dark blue velvet drapes.
The floor was tiled in white marble. At equal intervals
on either side of the room, six circular daises were
arranged. They were about a foot off the ground and
two feet in diameter, painted in a blue that matched
the drapes. Above each hung a white rope, to the end
of which was attached a chrome hook. The ropes disappeared into the ceiling. The ceiling also housed
rows of spotlights grouped to illuminate each dais.

On one of the diases was a long-haired blonde. Her
hands, imprisoned in cuffs identical to those Melinda
was wearing, were pulled up above her head by the
chrome hook and white rope. Her outfit was identical
too, her ample body – large fleshy tits, a big plum-
shaped arse, wide shapely thighs – straining against
the tight transparent nylon and Lycra.

238

Marion stood by the dais opposite the blonde. She wore a black business suit and white blouse, with her hair pinned up to her head.

'Over here,' she said to Cybele.

Melinda was led up and onto the dais.

'Hands above your head,' Marion ordered, not looking at her directly.

Melinda stretched her arms. The hook was just above her head. Marion stepped onto the dais and slipped the hook into the chrome links of the cuffs. She stepped down again. A small metal pedal was set in the floor by each dais. Marion's foot pressed the pedal and the rope wound upwards with a whirr of electric motors, until Melinda's arms were at full stretch above her head.

Almost immediately, the door opened again and Selene led a third woman in, a petite and freckled redhead, her body much less lush than the two blondes already in position, but nevertheless attractive. Selene attached the rope to the cuffs and operated the pedal until the new arrival too was stretched out on a dais, her body displayed under the tight catsuit.

It was some minutes before Hera brought in a fourth woman, an olive-skinned brunette, her breasts smaller than those of the other three, her pubis as dark as her long black hair. Of all the women, the brunette seemed least at ease. She refused to put her hands above her head and Hera had to enlist Cybele's help. Once she was stretched like the others, however, her rebelliousness seemed to disappear and she lapsed into a sullen acceptance.

Marion and the chatelaines left the room.

Melinda looked at the other women. She had not been aware of anyone else in the house, but it was obvious the stable block was equipped to take more than one occupant. Had these women been entertained by the Master on the nights Melinda was left alone and bound in her cell? They were each beautiful in their own way.

She looked at their bodies and saw them looking at her. It was the olive-skinned brunette who particularly attracted her. She caught her dark brown eyes, but knew better than to speak. Each woman obeyed the rule of silence, even the brunette who had struggled, though each clearly yearned to talk.

A movement caught Melinda's eye. She looked up to see a video camera moving position. She examined the ceiling. Four cameras were placed in each corner of the room.

How long they were left there, their shoulders strained and taut, their muscles aching, waiting, it was impossible to know. Like everything else in the house, time was something over which they had no control.

In fact, it was an hour before the Master opened the door and strode purposefully into the room, followed by Marion and the chatelaines. At the far end of the room, the end opposite the doors, was a raised platform on which was a long desk littered with telephones. To the side of the desk was a lectern.

The Master took up position behind the lectern. Melinda saw one of the video cameras training itself on him.

Each of the chatelaines sat behind the desk, with a telephone in front of them.

'Gentlemen. Welcome. Welcome,' the Master said, looking up into the camera. 'You have all received the videos. So without further ado shall we start with C.'

Marion took a large yellow card from the desk and went to stand by the brunette.

'C, gentlemen. In need of training as you will have seen. What am I bid?' Again, the Master looked into the camera as he spoke.

Melinda could see that set into the lectern was a computer display. This was an auction. They were being auctioned! No wonder the Master was going to miss her.

Bids appeared on the computer, scrolling up on the screen in order, the largest at the top.

'Is that it, gentlemen? Very well.' The Master called out a number and Hera picked up the phone and dialled.

'Yes,' she said, as soon as the connection was made. 'Fifty confirmed,' she said to the Master.

'Right, gentlemen, fifty confirmed. Any advance?' He looked into the camera then down at the computer screen. 'All done at fifty then,' he said, like an experienced auctioneer.

Melinda's mind was reeling. There was no doubt about what was happening now. The Master was going to sell her, like a valuable painting, to the highest bidder.

The bidding for the redhead was over quickly. Selene was given a number to dial and confirmed a price of twenty, though twenty what was not specified.

'And now, gentlemen, we come to M . . .'

Marion took a yellow M from the desk and came to stand by Melinda. Melinda sensed a reluctance in her step, just as she did in the Master's voice.

The Master's eyes scanned the screen. He gave Cybele a number to dial. It was a long number.

'Seventy-two confirmed,' Cybele announced when she got through.

'Seventy-two confirmed, gentlemen. Any advance?'

He looked down at the screen set in the lectern. Immediately, he saw a change, and gave Hera a number to dial.

'Ninety confirmed,' Hera declared, as soon as she was connected.

'Ninety confirmed,' the Master repeated into the camera.

'One hundred,' Cybele said, her ear still to the phone.

'One ten,' Hera entoned.

'One twenty.'

'One forty.'

Cybele said nothing this time. She put the phone down.

'One forty, gentlemen,' the Master said, looking at the computer. 'All done at one forty.'

They moved on to the other blonde. She reached seventy.

'Thank you, gentlemen. Please fax your instructions immediately. That concludes the business for today.'

'There was very stiff competition for you,' the Master said. 'The Egyptian, well I thought he was going to bid more. But the Spaniard came up trumps. I know him, Melinda, you'll be safe with him.'

Melinda was naked again. Hera had taken her back to the cell, stripped her out of the catsuit and taken her to the bathroom where she had been allowed to soak in a bath, easing her aching shoulders and tortured muscles. After she had dried herself she had been led out into the gardens, across an immaculately manicured lawn, to what looked like a large garage complex. Inside, Melinda found herself in a neatly arranged workshop at the back of a large garage. A van was parked in the garage, its rear doors open. In the centre of the workshop floor were two large wooden boxes, for all the world like coffins.

The Master had come in behind them and now sat on a plain wooden chair, his eyes, as ever, seeming to bore into Melinda's soul. 'I think one forty is a record too,' he concluded, though he did not smile.

Cybele was already in the workshop. She lifted the top off one of the boxes. Inside, Melinda could see the outline of a human form, marked out by heavy padding on all sides, especially around the head. Numerous leather straps lay unbuckled in the box.

'Put these on,' Hera said. She handed Melinda a pair of plain black panties, made from silky nylon.

Melinda took them in her hands. As she pulled them up over her thighs she realised it had been weeks since she had worn anything to cover her sex, with the exception of the transparent catsuit earlier today. It felt strange. She smoothed the panties into place.

Her hands were trembling. The box frightened her. Really frightened her. She looked at the Master, trying to use her eyes to show him her fear. She did not want his last memory of her to be disobedience. She wanted to submit, but at the moment her fear was overwhelming her.

The Master had expected her reaction. He had seen it before in many other women.

'You have one final request,' he said. 'Is there anything you would like?'

The question was so unexpected, Melinda could hardly find the words to answer.

'You're allowed to speak,' he said.

She wanted to beg him not to send her away. But that was pointless.

'My breasts,' she stuttered. 'What have you done . . .?'

243

Most of them asked the same question. They were ready. Cybele came around behind her and lifted her breasts up, holding them just as the plaster had held them last night. Hera held a mirror, angling it so Melinda could see. Centred neatly beneath each breast, Melinda read the letter W in a purplish ink. The mirror inverted the letter. It was of course an M.

'Master . . .' Melinda murmured.

'Melinda and the Master,' the Master corrected. 'Now you must get into the box.'

'I'm frightened, Master.' It was the only time she had spoken unbidden.

'Don't be. You have nothing to be frightened about.'

She looked into his eyes. They were hypnotic. She felt her fear melt. He was her Master.

Unsteadily, she stood in the box then slotted herself into its padding. It was a tight fit.

Hera and Cybele fastened the straps, endless numbers of straps holding every part of her body tight.

When finally they were finished, the Master came and knelt by the box. He had a white pill in his hand.

'This will make you sleep,' he said. His voice sounded far away, muffled by the padding that held her head firmly on both sides.

He put the pill in her mouth. She held it on her tongue. She could spit it out. She could scream and scream and they would release her, let her go, out of the box, out of the house, out of the system. It was her choice. It had been her choice to put on the strange bra and knickers in her bedroom weeks ago; her choice to walk through the gates; her choice to be bound and spread and fucked and sucked and buggered. Her choice.

244

There was no turning back now. It was time for the final submission. Melinda swallowed the pill. She belonged to the Master. To be bought and sold like anything else he owned.

She saw the two chatelaines manoeuvring the lid of the box. Then it was too much of an effort to keep her eyes open and she let darkness engulf her. There, before sleep overtook her, she felt her body pulsing, a damp wetness spreading over her sex, the last thing she was conscious of.

She had no idea where she would wake up, but she knew what would be done to her when she did. That was the point. To be done to, not to do.

Dear Readers

Deck the walls with belles and holly . . . My helpers and I have been working especially hard this month to ensure you get some wonderful Nexus Christmas presents. I've got enough caffeine in me to keep an American Football team up for a week! Not that I usually *need* coffee to do that, mind . . .

Yes, there are some wonderfully sexy surprises in my Christmas stocking this year. First of all, from the creator of Stephanie comes a new and equally gorgeous character called Melinda. In her first adventure, *Melinda and the Master*, she starts out happily married to a high-flying lawyer. But her husband's fortunes turn, and when he receives an indecent proposal from a wealthy and lecherous client, he finds it hard to refuse.

Fans of corporal punishment will be pleased to learn that our other offering this month is *The Fantasies of Josephine Scott*. In explicit detail, it recounts the experiences, both real and imagined, of one of the best-known writers (and practitioners) of chastisement. A veritable welter of spanking stories! Now there's something I wouldn't mind turning my hand to.

The Black Lace book for December is *Black Orchid*. What I wouldn't give to be a member of the Black Orchid Club! It's a hotbed of pleasure where wealthy ladies go to indulge their every sensual whim, and men only exist to serve. Anything – and everyone – goes! Young Maggie enjoys it so much, she decides she wants a piece of the action. It's sure going to be a White-Hot Christmas for Nexus readers!

Goodies for the New Year kick off with *The Passive Voice*, the story of a tyrannical mistress, Harriet, and her meek but willing prisoner Hilary. If you're into bondage, these two are bound to please!

Next up there's *Heart of Desire*, documenting the antics of Sarah, an actress who has to research a role as a dominatrix. Instructing her is the unimaginatively named Dominique, who ensures that she plays her part with more gusto than usual. *Heart of Desire* is the latest sizzler from the author of *The Institute*, *Paradise Bay* and *Obsession*.

January brings exciting news for our female readers as well as the men. The Black Lace series has been so successful, that from January, we're producing two a month! First there's *Odalisque*, in which we meet Auralie, a designer, and part of a powerful, sophisticated family. She's soon hatching designs of a different kind as she begins to persecute her innocent cousin Jeanine. What does she hope to gain by victimising this beautiful young thing? And is Jeanine as virtuous as she seems?

Outlaw Lover takes us into the world of the future. It's the year 2075, and society has been divided — literally — into communities of rich and poor. Fee Cambridge is one of the lucky ones; she's got everything she could wish for. Everything, that is, except a decent sex life. Perhaps she can find the excitement she lacks on the other side — where the vicious pirates lurk . . . If you think that sounds familiar, then you could be right. Nexus issued a similar book called *Wicked* a while ago, so if you've already got that, it's probably not worth your while buying this one.

Well, that about wraps it up for this month. Which is good, 'cos now we can start the unwrapping . . . Merry Christmas!

Esme ♥

THE BEST IN EROTIC READING – BY POST

The Nexus Library of Erotica – almost one hundred and fifty volumes – is available from many booksellers and newsagents. If you have any difficulty obtaining the books you require, you can order them by post. Photocopy the list below, or tear the list out of the book; then tick the titles you want and fill in the form at the end of the list. Titles marked 1993 are not yet available: please do not try to order them – just look out for them in the shops!

CONTEMPORARY EROTICA

AMAZONS	Erin Caine	£3.99	
COCKTAILS	Stanley Carten	£3.99	
CITY OF ONE-NIGHT STANDS	Stanley Carten	£4.50	
CONTOURS OF DARKNESS	Marco Vassi	£4.99	
THE GENTLE DEGENERATES	Marco Vassi	£4.99	
MIND BLOWER	Marco Vassi	£4.99	
THE SALINE SOLUTION	Marco Vassi	£4.99	
DARK FANTASIES	Nigel Anthony	£4.99	
THE DAYS AND NIGHTS OF MIGUMI	P.M.	£4.50	
THE LATIN LOVER	P.M.	£3.99	
THE DEVIL'S ADVOCATE	Anonymous	£4.50	
DIPLOMATIC SECRETS	Antoine Lelouche	£3.50	
DIPLOMATIC PLEASURES	Antoine Lelouche	£3.50	
DIPLOMATIC DIVERSIONS	Antoine Lelouche	£4.50	
ENGINE OF DESIRE	Alexis Arven	£3.99	
DIRTY WORK	Alexis Arven	£3.99	
DREAMS OF FAIR WOMEN	Celeste Arden	£2.99	
THE FANTASY HUNTERS	Celeste Arden	£3.99	
A GALLERY OF NUDES	Anthony Grey	£3.99	
THE GIRL FROM PAGE 3	Mike Angelo	£3.99	
HELEN – A MODERN ODALISQUE	James Stern	£4.99	1993
HOT HOLLYWOOD NIGHTS	Nigel Anthony	£4.50	
THE INSTITUTE	Maria del Ray	£4.99	

Title	Author	Price	Year
LAURE-ANNE	Laure-Anne	£4.50	
LAURE-ANNE ENCORE	Laure-Anne	£4.99	
LAURE-ANNE TOUJOURS	Laure-Anne	£4.99	
Ms DEEDES ON A MISSION	Carole Andrews	£4.99	1993
Ms DEEDES AT HOME	Carole Andrews	£4.50	
Ms DEEDES ON PARADISE ISLAND	Carole Andrews	£4.99	1993
MY SEX AND SOUL	Amelia Greene	£2.99	
OBSESSION	Maria del Rey	£4.99	1993
ONE WEEK IN THE PRIVATE HOUSE	Esme Ombreux	£4.50	
PALACE OF FANTASIES	Delver Maddingley	£4.99	
PALACE OF SWEETHEARTS	Delver Maddingley	£4.99	
PALACE OF HONEYMOONS	Delver Maddingley	£4.99	1993
PARADISE BAY	Maria del Rey	£4.50	
QUEENIE AND CO	Francesca Jones	£4.99	1993
QUEENIE AND CO IN JAPAN	Francesca Jones	£4.99	1993
QUEENIE AND CO IN ARGENTINA	Francesca Jones	£4.99	1993
THE SECRET WEB	Jane-Anne Roberts	£3.99	
SECRETS LIE ON PILLOWS	James Arbroath	£4.50	
SECRETS TIED IN SILK	James Arbroath	£4.99	1993
STEPHANIE	Susanna Hughes	£4.50	
STEPHANIE'S CASTLE	Susanna Hughes	£4.50	
STEPHANIE'S DOMAIN	Susanna Hughes	£4.99	1993
STEPHANIE'S REVENGE	Susanna Hughes	£4.99	1993
THE DOMINO TATTOO	Cyrian Amberlake	£4.50	
THE DOMINO ENIGMA	Cyrian Amberlake	£3.99	
THE DOMINO QUEEN	Cyrian Amberlake	£4.99	

EROTIC SCIENCE FICTION

ADVENTURES IN THE PLEASURE ZONE	Delaney Silver	£4.99	
EROGINA	Christopher Denham	£4.50	
HARD DRIVE	Stanley Carten	£4.99	
PLEASUREHOUSE 13	Agnetha Anders	£3.99	
LAST DAYS OF THE PLEASUREHOUSE	Agnetha Anders	£4.50	
TO PARADISE AND BACK	D.H.Master	£4.50	
WICKED	Andrea Arven	£3.99	
WILD	Andrea Arven	£4.50	

ANCIENT & FANTASY SETTINGS

CHAMPIONS OF LOVE	Anonymous	£3.99	
CHAMPIONS OF DESIRE	Anonymous	£3.99	

Please send me the books I have ticked above.

Name   ....
Address   ....
            ....
            .... Post code   ....

Send to: **Cash Sales, Nexus Books, 332 Ladbroke Grove, London W10 5AH**

Please enclose a cheque or postal order, made payable to **Nexus Books**, to the value of the books you have ordered plus postage and packing costs as follows:

UK and BFPO – £1.00 for the first book, 50p for the second book, and 30p for each subsequent book to a maximum of £3.00;

Overseas (including Republic of Ireland) – £2.00 for the first book, £1.00 for the second book, and 50p for each subsequent book.

If you would prefer to pay by VISA or ACCESS/MASTERCARD, please write your card number here:

— — — —   — — — —   — — — —   — — — —

Signature: _____